Royal
RELUCTANCE

LOVE IN LAANDIA
SWEET ROYAL ROMANCE

HOLLY KERR

Also By Holly Kerr

Royal Rumble
Royal Retelling
Royal Rising
Royal Reluctance
Royal Rebel
Royal Replacement
plus
Suitor Science series
Love &Alliteration series
Don't series
Charlotte Dodd series

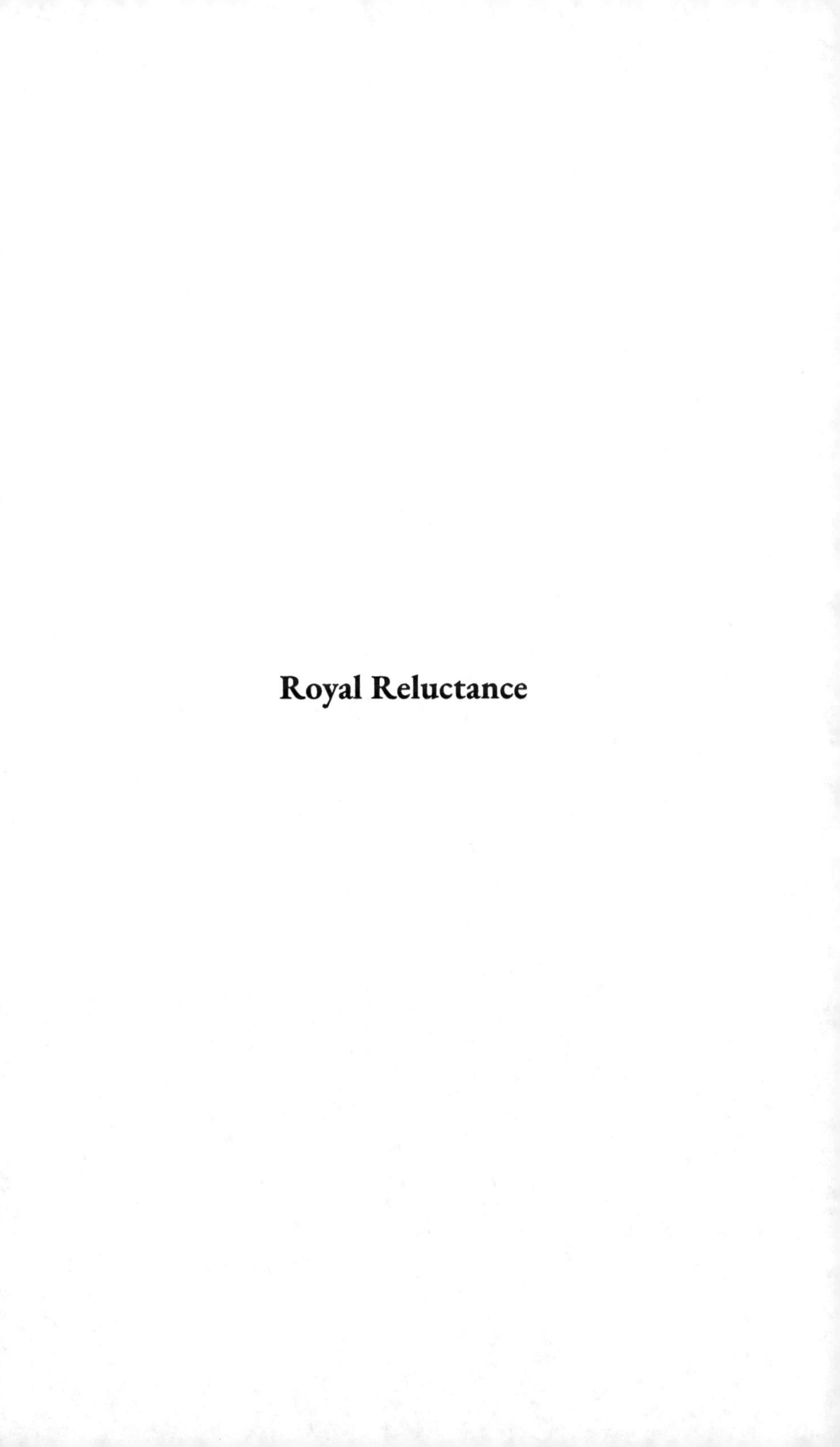

Royal Reluctance

To all those who found a first love...
and managed to keep it

Prologue

EIGHT YEARS AGO...

Once upon a time, a prince went to talk to his queen.

But this isn't a fairy tale. At least it doesn't start out as one. Because if this was a fairy tale, I shouldn't be so nervous about talking to my mother.

All the happiness of the last two days disappears as soon as I enter the castle.

The last place I want to be is here, but if my father taught us anything, it was duty. And to take responsibility for your actions.

That was what I was here to do. To confess and take responsibility.

Standing in front of the door of her sitting room, I lift my hand to knock, then pause. This is my mother, I tell myself. But she's also the queen of Laandia. And I am Prince Bowden Eugene Jerome Leif Erickson—third son of King Magnus and Queen Selene.

And mother or queen, I know she's going to be pissed off with what I'm about to tell her.

I don't have the dumb luck or blind faith of Gunnar or Lyra, the certainty that whatever they try, it'll all work out. I lack the intelligent rationale of Odin that helps with the knowledge that mistakes can always be fixed. I especially don't have the straight-up courage of Kalle, because knowing you're going to be king some-day takes a special kind of bravery.

I may not have the traits my siblings do, but still, not a lot scares me.

My mother does.

And I know that if anyone else was about to tell her what I have to tell her, they would be terrified too.

I steel my nerves, fist my hand and knock twice on the door. "Come in," Queen Selene calls.

Deep breath… and go.

My mother sits on one of the delicate wing chairs that flank one of the fifteen huge fireplaces in the castle. The chairs are a cause for concern for me and my brothers because they really don't look strong enough to hold a male of our height and weight.

They birth them big here in Laandia.

My mother smiles as I enter; smiles with her eyes and her mouth and looks like I am her very favourite person. I'm not—Mom loves me as much as she loves my brothers and Lyra, but it's just the way she smiles at everyone, from Duncan, Dad's right-hand man, to the castle chef and even that obnoxious buffoon of a man running America.

She smiles at my father a little differently. And my father still looks at her like she's the only woman in the world. It's nice to see; together for twenty-five years and more in love than when they met.

Which isn't hard since it was kind of an arranged marriage. Magnus needed a wife; Selene wasn't thrilled about the coupling but didn't have much choice in the matter.

It all worked out and quickly turned into a love match, one that is celebrated all over Laandia. It's the kind of marriage I want. The love match, not the arranged marriage.

"Bowden," my mother says in that way she has that makes you believe everything is going to be okay. My little sister Lyra has the same gift. "What's up?"

Mom is the only one who calls me Bowden. To the rest of the family, Laandia, and even the world, I'm Prince Bo.

Newly anointed People Magazine's Sexiest Man of the Year.

I bring that up because the magazine is right there on the table beside Mom's chair, as if she was perusing it and put it down when I knocked.

My face heats *again*, like it's been doing since the stupid issue came out. Nobody should want their mom to see pictures like that. Plus, I have no clue why they picked *me* over my brothers. Or anyone else in the world. "You can throw that out, you know," I mutter.

"Oh, no." Mom laughs as she taps the glossy cover. "I'm going to frame it. 'Sweet, Stoic and Sexy—What Really Goes on in the Forests of Laandia?'" Her blue eyes twinkle with delight as she recites the copy from memory. "Your brothers are never going to let you live this down."

"I know."

"Poor Bo." And she laughs again.

But the headline on the magazine brings back a wave of unease. Things do go on in the forest, and I'm here to tell my mother about them.

Not all of them, just the most important one.

Mom's smile drops into a frown. "Is this about more than the magazine? I didn't expect you back for another few days. Did something happen in Wabush?"

The royal family has a hunting lodge in the forest, halfway across Laandia. As soon as I could make the trip—first making the eight-hour drive with Kalle, and then getting my pilot's license at seventeen so I could fly—I would disappear into the woods for as long as duty let me.

I rub the back of my neck. "I gotta talk to you."

"Then you better come and talk then." She motions to the couch beside her. "But I have to warn you, I need to leave in a few minutes to pick up Lyra."

"I can wait," I say automatically. That might be better because I have no idea how I'm going to get the words out. How is it possible that talking to my own mother is more difficult than talking to that reporter for the magazine?

She studies me carefully. "No, I don't think you can. What is it, Bo? Did something happen?"

"It's about Hettie."

I don't recognize the flash that crosses her face. My mother assured me she's happy that I'm with Hettie, but there's no ignoring the chaos of the Crow family. If I were a regular guy, I could fall in love with whomever I wanted to, but because I'm a prince, there's so many things to consider.

Not that Mom would ever bring them up, but everyone in Battle Harbour is well aware of Hettie's two brothers in jail, her uncle who protests everything Dad stands for, and a grandmother who refuses to seek help for substance abuse and would rather live on the streets of nearby Mary's Harbour than let anyone help her.

Mom would never say anything, but Hettie would—and has, on many occasions. It took me nearly a year to get her to agree to go out with me. Even now, she still reminds me how we shouldn't be together, how it looks bad for the royal family.

I tell her I don't care. I love my family, but I would rather be anything other than a prince.

"How is Hettie?" Mom asks politely. Hettie has refused every invitation to the castle, so Mom has never met her. Not officially, anyway. Not as my girlfriend. And not as my—

"She's good." I press my palms on my knees and take a deep breath. "I married her."

The tick of the clock is the only sound in the room. Mom sets her tea cup gently on the coffee table before responding. "I'm sorry?"

"We got married."

A deep inhale. "Bo... Okay. When?"

"Two days ago."

Her face is expressionless and I know she's in queen mode, not mother mode. Which is better because I'd much rather disappoint Queen Selene than my mom. "Was it a real wedding?" she asks.

I frown at the question. "What do you mean? I said 'I do.' So did she."

"Who did you say it in front of?"

"A justice of the peace." I pause again. "And Spencer."

"Then it's legal." I can't read anything on her face. Is she furious? About to throw me from the room? Call for my father, which would be better because he'll be much easier to tell.

Spencer, the lawyer-to-be, has followed in his father's footsteps in protecting the royal family and already makes it a point to ensure *i's* were dotted and *t's* were crossed. Although many would say letting me go through with a wedding to Hettie Crow isn't really protecting the family. "It's legal," I say gruffly. "She's my wife."

Even saying the words brings about a rush of happiness. It also brings on another wave of terror, but still—happy. About my wife.

Hettie is my wife.

"Why?" Queen Selene? Or maybe this is Mom.

I'm not sure because there's real distress in her voice. I knew Mom would be angry but that she'd eventually understand—because she always understood. "I love her," I say because there's no other reason. I love Hettie. Hettie loves me. Marrying her was the one way I could show her that she truly mattered to me, that she was my life.

She's the most important thing in the world to me and now everyone will know.

"I know, Bo, but why not get engaged, get used to the idea of a future with her? This is such a big step."

"I didn't want to wait. Her brother is in trouble again—she was going to leave me and I couldn't let that happen. And I didn't want a big wedding. A royal wedding. I can't handle that."

"Oh, my sweet Bo." Mom—not Queen Selene—shakes her head. "You can handle more than you think you can. Being part of this family isn't the prison sentence you make it out to be."

"I don't like it," I mutter.

"Neither does anyone else," she admits with a rueful smile. "Except maybe Gunnar likes the attention. You learn to deal with it, rather than go into hiding. You were born into this family, and while you had no choice in that, your father and I have given you many choices in how to deal with the attention and the responsibilities. We've never forced anything on you." She taps the magazine again. "You dealt with this, so don't tell me you can't do anything."

"That's not the same. How could I say no?"

"Thank you, but no," Mom says quickly. "You didn't even tell anyone until it was published, so there was no way we could prepare you for it. You must be going crazy with the attention. Duncan can help."

She does have a point. I've turned my phone off because of the constant calls from friends and strangers alike, all wanting a comment. And it would have been nice to have been prepared for the media storm, but that's on me because I never mentioned the magazine had even contacted me until a few days before the issue was published.

The same way I never told anyone of my plans to marry Hettie, not until it was too late and there was nothing anyone could do.

Mom sighs. "You really married her?"

I nod, shoulders hunched. "I love her," I say helplessly.

"Well, that's good because you've made this very difficult for yourselves. The press..." She shakes her head and stands. "I'm sorry, but I need to get Lyra. We'll talk about this when I get back. And we're going to have to tell your father."

"I know."

"I have no idea what he'll say." Mom stares out the window at the icy rain that falls in sheets. The weather had been a beautiful early October day when we left Wabush this morning, but the storm had blown in arrived soon after, along with a cold front blowing down from the Arctic. Snow and ice are expected tonight, which means I won't be heading back with Hettie.

I stand as she moves toward the door and Mom touches my arm with a tired smile. "I'll be back as soon as I can. Make sure you're still here, please. No flying tonight."

I nod.

Only my mother never came back.

1

Hettie

"A RE YOU SURE YOU'RE ready for this?" Mabel asks.

The air is cold on the very edge of Laandia, but the water is colder. I forget how long it would take to get hypothermia in the water, and I also forget how long it has been since I put a toe in the Atlantic.

My sister and I walk along the beach on the edge of town. When people think of Laandia, no one gives the beach much thought. It's a fishing village—town, these days—and the pier is the heartbeat of Battle Harbour. But it's on the eastern edge of North America, and where there is ocean, there is beach.

My toes, already chilled from my inadequate boots, itch to walk along the sandy strip. It's the only beachy beach in all of Laandia; the rest of the coastline is either sharp rocks jutting up from the water, making it disastrous for boats and swimming, or strips of pebbles, worn smooth from the constant waves that will easily knock you down if you go in the water the wrong way. But it's a beach and I love it. Even though I've lived in British Columbia for years, with beaches full of sand and calm water, I still love Battle Harbour's beach best of all.

I sometimes wonder how the Vikings ever thought this country would be habitable but then I think of the prettiness of the harbour. They must have come ashore in their longboats at just the right spot.

This morning, the first morning in eight years that I've been back in my home country, I woke to find all the carefully constructed walls in my mind had crashed and burned. One night in Battle Harbour, and I can't get away from Bo.

He's in my mind. He's all over my mind. Everything reminds me of him—the trees surrounding the town, standing tall and unyielding, the roads we travelled looking for the perfect spot to confess our love, the castle on the hill where he grew up.

The spot behind the high school where he told me we should have never gotten married.

When I woke up this morning, the school was visible from the window, and that was the only thing I could think about. Replaying the moment Prince Bo of Laandia—the man that only a short time earlier had professed his undying love and commitment to me—broke my heart.

I hadn't even wanted to get married but Bo convinced me. I loved him but my life was far from a fairy tale, and the only place a girl like me got the prince was in a fairy tale.

But I went along with his wild plan because I loved Bo Erickson more than anything.

And still, he broke my heart. Crushed it really. Saying marrying me was a mistake, that he never should have thought it would work out, that we couldn't be together.

It was like when I was swimming and got caught in the undertow. I didn't fight or flail because I knew there was nothing I could do but surrender and let it drag me down. Listening to Bo say those things, I let myself be dragged down.

Until Mabel pulled me up.

She dragged me to my feet after Bo. It was Mabel who told me to get out of Laandia. Granted, she had been telling me that all of my life, but this time I listened. And Mabel worked with someone in the castle to help because the press was still swarming after Queen Selene's death and to see the girlfriend of Prince Bo fleeing town like a criminal would have led the swarm straight to me.

Bo had always hated the press. The lack of privacy. The demands that the people have a right to know more about him, intimate details that he doesn't want to share.

No one should want to share their first kiss with the public.

I hunch my shoulders, my hands digging into my pockets. Eight years away will make you forget just how brutally cold a March wind can be blowing in from the Atlantic. The sun is bright but offers no warmth. I clearly don't have enough clothing packed to keep warm during my visit and I never even thought to bring gloves.

I am not ready for any of this. I'm not ready for the cold, I'm not ready to deal with my family, and I'm definitely not ready to see Bo.

"How did you get the job at The King's Hat?" I ask instead. There were a few surprises when I got back into town yesterday, but one of the big ones was that my big sister Mabel is now the manager of the pub owned by Prince Kalle.

Mabel smirks, well aware of my dodging of her question but always willing to have the attention focused on her. "Edie hired me. She's going to be queen, you know? Guess there's not enough time to run a bar and prep for that."

"Yes, we get news of the royal family of Laandia all the way over in British Columbia," I tell her drily.

"I didn't know if you ignore news about them like you do our family." There's no bitterness or disappointment in Mabel's tone. I don't have much in common with Mabel, and never have, but one thing we can agree on is that we'd much rather be part of any other family than the one we are saddled with.

And she does have a point. I haven't gone out of my way to search for news of King Magnus and his family since I left, but I don't turn off the television when there is a story featuring them either.

Like Prince Kalle's engagement to Edie England. I also watched coverage of Prince Odin's wedding to Lady Camille and his subsequent abdication.

I couldn't help thinking about how I would have been at that wedding if things had been different.

"I don't ignore news about the royals or anyone," I say.

"You should," Mabel scoffs. "You're how far away from here? It's a lot easier to pretend the fam doesn't exist from there than be like me and try to hide my head in the sand every time one of our idiot brothers breaks into somewhere else, or starts a fight. Or refuses to pay their pay tab."

I sigh. "Yeah."

"So?" she presses.

"I don't know if I'm ready," I admit. "But it's time, don't you think?"

Mabel snorts. "I think it's way past time. But why now?"

I've kept in contact with Mabel over the years, but she doesn't know what the years have been like for me.

I'm not about to get into it now.

And Mabel knows I'm not about to talk about it. "And Abigail came back with you?" she asks instead.

Abigail Locke has been my best friend since I was born, seeing as her mother shared a hospital room with mine. We were born seven hours apart and not a day has gone by where we haven't talked. When I made the move to British Columbia, Abigail never questioned whether she would come with me—she just quit her job and bought a one-way ticket.

"She did. She's at her mom's. I'm staying there."

"I would."

The house we grew up in had always been full of tension and toxicity, and the one good thing about leaving had been knowing I didn't have to live with that any longer.

Mabel wouldn't let me feel guilty about leaving her behind.

I crouch and pick up a piece of blue glass worn smooth from the waves. Mabel would always bring me here when things got bad at home.

They were bad a lot.

Seven children, Mabel and I being the only girls.

Our father tried, but he is and always has been a fisherman, often heading out in the boat for weeks at a time. And when he wasn't on the ocean, he was in a bar dealing with the heartbreak of our mother running out on him and leaving all of us, including five-year-old Earl.

She left the day my little brother started kindergarten. She dropped him off and never came back to pick him up.

The two oldest Crow brothers—Hank and Lloyd—had already left home by then, and we heard about them more than we saw them: the fights, the breaking-and-entering arrests, stealing cars. Hank now owns a garage in nearby Mary's Harbour, but Lloyd is serving a twenty-year sentence for manslaughter.

My other brother Reggie is also in prison for starting a fire that burned down two farms and at least ten acres of forest. It had been expected that he would end up in jail for something.

Mabel was six years older than me and took care of the rest of us the best she could. Earl, the youngest, is now a fisherman like our father and, also like him, spends his free time in the bars of Battle Harbour. Tommy was the one who got away—he lives in Halifax now and we exchange Christmas emails.

"When are you seeing him?" Mabel asks as I slip the piece of glass in my pocket.

Bo, not Tommy. It's been eight years since I've seen my husband.

Husband.

I've hidden the fact I have a husband for years. I pull it out now, like a folded receipt you find in an old jacket.

"Tomorrow." There is a note of determination in my voice that I don't feel. I'm not about to let Mabel know how much I'm dreading this.

And how excited I am.

How terrified and yet looking forward to seeing him in person. Has he changed? What is he like now?

How does he feel about me?

That, though, is not a question I should ask anymore.

I left, Bo didn't stop me, and our lives have gone on.

It's for the best.

2

Bo

O NCE AGAIN, I'M YANKED out of sleep by the screech of metal that sounds like it's being dragged around the room. And the scream, the second scream is too loud to have just been in my head.

I can *hear* the rain beating down on the crumpled car, steam rising, making the pavement even more slick.

I never saw the accident, so why do I keep dreaming about it?

Drawing a shaky breath, I blink into the darkness, confused and so sad, just like every other time I've had the dream. And there's been more than a few times that it's haunted my subconscious over the years.

Kody stirs on the floor by the bed. I like the quiet, but sometimes the silence gets to me. "I'm awake, boy," I tell my dog, just to hear the sound of a voice.

The thump of his tail answers me. I lie in the dark until the outside is more grey than black, and then I pull myself out of bed.

Dreaming about the accident that killed my mother happens often enough for it not to be a surprise, but it still throws me, even after all this time. And each time, the nightmare gets harder to shake off.

But I can shake it off. Coffee will help.

Kody follows me into the kitchen, watching from his spot by the door as I measure coffee grounds, add water, and wait for it to percolate. One thing I really miss about Battle Harbour is the coffee. Silas makes the best. When I stopped in over the holidays, I mentioned if he could somehow supply a bag for me, I'd be willing to pay any amount.

His new girlfriend, Fenella, overheard the request and promised to come up with something for me.

Even if I used the same beans and machine, it's the way Silas makes it that has the Coffee for the Sole brew taste so good. I haven't found anything to compare here in Wabush and I've been living here full time for almost six years now.

Coffee made, I shrug into my coat, taking a cup out to the porch along with Kody so he can do his business.

Wake up. Coffee. Let Kody out. Eat, and then chop. My morning routine may be comforting but it still... lacks.

I know exactly what is lacking, but I'm not ready to do anything about it.

The sun hints at the horizon. Laandia may be on the edge of the Atlantic, but we're pretty far north so the sun is a rare commodity during the winter months.

The cold seeps through the flannel of my pants and quickly chills my bare feet in the fuzzy yellow Crocs Lyra gave me last Christmas, but I'm used to the temperature. Winter in Laandia is unforgivingly cold, and you accept it. Or you leave.

Through the trees, I see the light wink on and time how long it takes for Fred to gallop through the forest for his morning visit with Kody.

My neighbours, Jean and Buck Marsden, live five minutes away through the trees but a longer twenty if you take the road. Fred is a Lab/ beagle cross and seems to always know when Kody is outside.

"I'm glad you have a friend," I mutter as Kody races away for a romp with Fred.

Buck's father had been the groundskeeper when my grandfather would use the cottage as a hunting lodge years ago. No one in our family is a hunter, but the one-bedroom cottage made a great hideout when I was younger.

Buck and I expanded it over the years—it now has four bedrooms, three baths, with a porch wrapping around the building to join the screened-in section out back with the good view of the mountains. The screens help with the mosquitoes and the heaters help with the cold.

There's enough space for my brothers for a visit even though it's been a while since anyone has been here. I usually go back to Battle Harbour when I'm summoned, or someone needs me. Or when I miss my family.

My brother Gunnar isn't the only pilot in the family. As soon as my father took me to the cabin, I knew I had to find an easier way to get there than the drive across Laandia. I bought the secondhand Cessna 206 about five years ago, so it's an easy flight back home when I need to be there.

The barking of the dogs treeing every squirrel in the vicinity follows me inside. I see the odd deer and the coyotes roam through the trees but they steer clear of the house. The bears keep to the north, so the only wild things I have for company are the squirrels and the raccoons.

I like the solitude. At least that's what I tell myself.

I like living in the woods, far away from the demands of being part of the royal family. No one bothers me here, no one expects anything from me but a load of firewood. I have no responsibilities or duties other than at the animal reserve about half an hour north that I work at a few days a week. There's no strain of being told to smile, give my opinions, or show up dressed in a tuxedo to be fawned over.

I have my trees. I have my books, the homemade shelves filling one wall. I have friends in Wabush when I'm in need of conversation over a beer.

There are women if I'm in need of more than conversation, but I've never brought anyone here.

This is my space. My sanctuary, full of great works of literature and a whole pile of regrets.

The sunken living room is dark, but my eyes still land on the painting hanging on the wall: the back of a woman walking through the pine trees, wearing a short pink dress with flowers in her red hair, Kody by her side like he's escorting her. She walks along a thick carpet of rose petals that I laid down because Hettie preferred her feet to be bare, even in the forest.

It took bags and bags of petals to make the path from the house to the spot in the woods, and a lot of praying that the wind wouldn't pick up.

It's truly amazing what you can order on-line.

I commissioned the painting years ago because there were no pictures of that day and I wanted to remember what Hettie looked like when she walked toward me. The artist couldn't get her face perfect and it hurt too much for me to see it, so we went with the back view.

Her face haunts my dreams more than the accident, so I don't need to see her smile every time I walk into the room.

I still remember the way the corners of her mouth curved up, always ready for a smile, how her eyes would shine when she looked up at me. The tiny spatter of freckles across her cheeks. How it felt to have her hand folded into mine, her body pressed against me.

Missing Hettie has been a constant over the years. Some days it's bad. Some days it's bearable.

Today, after dreaming about the accident, it feels like a bad day. I make myself eggs and toast and then head out with my ax to stop myself from thinking about her.

Some days it works.

3

Hettie

Buck Marsden gives me a ride to Bo's.

He was the first person who I saw when I got off the plane, almost like he knew I was coming.

He didn't; I asked.

But he recognized me right away, even before I was off the tarmac. Now that I've seen more of the world than just Laandia, I realize just how small the Battle Harbour airport is. The one in Wabush is even smaller.

But it's the quickest way to get to Bo. Driving across Laandia would take at least a day when the weather is good, and that's only because one of King Magnus's first priorities when he took the throne was to create a trans-Laandia highway.

It's one country, but there's a lot of land to travel from Battle Harbour to Wabush. Hence, me being on the first flight out of Battle Harbour this morning.

With any luck, I can sort things out with Bo and be back on the four o'clock flight back home.

Not that Battle Harbour is home. It hasn't been for a long time.

Almost as long since I've seen Buck.

Bo used to bring me to Wabush as often as we could get away, to stay at the cabin in the middle of the woods. Buck Marsden and his wife Jean lived next door, looking after things for the royal family.

They were at my wedding.

So it wasn't a big surprise when Buck came up to me as I crossed the tarmac and took my small bag from me. He said he'd run me over to "the prince's."

He let me hug him, and didn't fuss when I held on too tight.

I hadn't thought much further than getting to Wabush but I knew I'd be able to find someone to give me a ride to Bo's. Buck is perfect because he doesn't say a word during the thirty-minute drive. And he agrees to let me off at the end of the road so I can walk in through the woods.

I need to figure out what I'm supposed to say to Bo.

Maybe being around the trees will help. I know the forest has always calmed Bo when he was upset. He'd disappear into the trees for hours at a time when he was thinking about something, ax over his shoulder and a pair of leather gloves tucked into his belt.

When I left Laandia eight years ago, I never really expected that it would be the last time I'd speak to Bo. I was angry and hurt, but I never thought that would be *it*. I waited for a letter or a phone call. I honestly expected him to come and find me.

He didn't.

Days turned to weeks, and then months. I knew Bo was dealing with the loss of his mother but I didn't think he'd forget about me. I was his wife, the woman he loved.

After the accident, it was like I never existed. And it hurt.

And because the hurt was so all-encompassing, I couldn't reach out to him.

Regrets? There are a few, but we were kids. Things have changed. Maybe Bo is a completely different person now. I know I am.

The path through the woods to the house is the same, however. The trees are still as dense, the leaves in the summer blocking out the heat of the sun. But now, in the middle of March, the dead leaves are covered by a crust of snow and only the pine trees offer a burst of colour. The sap is already flowing inside the trees, and tiny bubs will be showing soon, but on the outside, the forest is still winter bleak.

The path runs alongside the driveway of the cabin, veering off into the cleaning where I married Bo. If I kept walking past it, I'd get to Buck's place.

Bo wanted to get married in the woods because he loved the trees, and back then, I would agree to anything that made him happy. He escaped among the trees when he was upset, and retreat to the cool shade along the path when he was happy.

He kissed me in the woods, my back against the bark of a tree, leaves falling in my hair.

I hear the *thwock* of the ax hitting wood when I get close.

The trees might soothe Bo, but they do *nothing* for me. My stomach is nauseous with nerves and I still have no clue what to say to him. How do you begin a conversation after eight years?

Shoulders hunched with dread, I exhale loudly, my breath visible in the cold air, and I pause just before I step into the clearing.

This is where I got married.

It had been early October; the leaves were turning, but that day had been as warm as summer. It made it more magical, a surprise just for us. We planned it for the end of the day when the shadows lengthened, just before the air chilled. I had come from the cabin; Abigail and I had spent the afternoon giggling as she curled and braided and set flowers in my hair, turning me into a wood nymph worthy of Prince Bo.

There had been a path of rose petals, all colours, soft against my bare feet. I slowed my steps when I walked to meet him— not because of nerves or cold feet but because I wanted to savour every single moment of this day.

Bo and Spencer had hung strings of fairy lights among the lower branches, soft sparkling white lights that suddenly turned blue as the justice of the peace greeted us, and then green. Bo had been so flustered that I had to kiss him right then, before we were even declared husband and wife because I was so happy.

It seems like a lifetime ago. It seems like it happened to another person—another Hettie who stumbled into a fairy tale and got to have her happy ever after with the prince.

That obviously didn't happen.

I step into the clearing, wiping all thoughts of that October day out of my mind. Not that I have to try very hard because once I see Bo, all conscious thoughts vanish because Bo...

Bo is...

He's...

My inhale is shaky and after that I think I forget to breathe at all.

Bo holds the ax over his head and swings it down to neatly split the log. It used to mesmerize me when I watched him dismantle a tree, the sound of the ax, the crack of wood surprisingly soothing.

Despite the cold air, he's only wearing a long-sleeve T-shirt that clings to his arms and chest like it was smoothed on by an admiring female.

Arms and chest that seem... different... than when I last saw him in person.

Bo was always muscular—he was the first of the four princes to be named Sexiest Man—but he seems to have grown. Filled out.

Become more manly.

Very... manly.

And I drink him in like I'm in desperate need of water.

I have seen pictures of the prince, and for a while, I followed his lumberjack career as he travelled the world with his ax to compete in events like log chopping and speed climbing.

Watching the man climb a tree like some kind of oversized monkey is a lot sexier than it should be.

What I've seen of Bo in the last eight years didn't look real. He's beautiful and muscular, but it was like he was the Prince Charming of a fairy tale. One that liked to chop wood.

Not like the man I had been hopelessly in love with.

He doesn't see me and I stand in the shadow of the trees watching him, trying to come up with what to say. He splits log after log, the damp patches on his shirt the only evidence he's worked up a sweat.

He's wearing a black beanie on his head—could it be the same one he used to wear?

But there are other differences.

The beard is thicker, hair curling under his hat. The furrow between his eyes that appeared when he had a lot on his mind is more pronounced. What is he trying to forget about?

The bark of a dog jerks me out of my observation and for a moment I'm afraid, but then I recognize him and my heart swells.

"Kody!" I cry before I stop myself.

Bo whirls around as Kody thunders past him. I crouch, hands outstretched, focused on the dog. Kody bounces around me, and I swear he's smiling. I pat him everywhere I can reach until he calms for a moment and I can throw my arms around his neck.

He's thicker around the middle, with more white than black on his nose, but it's still Kody.

If this is what it feels like to be welcomed by a dog—

This is such a bad idea

But the thought of what's waiting for me back home urges me forward.

"Hettie?"

And with that one word, I know I'm not about to get the same reaction from Bo that I did from Kody.

Bo sounds choked, like there's something caught in his throat, and he coughs to clear it. "Are you...here?"

I sink my cold hands into the ruff of fur around Kody's neck because I'm suddenly so afraid to face Bo.

Taking a deep, albeit shaky breath, I finally stand up, eyes beginning to sting. I keep a hand on Kody for courage. "Hi," I whisper.

"Hi?" Bo carefully props his ax against a log and takes a step toward me. And stops. "You walk out of the woods like you're some kind of dream, and all you can say is *hi*?"

He is six feet away from me. After years of being a country apart, I don't know how to deal with his closeness. I can only stare and do my best not to rush into his arms.

That would be very bad. "What do you want me to say—?" I manage.

"You could start with what the hell you're doing here?"

It's like a slap. The heat of his words sends a cold shiver through me and I have to swallow around the lump in my throat.

He's angry.

I should be the angry one. I'm the one who has been ignored for years.

"Bo—"

"Where did you come from? Why didn't you call? Why didn't you tell me you were coming? Why are you here, Hettie?"

Bo has always been the quiet brother, the one who watches every word he says.

No one would know it from the questions he's peppering me with, and with each one he comes a step forward.

I take a step back into the trees. "I want a divorce."

Bo stares, his blue eyes studying me like I'm one of his precious books. Then his gaze closed like he doesn't know me. Then—

"No."

4

Bo

HETTIE IS HERE. HERE. She's here. *Here.*

I have to keep repeating the words in my head like I need to tell myself to keep breathing.

She shows up like a fictional character come to life. Because it's been so long since I've seen her that some days, I have to convince myself I didn't dream it all.

But why would I dream about the worst things that have ever happened to me? That would be a nightmare.

She looks different—longer hair, darker red and swirling around her head because she refuses to wear a hat. A coat I don't recognize. It might be warm enough for the West Coast, but she'll freeze here.

She's lost some of the softness in her face, turning her from a teenager to a woman.

But her eyes are the same, the mix of green and brown, and the quirk of her lips that makes her look like she's always on the brink of a smile.

She's here, and she wants a divorce.

"No," I repeat and turn back to the house.

"Bo," she calls after me, still caught in the shadow of the tree. Kody runs back and forth between us, torn between his master and the woman who loved him since he was a puppy.

"Don't walk away from me!" There's an edge to her voice that's new—the Hettie I knew would never speak sharply to anyone.

"I'm getting you a warmer coat," I snap over my shoulder, still mid-stomp toward the house. "Or else come in inside before you freeze."

She must be cold. I'll make her tea.

Tea, like it's a normal visit. Like it's not a heart-attack-worthy shock that my wife, who I haven't seen in eight years, has just shown up to say hi.

Or wants to say more than a hello.

My mind always shifts to Hettie when I dream about the accident, so when she showed up out of nowhere, I'd been already thinking about her. Thinking hard, the way no manual labour can wipe from my mind.

She says she wants a divorce. I don't blame her.

But no.

Hettie follows me reluctantly, a far cry from an over-excited Kody. I let them both in the house and kick the chew rope toward the dog to distract him as I toe off my boots. "How did you get here?"

I don't look at her as I head to the kitchen area to fill the kettle but I can hear as she takes off her boots, says something in a low voice to Kody.

She's in my house. *Our* house—the one I planned to build for us.

I push down all of my feelings, and there's a lot of them. I push them all down and fill the kettle like it's a normal day and Jean's come over with cookies.

I can tell she's in the kitchen because she steps on the floorboard that I haven't gotten around to fix, and also because of her scent. Sweet, like spring blossoms. Different from what she used to smell like.

I sound like some sort of dog able to sense her through scent and hearing.

"I flew," she says, and my hand tightens on the handle of the kettle at the sound of her voice. That sweet, soft voice; always cheerful, always understanding.

Hettie is here. She's in my kitchen. She wants a *divorce.*

"I took a plane," she adds. "Two planes, actually, since you can't fly directly from Victoria to Battle Harbour. And then I took another plane here."

That finally makes me look at her. The sarcasm is new.

"I meant, how did you get here from the airport?" My voice is strained with the effort of holding all of it in. I clench my fist before I reach for the mugs.

"I don't need tea," she says. "You don't even like it."

"How did you get here from the airport—and please don't say you walked?"

"Buck gave me a ride."

I stifle a groan. If Buck brought Hettie here, then Jean will know she's in town, and that means that she'll, first of all, tell everyone, and second, be over any minute now to find out everything.

I keep my back to Hettie, waiting for the kettle to boil and listening as she moves around my kitchen. I can't look at her—not yet. Not when all I want to do is grab her up into my arms and not let her go.

The urge is so strong that I grip the edge of the counter to stop myself.

"How are you?" Hettie asks. She's in the middle of the room, within touching distance.

I screw my eyes closed. I can't do this. "I like tea now."

"You—oh. I'm happy for you. What are—?"

"I think we're beyond basic small talk, don't you?" I ask in a gruff tone.

"You never liked it anyway." The smile in her voice almost breaks me but I steel my shoulders. I still can't look at her, because if she does turn out to be a dream, or some figment of my imagination brought about by being alone all the time, I don't want her to vanish.

"Talk to me," Hettie orders. Before, she would ask, plead. She would almost beg for me to share my feelings with her. Now it's an order.

"There's nothing to say," I tell the cupboards.

"There's everything to say." My retort chokes in my throat. "Why didn't you come and get me, Bo?"

I finally turn to face her. I need to see her face for that question. "It's been eight years, Hettie, and that's what you want to know?"

Big hazel eyes stare up at me. There is strength there, more than I ever realized. And hurt.

I did that.

And her eyes also swim with tears. I did that too.

Hettie swallows but keeps her gaze trained on me. "I want to know a lot of things. I deserve to know. But I guess the first should be: why won't you divorce me?"

The kettle begins to whistle, like it wants no part of this conversation. "Not now, Hettie."

"Not now? Then when? It's been eight *years*, Bo. We had two days together, and it was perfect. And then we went back home, and it was like you became a different person."

"I didn't."

"You *did*. You treated our love like a dirty little secret, like it was nothing, even though I was wearing your ring. You told me it was a mistake, that you never should have done it. And then I left, and you pretended like I didn't exist." Hettie takes a step forward, eyes shining with tears. "I saw pictures of you, Bo, pictures of you with other women. So yes, I want a divorce."

There's a steeliness in her voice that wasn't there before. A toughness that reminds me of her sister, Mabel. Hettie was always the sweet one; she was soft, delicate.

I changed all that. It's all my fault. But still—

"No." It's almost a groan.

Because what else am I supposed to say?

Two steps and she's right there, her fist raised against my chest like she wants to pound on it. Instead, she rests it over my heart. "If you don't want me, let me go," Hettie whispers, her voice a mix of sadness and longing.

I cover her hand with mine, as the kettle continues to scream a protest. "When did I ever say I didn't want you?"

5

Hettie

THERE'S A RAWNESS TO Bo's words that makes me lean into him. My hand is already on his chest, and the way his is covering mine—strong and callused, but tender.

The way he's looking down at me is like an ax sliding down the old break in my heart, splitting it open like one of Bo's logs.

"Bo," I plead in a tiny voice.

He breathes my name. "Hettie."

And then my arms are around his waist, and his arms are cradling me and I'm clutching him as tightly as I've ever held anyone.

It's a moment, and it's *good,* despite the fatal crack in my heart.

Suddenly he lets go, opening a gaping, cold space between us—and unzips my coat— pushing it off my shoulders. I shrug out of the sleeves, letting my jacket fall onto the floor behind me, desperate to be back in his arms.

His hands are on my back, in my hair, moving like he's trying to convince himself that I'm real.

I know what he's doing because I'm doing the same thing. The soft cotton of his shirt, damp and warm as it hugs the strong muscles in his back. The waistband of his jeans...

On the flight here, I told myself not to hug him. There would be no physical contact. There didn't need to be any touching. We would communicate as adults, like the friends we used to be, only without the affection, because that could lead to touching.

I promised myself I'd keep my distance but now, somehow, my cheek is pressed against his shirt, and all I smell is Bo—old leather and pine, and yes, sweat, because cutting wood does cause perspiration.

But I don't care because it smells like Bo. I breathe deep and tighten my arms around his waist, my hands fisting in the back of his shirt.

Kody nudges my knee with his chew toy, wanting attention.

Or telling me he likes what he sees. That it's about time.

That's when the heat in my eyes and lump in my throat gets to be too much and a sob escapes.

"Hettie... Hettie, don't," Bo begs as the tears begin to fall. He always hated to see me cry. The memory of this makes me choke back a laugh, which makes me cry harder, because we've missed so many laughs.

We've missed so much of everything.

Long minutes pass, Bo holding me as I cry, the kettle whistling as it boils. The sound becomes too much for the dog's sensitive ears, and Kody lets out a sharp yip of protest.

I pull back, wiping my cheeks and wishing for a tissue. "It's good to see you," I manage, my throat thick with tears.

Bo pulls the kettle off the burner and turns it off before handing me a sheet of paper towel. "Yeah."

I draw in a shaky breath. "I'm glad Kody... He hasn't changed." I wipe my eyes and do my best to control the sobs. "And Buck."

"No."

"This place has." I look around in an attempt to settle myself.

The cabin was once one room with a basic kitchen in one corner and a bed pushed into the other. Bo's family called it the hunting lodge, and maybe it was, but it always seemed to me that the little building in the middle of the Wabush Forest would have been perfect for a rendezvous with someone connected to the royal family.

I have no idea if Bo's ancestors used it for that; I'm certain his father never did.

I have a flash of memory of lying in the old bed with him, his body cocooned around me.

The first time Bo brought me here, for our first time, I couldn't help but think of other young lovers wrapped in each other in front of the fire.

It's different now.

The bed is gone.

Bo has his back to me as he makes tea, so I take the opportunity to look around. The kitchen is a new addition, still sparse but much bigger. The living room looks like a man cave with dark walls covered in shelves, and leather couches, and a huge flat-screen television mounted on the wall. There's a hallway where the bed used to be, possibly leading to bedrooms.

The fireplace has been expanded, enlarged, so big I could stand upright in it.

It's all very different now.

"I added on," Bo says needlessly, appearing with two mugs of tea. "Buck helped."

"You've got lots of room now. Do they come and stay with you?"

They being his brothers and sister.

"Sometimes." He brings the mugs to the coffee table, and I follow him, taking a seat on the far side of a couch with a full cushion between us. It's a large, long couch, because Bo is a big man. "But not for a while," he adds. "They're busy."

He's too far from me. Before, when we sat together, it was always hip to hip, me leaning against him. Bo was never fond of public displays of affection, but in private, he never stopped touching me—his fingers in my hair, his hand on my knee, my shoulder, splayed against my stomach. He was always kissing me, those lips—

That line of thought comes to a screeching halt because I'm not here to fall back into the memories of kissing Bo.

They haunted me for long enough.

"I can't believe Kalle is getting married." I sound remarkably chipper for someone whose eyes are still red and nose clogged from crying. "I watched the coverage of Odin's wedding—"

"You did?"

I only nod because I'm not about to confess to how I searched through the videos and pictures of the wedding looking for any sight of Bo. "Is Lady Camille nice?"

"She's great."

"He gave up his spot in the line of succession," I say even though Bo must be very aware of the fact. "That makes you—"

That makes Bo the next in line for the throne, after oldest brother Kalle. "Yeah. Not going to happen," he says in a gruff voice, picking up his mug of tea.

"I always thought it would be Odin." Neither Kalle nor Bo had ever expressed an interest in being king, and I—like most of Laandia—expected Prince Kalle to eventually step down and allow Odin to become the next king. It still would have pushed Bo forward, but Odin's children would have taken care of that. Now it's only Kalle standing in the way of Bo becoming the next king.

"So did everybody." Bo cups his mug in his hands, steam curling up. I don't want to think about those hands, because that brings more flashes of memory, and they hurt.

"I'm glad Kalle is going to end up with Edie," I manage.

"He didn't really have a choice. They belong together."

I reach for my cup. "Some said we did." The words just pop out and I wish I could stuff them back in. Along with the no-hugging rule I made for myself—and already broke—there was the strict no-talking-about-the-past vow.

Two for two already. I'm clearly not good at this.

"Why now?" His voice is choked, sounding angry, hurt, and confused. "Why are you here?"

He's probably all of those things. Me showing up out of the blue like this, literally walking out of the woods, must be...

I should have warned him. I should have given him time to process. I had weeks to plan, to tell myself this was the right thing to do. That I needed to end it. Shut the door. Closure. Move on.

Whatever it can be called. I needed to see Bo and finally talk to him after so many years.

"It's not because of the succession thing," I tell him quickly.

He pauses, looks over the rim of his cup at me. "I never thought it was."

I nod. I don't know how to tell him, because I know it's going to hurt.

Or maybe it won't. It has been eight years of no contact, so it's likely Bo has gotten over me long ago, met someone else, and is looking to move on with his life. Maybe this is a blessing for him, too.

"I met someone."

Bo jerks like I've kicked him, and tea splashes over the rim and onto his wrist. "Oh—hot! Are you okay?" I gasp.

He swipes at it with his sleeve. "It's fine."

"But you could burn—"

"Who?" he demands. Taking a breath, he sets the cup down. "Who is he?" he asks, softening his tone. His blue-eyed gaze meets mine, and yes, I falter.

There has never been another man since Bo. There has only been strong, solid Bo, who looked at me with so much love that he made me believe in happy endings. I trusted him completely because I knew he'd never hurt me.

Only he did. He broke my heart, and now I'm here, telling him about someone else.

"A man... He's from Victoria. Timothy." I draw in a shaky breath. "He's a good man. He says he'll take care of... me." It hurts to look at Bo, the way his jaw flexes, his fingers dig into his knee, but I can't turn away.

"You don't *say* you'll do that, you just do it," he says roughly.

You didn't. But I don't say that. I can't. Bo is... He's still wounded. If I had to guess, I'd say he's not over me, not by a long shot. I think deep down I've known that he wouldn't be. He's vulnerable, but pretending not to be. Like a branch that's beginning to rot from the inside as the bark gets tougher and thicker to protect it.

I have no idea if that actually happens to trees, but I can see it's how it is for Bo. "He's a good man," I repeat. "And it's been a long time."

"That's what you've been doing then? Meeting other people? Getting over me?"

No. I've tried to convince myself that was what I wanted—to forget Bo, to stop feeling all the feelings. To push away the hurt and disappointment and *anger*—yes, I am still angry with him, with myself, with the circumstances that brought us here, that I still don't understand.

"I've never gotten over you," I whisper into my tea. "But I had to move on."

"You never came home. You never let me explain."

"What would you have said?"

There's no response. Bo could have tried to explain before I left, while I was gone, but he didn't. He never said anything other than *mistake, shouldn't have happened* and *can't tell anyone.* He didn't stop his wife of less than two weeks, the person he promised to love and cherish for the rest of his life, from moving to another country.

Alone. Without him.

I wonder if he even understands it now. I know I don't.

I shrug into his silence. I have versions of what I might have said to Bo, dreamt up during sleepless nights when all I wanted was to see him one more time but I can't find the words now.

"You never came home," he repeats.

"Mabel came to visit," I offer, like he might have been worried about me being alone.

Maybe he was. I have no idea because I never heard *one word* from Bo once I left.

"I was with Abigail and my grandfather. Everyone else..." I don't have to explain about my family. I've never had to with Bo.

We both knew that was a big part of the reason I was able to leave.

"It would have been too hard," I add. "I didn't want to see you if we..." If we couldn't be together, I'm thinking.

Is he thinking the same thing? "Maybe we could have."

Could have what? There only would have been one possibility. If I had come back, or if I'd never left in the first place, I know where I'd be right now.

Not having this conversation, that's for sure. "You can't say that now," I whisper. "That's not fair."

"Nothing about this is fair."

He's got a point there. As much as I blame Bo for not coming to find me, for telling me the marriage was a mistake, I had been the one who got on the plane headed to British Columbia.

I'm the one who ultimately left. I could have stayed and fought for him, rather than cry through the entire flight.

There's a lot of things I can be blamed for too.

And I know Bo will blame me, as soon as it all comes out. "Bo... there's something I need to tell you."

"Yeah. You met someone." I've never heard him so bitter, so full of remorse. "You said that."

"No, it's…" I gulp my tea, scalding my mouth as I hunt for my courage. How do I do this? What do I say? Should I blurt it out and take the repercussions as they fall? Gently ease into it?

Bo turns to me, and looking into those blue eyes makes me lose my nerve. I can't find the words. I pull my bag toward me, find my phone. With my heart stuttering like an old car backfiring, I scroll through my pictures.

I hand my phone to him. "This is Tema."

He has to know. The smile… the reddish hair. Those eyes.

But he looks at me with confusion. "Who? What is this?"

"Bo, she's…" There's a moment of terror because how can I tell him? How could I have *not* told him?

"She's our daughter."

6

Ba

WHEN I WAS SEVENTEEN, I spent a summer working on a fishing boat. We all did, even Lyra. I remember this one time when we were out collecting the catch, somewhere between Laandia and the west coast of Scotland, and trying to make it back to the harbour before a storm hit.

I had been on deck, watching the dark storm clouds chasing us into land. The waves had already been so big that I couldn't keep my balance. Stumbling side to side, I kept trying to grab something to steady myself because the deck just wouldn't stop moving and the storm wouldn't stop knocking me down.

This moment feels like that. A lot like that.

I can only stare at Hettie, willing myself to understand what she just told me. "What did you just say?"

Hettie draws in a shaky breath and then another. She's on the verge of tears again.

For once, I don't care.

"I had a baby," she whispers.

Do I hear her correctly? Did she really say baby? As in...

I glance at the screen in my hand. She's—

She's Lyra when she was little.

Whoever that child is, she's a mixture of Lyra and Mabel and Hettie, and I think that's my nose. She's...

Mine?

Things start to spin. If I hadn't set down the cup after I burnt myself—there's a red patch on my wrist from the hot water—I'd have to now because I don't trust myself to hold anything at this moment. "Why?"

"Why did I have our child?" Hettie asks with confusion.

Our child. "Why didn't you tell me?"

Hettie stiffens, and Kody raises his head. I didn't mean to shout—or maybe I did because this deserves a shout. This deserves a roar.

Hettie jumps to her feet. We rarely argued, but I can still tell when someone is on the defensive.

There better be a good reason for her to try and defend herself.

"You sent me away."

That's not a good reason. "You left," I correct.

"Only because I had no choice. You might have married me, Bo, but you never wanted me to be a part of your life. You made me a part of your family that you hated being a part of."

"I don't hate my family."

"You hate being a prince. You told me that so many times. And yet you made me a part of your life, then pushed me away because you were afraid."

"I didn't want you to get hurt."

"But *you* hurt me. You destroyed me, Bo. You cracked open my heart—you made me love you even though I had no intention of letting myself fall for you—and then you *stomped* on it. You let me leave."

I flinch at the pain in her voice before I manage to steel myself. "She's a princess," I remind her with another glance at the picture.

"No, she's not."

"Yes, she is. Any child of mine is born royal. A princess. She's—my god, she's third in line to the throne."

Hettie looks at me with a steady gaze. She knows this and still kept it from me. Kept it from my family.

I stand up. I need to move. I have to be away from Hettie even as everything in my heart wants, *needs* her close to me. I want to celebrate her stepping back into my life at the same time I'm shaking with anger and confusion.

Our child.

It's been eight years.

I stare at the screen, not hearing what Hettie is trying to say to me. There's no point listening to her excuses, because regardless of her reasons, it doesn't change the fact that this little girl is mine. *Ours.*

"I need to meet her," I insist, cutting off Hettie mid-excuse. "And we need to tell my father."

She smells good.

Hettie smells good, and she looks great. She's wearing a pair of those leggings that hug everywhere, and a white sweater that hits at the waist. Her hair is longer and her eyes seem bigger with dark circles of sleeplessness.

I wish I could focus on that instead of the other... stuff.

Divorce and other men and... a child. My daughter.

Our daughter.

It's a lot.

I fell in love with Hettie Crow when I was fifteen. She sat in front of me in math class, which I almost failed because I kept staring at the back of her head, willing her to turn around and smile at me.

It took so long to get her to smile at me, and it finally happened in English class when I had the balls to stand in the front of the class and read a stupid poem aloud. Six months later, after I finally got to kiss her, I told her I wrote the poem about her.

I married her because after almost four years together, she still wouldn't stop talking about how she didn't deserve me. Her family... her family isn't the best but I never cared. I only wanted Hettie. Marrying her was the only way I could think of showing her that her family didn't matter to me. She mattered, and I loved her and I wanted to make her *mine*. I wanted us to be together forever.

I convinced her to marry me, forgetting for a few blissful days that I was also Prince Bowden of Laandia, with duties and responsibilities and a family who ruled a country.

It was good until it wasn't.

An hour after telling me that I have a child, Hettie is back at the airport. But this time I'm with her.

I leave Kody with Jean and Buck and we take my plane back to Battle Harbour.

I don't say much for the first half of the flight. Maybe she does, but I can't comprehend what she's saying. Something about reading and loving math and looking at the stars.

To be honest, I haven't understood much after I heard "our daughter." I saw the picture of her—Tema—saw her smile that is pure Lyra, and her eyes that are greener than Hettie's hazel but still look exactly like Hettie's sister Mabel's in shape and size.

The realization that I have a daughter—and she's in Battle Harbour, staying with Abigail and her family—is making me slightly nauseous. I keep taking deep breaths, which makes Hettie keep looking over, but I don't meet her eyes because then she'll start talking and then...

She didn't tell me. Hettie found out she was pregnant after she left and never told me. She had a baby and didn't think I deserved to know. That much I understand. She's raised our child while I was here, completely ignorant of the fact that I had a daughter.

These things running through my mind are why I tune out Hettie. Because I want to know *everything*, but not yet.

Hettie must know I'm having trouble with this because she eventually falls quiet during the three-and-a-half-hour flight back to Battle Harbour.

I've made the trip so many times I practically do it on auto-pilot, but I still keep my focus on the controls and the sky around us so I don't go completely ballistic on Hettie.

We have a daughter and she never told me.

It's not until the familiar rocky hills come into view that my stomach calms and I realize that Hettie is shivering beside me. The cockpit of the Cessna is cold enough that I left my bulky jacket and toque on, but Hettie only has her thin coat to wear.

I pull off the hat and thrust it at her. "Here. You're cold."

"Because it's frigid in here." Her lips are a faint tinge of blue and she doesn't protest as she tugs my hat over her ears.

"Do you want my coat? I can—"

"No, we're almost back. Just fly the plane." She sounds irritated. Why does she get to be irritated?

And then I forget it all as Hettie pulls her hair out of her coat, hanging long and reddish-brown over her chest, and begins to braid it.

She would always fidget with it when she was nervous. When she was writing exams in class, her fingers would tangle in the long strands without realizing it. The first time I took her for fish and chips, she put her hair up and took it down seven times.

I counted.

It's funny, the things you remember about a person. With Hettie, I have perfect recall about the way her eyes light up when she laughs. The scent of her perfume. The feel of her hair between my fingers—thick and silky, but a little coarser than mine.

I used to play with her hair whenever I got a chance. She taught me how to braid it a few times, but my fingers were too thick and clumsy and only resulted in a nest of tangles.

I remember all of those things and more, but I won't remember the touch of her lips against mine.

I'm pretty sure I tuned that out so it wouldn't play on repeat in my head.

"Your hair. It's... longer," I manage. Conversation might be better than me raking through my memories to dredge up one of me kissing her.

"I don't have much time to get it cut." She finishes with the first braid and a hair tie appears from somewhere before she starts on the second.

"No. I like it." Deep breath because my stomach is starting to roil again. "What do you do… there?" Hettie was the focus of my life for years and now I don't know how she spends her days. How she provides for our daughter.

I could have found this out years ago, with a few phone calls, but I never bothered. I could have had one of the castle security team, or even Spencer track Hettie, or Abigail, and I would know all of this and wouldn't have to ask like I'm making small talk with a stranger.

But I didn't bother because Hettie left me, right when I needed her most.

I made her leave, the voice inside me corrects.

"I work in a real estate office," Hettie says. "It's a good job. I'm happy there."

"You wanted to work in a library," I remind her.

"They didn't pay as well."

The fact that Hettie spent the past eight years alone raising our daughter eats at me, like squirrels destroying a pumpkin. Why did I never track her down? "They treat you okay?"

I hear her sharp inhale. "Yes."

"And Tema? What does… She's in school?" I silently thank her for not laughing at the inane question. Of course, she would be in school. She's seven-years-old, so that means she'd be in… "What grade is she in?"

"Grade Two. She loves reading and math. She takes after you with the books. I swear, she could bankrupt me for all the books she wants. Thankfully, we have a library close by."

"Do you want money? Does she need things?" Hettie has been providing everything for our daughter when I was sitting back in Laandia buying a *plane* and renovating the cabin. I could have been helping.

"We've managed. Me and Abigail."

"I could have helped." Now it's my turn to sound irritated.

"Bo—"

"What else does she like?"

This time Hettie's inhale is shaky, her fingers rebraiding her hair. "We tried dancing, but she'd rather fool around. She plays soccer. Baseball. She really likes that. I thought—"

"Kalle played baseball."

"So did you," she reminds me softly.

"Do people know you're married?" I demand.

She turns to the window, watching the snow-covered hills and tall pine trees reaching for the sky. "I don't broadcast it, no." Before I can think of how to respond—because what do you say to that?—Hettie reaches into her coat and, fumbling at her collar, pulls out a chain.

She shows me the ring on the end of the chain.

The ring in a simple gold twist, much like the braids in her hair. I have a plain gold band back at the castle.

It hurts too much to wear it. If I had it around my neck, I think it might burn me.

There was no time for me to find the perfect engagement ring for her. There was the proposal and then there was the wedding. Besides, Hettie told me she didn't want an engagement ring.

I think that was probably a lie.

We're silent as I fly over the familiar landscape because I really don't know what to say.

"Why?" I finally break down and demand as the top turret of the castle comes into view.

"Why what, exactly?" Hettie counters.

"Why didn't you tell me?"

Hettie sighs, a long, drawn-out breath that says so much more than she ever could. "Bo, you told me it was a mistake for us to get married. You didn't want to tell your family. You were afraid of their reaction and what the press would say about me and my family. You finally realized what I'd been telling you for years—I didn't deserve you. Hettie Crow should not be married to one of the royal family. It was insane to think we should be together."

"It wasn't insane."

"It was. The press would have eaten me alive. My family—You would have been ridiculed."

"You don't know what would have happened," I accuse. "You don't understand."

"I know I wanted to be with you," Hettie says quietly. "But you didn't want that."

"You don't understand," I repeat, fighting the controls as a gust of wind comes out of nowhere.

Much like this whole conversation.

"I don't," she admits, turning to the window.

I've wanted to tell her the truth for *years*. I've wanted to tell her everything, try to make her understand, but I couldn't.

I still don't know if I'll be able to say the words.

"I was willing to stick it out for you," she says, the steeliness back in her tone. "If you had wanted me. If you had been willing to tell your family about me. But you wouldn't, so how was I to know what you would have done if I'd told you about Tema?"

"I told my mother."

There they are. I hear myself say the words but I don't recognize my voice. I have never told anyone about my conversation with my mother.

Hettie gasps. "You did? But—when?"

I check the instruments as I prepare for the descent. I leave my truck at the airport so no one will need to know I'm back until I'm ready to tell them.

I do everything I can to postpone telling Hettie the truth.

I wait until the plane touches down; after I taxi to the private hangar at the end of the tarmac. I turn the engines off, and still, Hettie is sitting beside me, waiting for me to continue.

"When did you tell her?" she demands.

"I told her—and she died," I confess, my voice raw and rough.

I see the timeline flash across her mind, remembering the date of the wedding, the day when we came back to Battle Harbour full of nervous excitement. I had headed straight to the castle and promised to call for her as soon as I'd told them.

I had wanted her with me, but she refused, said it was something I needed to do alone.

Maybe if she had been with me...

I see the moment she puts the timeline together with my mother's accident. "Bo." Hettie shakes her head, hazel eyes wide with sympathy. "No."

I turn away. "I went to the castle and told her that I married you. And then she left to pick up Lyra and got in the accident. I told her, and then she died. She died because of me."

There's a ticking in the cockpit as Hettie processes my words. I see her eyes as she realizes I basically killed the queen of Laandia. My mother. What everyone would believe if I told them.

"You can't know that—" Even her protest is weak because she knows it's the truth.

"But I do," I cut in. "I do know that. I'm the reason my mother died."

7

Hettie

Bo's admission sucks the breath out of me in a whoosh. He thinks—he told her—the queen died...

It's as if the clouds suddenly part and the sun shines straight into my eyes, blinding me.

It all makes sense now.

The flight back to Battle Harbour had been painful, and not only because the cockpit is small, and Bo, with his broad shoulders spilling out of the seat, the harness barely containing him, takes up so much space. The memories of other flights with him haunt me; of Bo darting in and out of the clouds, of pointing out a pod of whales when we were over the Atlantic, of putting my hands on the controls and letting me fly for a few, glorious moments.

It's hard being trapped with him for more reasons than that: we're going back for him to meet Tema.

I never really planned for that, because I was never sure it would happen.

I wasn't thinking of our time together; I left those memories back at the cabin because it was too much, but now, to find out that he told his mother, and just before she died...

It explains so much.

The day when he met me behind the high school, I thought he was going to bring me to the castle. I had a bag packed. I told Mabel I wasn't coming home.

I didn't bother saying anything to my father or my brothers.

Bo had been happy; we had been in love, planning our future. Before the wedding, he had practiced with me how he would tell his parents and there had been a nervous giddiness when he left me the day we came back from Wabush. He would tell his parents by himself, and then he would come and get me and introduce us.

"They'll love you," he had promised.

"They won't love my family," I argued. It had been my biggest fear—my dysfunctional family would rob me of this chance to be happy.

"You are not your family."

But he never came to get me. The accident happened, and I thought he didn't have the chance to talk to them.

I never imagined that for years, Bo had been blaming himself for Queen Selene's death.

"Let's go," Bo says gruffly now, leaning over to pop the handle on my door. "Careful when you climb down."

"We have to talk about this," I protest as the door swings open. Cold air rushes into the cockpit.

"There's nothing to talk about." Bo's tone is as icy as the wind but I won't let that deter me. It's not right that—

"But, Bo, there *is*. You can't think—"

"Did you tell Abigail we're coming to see Tema?"

The abrupt veer into Tema territory has my thoughts come to a screeching halt. "Tema?"

"I'm meeting her. Now."

This is more urgent than sorting out the brainwash that Bo has been doing to himself for all these years. "You can't," I tell him, my voice high-pitched with fear.

"Why not?" Bo has never been anything other than a gentle, considerate man, but there's none of that Bo left. Dealing with the guilt of his mother dying—at least the perceived guilt—is enough, but throw in a child that he never knew about might be too much.

I didn't think enough about what this would do to him. *Is* doing to him.

"You can, but you need to wait. I need to prepare her," I counter quickly. "She needs time."

"You don't think I deserve time? This is why I came back."

"Bo, she's *seven*. She's—" But it's the look in Bo's eyes that stops me. There's anger and confusion, but also fiery determination—the same determination I saw when he proposed to me.

When he told me he wanted to marry me, that he wanted a life with me, he looked like nothing was going to stop him. My protests, my arguments that it wasn't a good idea fell on deaf ears. I always thought it was because I didn't really want to protest, that I didn't really believe my arguments, but maybe Bo has more determination than anyone ever gave him credit for.

"Seven years, Hettie. I don't want to waste another minute of not knowing our daughter."

I can't hold out any longer. "Okay. Let's go."

Bo had always been quiet—introverted, great one-on-one or in small groups, but he hated crowds. I understand that because I'm the same way. Both of our families had been full of big personalities, and being with Bo meant I was never pushed into the background.

We met when we were fifteen; it took him over two years to convince me that a Crow could be the girlfriend of a prince of Laandia. My family is... The Crows are known around Laandia and not in a good way. The daughter of a woman who abandoned her family and a father who cared more about his boat and how much fish he caught never ended up with Prince Charming in any of the fairy tales I read.

It wasn't until I was almost twenty that Bo told me he always considered himself like Rapunzel, trapped in the tower and I was the princess who rescued him.

It was an interesting way to look at his life.

I don't remember when he first talked about getting married, but he talked about it like it was a done deal. I never really believed it would happen, mainly because I wanted it so much and I was brought up never to trust that you'll get what you want, unless you take it. But then there was the summer when Bo turned twenty-one, and still kept talking about it. Kalle was playing baseball then, and it was all the family could talk about, as well as Odin's historical projects and Gunnar starting to race cars.

Bo didn't feel like he had a place in his family and he talked about having his own family, with me.

And finally when the summer blended into the fall, I gave in. "Okay. When?"

Less than a week later we were married in a secret ceremony at the cabin in Wabush with only Spencer Laz, my best friend Abigail, and Jean and Buck Marsden in attendance.

Two days after that, we came back. And then the crash that killed Queen Selene happened and changed everything.

Bo changed. Gone was the sweet and funny guy who always told me about the books he was reading, and who loved to challenge me in chess to see who picked the next movie we would watch. Who taught me about trees and the animals who lived in them, and would borrow planes to go flying early in the morning to see the sun rise.

Who wielded an ax like one of his Viking ancestors; only he attacked trees rather than his enemies.

Bo was haunted by his mother's death; the entire family was. The royal family was close, much closer than my family. They were all grieving.

But it was something more with Bo. He never let me comfort him. He wouldn't see me, talk to me. For four whole days after the funeral, I couldn't get hold of him. This was my brand-new husband and I couldn't find him. The castle didn't know we were married, and no one would tell me anything. I was frantic.

When he finally called, I burst into tears. I raced to meet him, so I could hold him. Comfort him.

Love him.

But instead, he told me that marrying me had been a mistake.

Looking back, I can see he didn't mean it, that he was hurting and pushing everyone away, but at the time, it literally broke my heart. Unable to eat, too numb to cry, write a best-selling-song-heartbroken.

But just like Bo, I didn't show him what I was really feeling because deep down, I agreed with him. I loved Bo more than anyone, but I couldn't see how we would work. And if he didn't believe in us...

I knew I needed to leave because it hurt too much to be around Bo. I picked the furthest spot to get away from him, following my grandfather to the west coast of Canada. Abigail came with me—my best friend since birth. We moved to Victoria, British Columbia, found an apartment, jobs, and I tried to move on from Bo.

And then I found out I was carrying his baby.

That was a very bad six months.

I wanted to tell Bo every single day, but I hadn't heard a word from him. Radio silence. Not even a text, or a DM, or a phone call. It was as if he had totally blanked out my existence.

The hurt was almost unbearable but it strengthened me—if Bo didn't want me, then he wouldn't want our child.

There was a bad moment when I was in labour, crying because I wanted Bo there, and Abigail held out my phone to call him but then the baby was coming and the phone was forgotten.

Holding Tema in my arms made everything better.

It was difficult, being a twenty-one-year-old single mother, but with Abigail's help, I managed. I had my grandfather as well, and Abigail's parents came to visit as often as they could. Mabel came twice, my brother Tommy stopped in once when he was in Vancouver, and that was my family. That was my daughter's family.

I told myself that was enough.

I have a wonderful little girl who I love more than anyone in the world, and I have kept her from knowing her father because he broke my heart. I convinced myself it was best for her, but the silence thickens as Bo drives us from the airport to the Lockes' house, and the guilt of keeping him from her almost makes me vomit. I knew it was wrong, but I did it anyway.

Watching Bo's face, watching the emotions pass over it—the clench of his jaw, the flutter of his eyes when tears threaten—I have never felt like such a horrible person.

How could I have never told Bo that he had a child?

How can I ever make this up to him?

8

Bo

THE ACCIDENT THAT KILLED my mother, Queen Selene of Laandia, happened two days after I secretly married Hettie.

After I confessed to what Hettie and I had done, my mother went to pick up Lyra.

I can't blame Lyra for this; we all hated when a castle driver came to get us from an activity or friend's house, Lyra most of all. She was having friend issues back then and didn't want any more unwanted attention.

Mom's death did damage to all of us, but none more than Lyra.

But the fact was I told Mom I was married; she got in a car and drove to Eliza Liu's house to get my sister, after which she got into an accident and she died.

It doesn't take a rocket scientist to figure out the accident was my fault. She was upset when she left, probably distracted. If I hadn't told her, she would still be alive today.

If I hadn't married Hettie, she'd be fine.

If I hadn't married Hettie, I wouldn't be finding out that I have a daughter, years after she was born.

I have a daughter.

Those words swirl around my brain like a tornado, touching down every so often to give me such a severe jolt that I tighten my hands on the steering wheel of my old truck.

I have a daughter. I'm going to meet her.

Hettie has been quiet but I feel her watching me. I'm not sure yet what to say to her about all this. What I want to say could very well involve shouting and anger and saying things I don't mean and might not even intend to say. So many of my emotions are connected to Hettie Crow and I've let them tangle too long so that the knot is too tight to be unraveled.

I don't want to untangle them because what do I do then? Figure out how I feel about her, only for her to leave again? What good would that do?

"What did you tell her about me?" I don't think to ask until we're in the car on the way to Abigail's parents' place. I hate the thought of Hettie leaving our daughter to come and talk to me. I wish she had told me she was in town and I would have flown home and met her.

But I know how close she and Abigail have always been. She left home with Hettie, with the Lockes' full support.

I know that because a month or so after they left, I ran into Mrs. Locke in town and had to endure a lecture about how I forced Hettie to leave. She was always more of a mother to her than Hettie's own.

They didn't know we had married, just that my actions had broken us up. As far as I know, only two people still in Battle Harbour know that Hettie is legally my wife—Spencer and Mabel Crow.

I'm going to have to tell my family. Not looking forward to that.

"I told her your family was important, and that you had a lot of responsibilities that kept you away," Hettie says carefully. "That you might not be around, but that didn't mean you didn't love her."

"So you forgot to mention to her that you never even told me that I had a daughter." I can't keep the sarcasm from my voice. It's not a good look for me.

"No, I didn't tell her that. She's seven. She wouldn't understand."

"You don't know that. I've heard kids are resilient."

"Bo..."

Hettie sounds guilty. She sounds... upset. But after eight years apart, I can't be sure of anything about Hettie now.

There is only silence until we pull up in front of the Lockes'. I was here so often when I was younger; the three of us spent a lot of time together and the family welcomed me as much as they did Hettie. Abigail was my friend too, and I missed her when she left.

I was also angry because she could be with Hettie and I wasn't.

I grip the wheel and stare at the house. The last time I was here, I was driving the same truck. It had been brand new and I had been so proud of it. Mr. Locke had come outside so I could show it off.

I have no idea what to say to him now. I have no idea what to say to my daughter.

How do you meet your own child after never knowing she existed?

"Are you all right?" Hettie asks hesitantly.

"Not really, no."

She sighs, and out of the corner of my eye, I see her hand move toward my fingers. It stops before she touches me.

It seems crazy that I'm still desperate for her to touch me.

"We don't have to do this now," she says gently. "You can take your time. In fact, it might be better—"

"Were you coming back to tell me?" I interrupt, voicing the thought that has been dancing around my brain like a merry-go-round. "If I had said I'd divorce you, would you have left without telling me about her?"

"No." Her reply is too quick. Even after all the years away, I can tell from her expression that's not the truth.

"You're lying," I say flatly.

"I don't know what I would have done," she confesses. "It's just... I don't know. I have to think of Tema."

I'm thinking of Tema, too, but I don't say that. It's only been hours but already she's important to me. There's a connection there, has been since I saw her picture. Maybe it's because she looks like a little Lyra, but I will not allow her to be hurt. I don't doubt Hettie is a good mother but she hasn't had the best example from her parents.

But I can't assume I would be any better.

What am I doing? Is this a good idea? I don't know this child—I don't know Hettie. I never would have believed she would have kept this from me. I knew she would move on, meet someone else but to hear her ask me for a divorce—? What will that do to Tema?

It'll do nothing because she doesn't even know me.

The cab of the truck seems too small, too close to be having this conversation. The console separates us, but it would be easy to take my hand off the steering wheel and touch Hettie's knee. Turn just a bit and cup her cheek. Reach out with both hands and draw her close.

I keep my hands firmly where I can see them. "Do you really want a divorce?" I ask, my voice rough like I haven't used it in a while.

Another sigh like she's the wronged party. Technically, she is… but so am I. "Did we even have a marriage?" she asks in a small voice. "I know it was real…"

"Justice of the peace. And it was… consummated."

I cannot think about how it was consummated. About how it felt to hold Hettie that last night, never dreaming it would be the last time. We planned our life together—

We made a baby that night. We conceived a child. I swallow the lump in my throat. "That's not what I'm asking. Are you really in love with this—what's his name?"

Timothy. She told me what his name is.

I hate that name.

"Timothy," Hettie says. I hate the way it slides over her tongue, like he matters to her.

I hate that he matters to her.

I hate that I let that happen even more.

"Yeah. Him."

"I care about him," she says carefully, like she's crossing a river by stepping on wet stones.

"That's not what I'm asking," I say again.

"Bo—we shouldn't talk about this now."

"Should we go back to why you didn't tell me about her, then?" I ask. I heave a deep breath. There's nothing to gain by arguing with her. It's only going to strip me of more time. "Tema. Where did that name come from?"

"There's a girl at the school where Abigail works. She talks about her a lot and I fell in love with the name."

"Is Abigail a teacher?" I ask, confused. I should know this. I should know all of this.

"Teacher's assistant. She wouldn't take the time to go to teacher's college."

I should know all of this. My knuckles turn white.

"Bo? Do you want to go inside?"

"I don't know how to do this," I admit. "I don't know what to say, how to be a dad."

"You don't have to be anything."

"I am her father." It comes out as a snarl, like when I try and take one of Kody's chew toys away from him.

"But Tema doesn't know that. You're a stranger to her, so you don't have to worry about doing dad stuff right away."

"Will I have to worry about it later? Are you taking her back? Is this the only time I have with her?"

Hettie closes her eyes. She may have changed, but I can still read her like a book.

She had no intention of telling me about her. She came to get a divorce, and then she'll take my daughter back to her life with this Timothy.

I'll be asking castle security to check up on him as soon as I can. In the meantime, if this is my only chance to meet her—

I open the car door and without waiting for Hettie, head across the lawn. My boots make dark imprints along the melting snow.

Abigail answers my knock, as Hettie hurries to catch up. "Bo," Abigail breathes, looking around for Hettie. "What are you—?"

"It's okay," Hettie tells her but Abigail doesn't move aside.

"Is this a good idea?" she demands. "It's not what we talked about, Het."

"I wasn't part of that conversation," I say. "I haven't been part of *any* conversation, so I think it's a great idea."

Abigail stands in the doorway, having a silent argument with Hettie. I'm not about to push past her or lay a hand on either of them to move aside, so I wait. Impatiently.

She looks different, not like the Abigail who had been my friend. The hair that had been a rainbow of colours over the years is back to basic black, cut short and sharp at her jaw. Her glasses are purple now, and there are more studs in her ears than when she left.

It's her eyes that are the most different: still bright green, but no longer full of laughter and adventure. She looks at me warily, coolly appraising me.

I've never not been welcome in this house. Or anywhere in Laandia.

Finally, Abigail moves aside and I step into the house.

At least the house looks the same and I half expect Mrs. Locke to greet me with a snack and questions about my family.

But it's only Abigail to greet me... and the sounds of girlish laughter.

"Bo..." Hettie puts a hand on my arm. "Let me first—"

"Do it now," I plead. "I can't wait any longer."

I think she's about to argue, but with a shake of her head to Abigail, she leads me down the hall to the living room at the back of the house.

It's like I've stepped back in time. The place still smells like apple candles and cookies. The pictures on the walls are the same—photos of Abigail and her brothers over the years, the family grouped together with big smiles and funny expressions.

Hettie is in a lot of the pictures.

I've been here countless times with Hettie, with Spencer. This was where we hung out; a safe space away from me being a prince and from Hettie's family.

I catch my breath before I step into the living room. Plants fill the windowsill, but I don't go there because out the window, I can see the castle in the distance. The couch is new, but the comfortable recliner where Ted Locke would sit and talk books with me is the same.

Hettie and I, along with Spencer, would sit with Abigail and her parents, crowding around the coffee table or the kitchen table, and play games—Abigail loved board games. There is still a shelf full of them behind the new couch. Scrabble and Monopoly, Risk and Ticket to Ride.

Twister in the basement the night Spencer brought beer. The silly Ouija board Hettie demanded we try and then got scared when the thing moved.

But I'm not here to play games. And I'm no longer seventeen.

The television is on. She—Tema—is sitting on the floor playing with LEGO. I don't make a sound. My heart stutters as Hettie lets me drink her in.

She's—she's beautiful.

Dark reddish hair caught up in an easy ponytail with frizzy curlicues surrounding her face. Pale pink Taylor Swift sweatshirt over bright purple leggings. Round cheeks in a heart-shaped face that is all Hettie.

She smiles at something on the TV, completely caught up with her life at the moment. A kids' show on television, toys to play with. Her tiny hands press the colourful blocks together.

She's mine? It doesn't seem possible. This tiny person came to be because I loved Hettie, loved her so much that we made a baby.

That I knew nothing about.

I make a noise deep in my throat, full of pain and fear and anger—why didn't she tell me? How could Hettie keep her from me?

What am I about to do to her life? How can I just show up and tell her I'm her father?

How do I even be a father to her?

Hettie puts her hand on my arm, which is a good thing because I was just about to bolt. This is *a lot*. This is a child—my kid.

How can I be a father if I couldn't even be a husband?

"Okay," Hettie whispers, giving my arm a squeeze. It's not a question or a request, it's a *let's do this*, and I stuff all my emotions back into the dark place and take a breath.

"Tema," Hettie says.

The little girl looks up and her face brightens. "Mommy. You're back."

She looks straight at me, and everything shifts. There's no fear or trepidation. Green eyes meet mine with a hint of a smile. "Hey," I croak.

"You're Prince Bo," Tema states.

I start and glance at Hettie. "You are part of a famous family," she says under her breath.

"Yeah, but—"

"Are you my father?" Tema asks.

9

Hettie

ALL THE AIR IS sucked out of the room with Tema's question.

How did she know?

Abigail crowds in the doorway with us, clutching my arm. "We need to—"

I have no clue how to respond.

But Bo does. He manages to react before I can even begin to process what is happening.

"Yeah," he says in that quiet way he has. And then he steps into the room, right where Tema is playing on the carpet, and settles on the floor beside her. He manages to fold his long, muscular body into a cross-legged position like he sits like that every day.

I don't know. Maybe he does.

But I know he isn't faced with a child he didn't realize existed every day, and the ease with which he just admitted that is mind-boggling.

Tema watches him sit down. I've been a mother long enough to understand that her comfort with the situation has everything to do with how Bo is reacting.

And me: only I'm not sure I'm handling it very well. Because I'm not handling anything, just watching it all unfold like I don't have a vested interest in these two people meeting each other for the very first time.

"What are you making?" Bo gestures to the blocks in Tema's hand.

"A boat."

"Do you like boats?"

Tema cocks her head. "I feel like I should," she admits, sounding older than her seven years. I may be biased, but I've always thought she is mature for her years. It might have something to do with being an only child, or I just might have an amazing kid on my hands.

I think both.

Bo doesn't even blink at her reply. "Why's that?"

"Mom says my grandpa has a fishing boat."

Please, please please don't mention her other grandpa is a king! I'm not sure who I'm silently asking this of. Maybe me?

"And we live near the ocean," Tema continues, and I'm forever grateful my filter worked and I kept that inside. "I swim a lot."

"Swimming is good. Boats are cool, too."

Tema searches for another block as if this were an everyday occurrence for her. "I'd like to go out on one to see what it's like."

"Might be a little cold for that now. But sometimes you can see whales."

"I like whales. Do you have polar bears?"

Bo nods. He still hasn't looked at me for—what? Approval? Reassurance? He doesn't need either, since he's doing better than I am. I'm waiting for Tema to run screaming away from Bo.

I shouldn't be, because Tema would never do that. My daughter is the bravest person I know.

"In the north."

Tema's eyes widen. "Have you ever seen one?"

"Couple of times. Big." He points at Tema's sweatshirt. "Did you see her in concert?"

"No," Tema says scornfully. "Mom says I'm too young."

"Maybe a little. You'll see her next time she tours."

Tema scoots closer to him. "Really?"

Bo shrugs. "We've been trying to get her to play here for a while."

"That would be *excellent*. Are you really my dad?" She stares at him, not upset or confused, just curious. And she seems pretty cheerful about the conversation there on the floor.

He glances up at me and I shrug. I had no clue how it would be, telling my child about her father, but I have to say, it's going *much* better than I expected. So much, so that I'm able to start breathing normally.

"Would that be okay if I was?" Bo asks her.

Tema laughs. She *laughs*. "You're a prince, so *yeah*. You have a castle and a king for a dad and a—I'm sorry about the queen. I heard she died."

"Tema—"

"Thank you," Bo says gravely. "She did die. I miss her."

And Tema, my brilliant, beautiful little girl, puts her little hand on Bo's knee. "It's hard to have only one parent when everyone else has two. Or three—my best friend Adam has a mother and a father *and* a step-father and they all live next door to each other."

Bo smiles. "Sounds like it's a good setup."

"Do you live in the castle all the time?" she asks, pushing her pile of blocks closer to him. "Abigail showed it to me when we went to get coffee. She really likes coffee. Because maybe you could live next door to us in Victoria. Or would that be too hard if you're a prince here?"

I can barely follow the conversation. My brain spins with the sight of Bo just sitting on the floor beside his daughter and how Tema has just accepted it. Him. This entire situation.

How can she be smiling about it when I'm completely freaking out?

Add in the crushing guilt and shame that I kept this from both of them, and I'm not in a good place right now. Plus—

I swipe my finger under my eye and it comes back wet. I'm crying. It's too much. And Bo...

"I don't live in the castle all the time," he tells her, picking up a few LEGO pieces and pressing them together. "I live in the woods most of the time."

"But you're a prince, so you should—"

"He's more than a prince, Tema," I interrupt.

"But you *are* a prince, right? Does that mean I'm a princess?" She claps her hands. "I think it'd be fun to be a princess."

"Sometimes it's fun," Bo agrees.

"He's doing great," Abigail whispers into my ear. "This is really good."

Abigail is my best friend, but she never truly gave up her loyalty to Bo. She's always been on my side but never fails to give me a reason or an excuse for Bo's behaviour. Even after all these years, Abigail is convinced Bo had a good reason not to ask me to stay.

I need to tell her she's been right this whole time.

I nod. "I didn't know what to do. He wanted to meet her. How could I say no?"

"You couldn't." Abigail squeezes my shoulder. "You did the right thing. He's a natural."

How can Bo be a natural when he's had only four hours to get used to the idea that he has a daughter?

"Do you think I'll make a good princess?" Tema demands and my heart stops. My daughter is *third in line for the throne of Laandia.* She always has been, but it was easy to ignore the fact when Bo or the rest of the royal family didn't know about her.

"Well." Bo studies Tema, his head cocked to the side. "You like LEGO, and polar bears, and maybe boats. And Taylor Swift. Do you like to read?"

"Yes! I love to read. My favourite books are Junie. B. Jones now, but I have all the Fancy Nancy books. It's quite the collection."

My heart swells and Bo doesn't even blink. "I don't know who they are but it sounds really cool. I think if you like those things, then you'll be a good princess."

"Can we visit the castle?" Tema bubbles. "I want to meet the king."

The king, her grandfather. I don't think she's really gotten the connection, but she's seven. She's doing better than I would under the circumstances. Than I am doing.

I still hold my breath at every question, wondering how Bo will react.

"Maybe we can ask your mom if you can stay there." Bo turns and looks at me. He really is asking. He's not about to pick up Tema and steal her away into the night, locking her up where I can't get to her.

I never thought Bo would do that.

Only I did, because in my mind, Bo had changed so drastically, I never knew how he would react when I told him about Tema.

But now I see he's still the Bo I used to love.

Used to. I repeat that to myself for good measure.

"Mommy!" Tema scrambles to her feet, little LEGO pieces falling as she dances over to me. "Can we go? Can we stay at the castle?"

I hiss under my breath. "Baby, can I talk to Prince Bo for a sec?"

"He's my dad so I don't think you have to call him 'Prince'," she says matter-of-factly.

Bo stands and his face is positively glowing. I know Tema's easy *he's my dad* is playing on repeat in his head.

"No. Well, let me talk to him for a minute. Why don't you clean up your LEGO?" I motion to Bo to follow me into the kitchen.

"Do you want me to turn up the TV so I can't hear your talking?" Tema calls after us.

Bo chuckles.

"That'd be great, thanks," I say over my shoulder.

Abigail waits for us in the kitchen, arms crossed as she leans against the counter. And as soon as Bo steps in, she launches herself at him.

"I should be so mad at you, but I'm so happy to see you," she says into his chest.

I wish I could hug him so easily.

Bo tightens his arms around her waist. "It's good to see you, Abigail." The tension from earlier has disappeared, his shoulders no longer fixed at his ears.

"It's been a long time." She pulls back and I notice her cheeks are damp like mine. When she came with me, Abigail left her family behind, but also her friends. Bo was her friend, too. And Spencer. She gave both of them up for me.

Bo nods with a hint of a smile hiding in his beard. "Thanks for helping Hettie with everything."

"Of course." Abigail turns to me, swiping at her cheeks. "That's it? That's the big reveal?"

I know how she feels. How can something that has caused so much concern and sleepless nights end up being so anti-climactic? Seeing Bo with Tema... seeing how Tema just took it all in stride... "I don't know what to say," I admit. "I didn't expect—"

"It to ever happen?" His lips quirk. "She seems cool."

"She is amazing," Abigail emphasizes.

"Yeah, but you've spent her whole life with her. I want to get to know her." He turns to me. "I'd like you to stay at the castle while we figure this out."

My heart stops beating because this is when Bo takes her from me, using his royal power to take my daughter—

"Both of you. You're welcome to stay at the castle as well." He gives Abigail a sideways glance. "Since I bet I'm not going to be able to keep you away from her."

"I've spent every day with her," Abigail retorts. "I love her more than life itself."

"I'm glad. But you say that like it's my fault. I didn't even know that kid existed until a couple of hours ago. Now I want to make up for lost time as quick as I can."

"You sent Hettie away," Abigail points out before I can say anything. She's always been my protector, but this is my fight. "That makes it your fault."

"No, I actually didn't." Bo's shoulders slump. "But I didn't do anything to make her stay, either." He glances at me. "Stay. At the castle."

My heart stutters to a full stop at the word *stay,* but I don't let on. "I wish you'd spoken to me first before you said anything to Tema. That's a big part of parenting."

"I wouldn't know."

He says that with no expression, like it's not even a dig at me.

"But I'd like to," he adds. "My father isn't back until tomorrow morning. I'd like him to meet her."

"Just like that? You're not going to give him any warning?"

"I thought I'd talk to him first. This is something you do face-to-face. But why don't you come with me and get settled?" Bo pauses, his gaze locked on mine. "Please."

10

Bo

I THOUGHT HETTIE WOULD put up more of a fight, but she doesn't even give it much thought before she nods sharply.

"I think that's a good idea," Abigail says.

Hettie's eyes widen. "Really?"

"It's time," she says firmly, and that's when I know Abigail might be a little on my side with this.

We were good friends once, and maybe someday—

I can't let myself think about someday. One day at a time here.

Hettie tells Tema we're going to stay at the castle for the night, and the kid erupts like a firecracker, bouncing up and down as her LEGO creation breaks into pieces. I help her clean it up as Hettie and Abigail have a whispered conversation.

"They're talking about you," Tema says, crawling around on hands and knees to get the last of the pieces.

"Yes," I agree, dumping a handful of bricks into the box.

"They think I don't hear them." She rolls her eyes. "That I don't know exactly what they're talking about. But I do."

"Yeah, well, sometimes adults forget kids have ears." And before I stop myself, I tug on her earlobe, the first time I've touched my daughter.

She has earrings. Hettie pierced our daughter's ears without telling me.

"I have very big ears," Tema informs me. "Or so Mommy and Abs always tell me."

They're a family. They're a family, and I'm not part of it.

But there is no surge of anger. There's only a determined *yet*.

Suddenly, my world has turned upside down. With one *he's my dad* comment, I am ready to move mountains for one little girl. She is going to change everything, and I'm fine with it.

I want it.

After the LEGO is picked up, I wait outside as Hettie packs their things for the move to the castle and Abigail calls her parents to explain what's going on.

How much do they know? And if they know everything, how did they ever keep it a secret?

Questions for a later time because there's something I need to do first.

This isn't something you text to someone, so I call Spencer. "I need a favour," I say when he picks up.

"Hello to you too."

Spencer Laz is like my fourth brother. Along with his father, Duncan, they're both unofficial members of the royal family. Spence has a good relationship with every one of us, but I'm the only one who knows he calls me his best friend.

"Hey. Hettie's here," I tell him with no preamble.

"What?" There's a crash in the background. "Dammit, you made me spill my coffee. Say that again."

"Hettie is here in Battle Harbour," I say, staring at the house as I pace around the car. "I'm with her."

I hear Spencer's swift intake of air. "Are you with her, with her?"

"I'm currently standing outside Abigail's parents' house, where Hettie has been staying." I stop my pacing on the side of the car. If any of the neighbours could see me, they'd call the cops on this stalker for sure.

"You didn't know she was coming?" There's surprise in Spencer's voice, but he's already switched into fixer mode. It's always been like that with him—if something goes wrong, call Spence.

"I had no clue."

I lean my head on the car roof. This is a blindside worse than any done on Survivor. I feel like I could sit right down in the snow and close my eyes.

I'd only do that if closing my eyes would make this all go away.

But do I want it to go away? "There's more," I tell Spencer reluctantly.

"She finally wants a divorce?"

"How did you know?" I demand.

"What other reason would she have for coming back?"

Me. But no. "Well, yeah, but there's *more.*" I take a deep breath. "She has a little girl. I have a daughter."

Even saying it sounds strange. Surreal. Unbelievable.

Silence for a long beat. "Are you serious?" Spencer finally says.

"Do I ever joke?"

"You've got a point there." I hear the click of a keyboard. "You'll need a paternity test. I'll set it up with the lab and make sure they know—"

"Dude, she looks just like Lyra at that age. It's obvious she's mine."

"*Damn.*" I can tell Spencer's lawyer brain is working, frantically trying to catch up to the events. "What do you need?"

"I'm bringing them to the castle. I want them staying there. Abigail too."

"I'll meet you there."

"No. But can you call Mrs. Theissen and ask her to make up a couple of rooms. I don't know what I'm supposed to tell her. Or anyone." I grip the back of my neck like holding on can make it all stop spinning.

"Done."

"And then... I'm texting the others."

"Odin is in town," Spencer says, and for the first time today, I feel relief. Odin has a way of looking at things that is almost as good as Spencer's. "We'll meet you at Kalle's place?"

"Yeah. Maybe two hours?"

"Are you just going to dump them there and leave?"

"I don't know what to do, Spence. This is... this is a lot." I gasp for a breath. "She shows up out of nowhere, just walks through the trees when I'm splitting wood. Eight years, and she shows up with no warning to tell me she wants a divorce because of this other guy. And then lets it slip that we have a kid. And then the kid—her name is Tema—she looks at me and she's like 'You're Prince Bo. Are you my dad?' She just *knows*. What kind of kid does that?"

"Scary kind, but to me, all kids are scary. Did Hettie tell her?"

"No. Just that I'm from some famous family and the kid put it together. She's really smart. And... cute." Tema's heart-shaped face is burned into my mind, and just thinking about her makes me smile.

After all that's happened today, I'm still smiling.

"And yours?" Spencer prompts.

"I don't think she'd lie. Plus, wait till you see her. It's Lyra."

"Okay. Okay." I can hear Spencer typing again. "Sent word to Mrs. Theissen and security that you're coming with guests. I'm going to loop in Kate when I get off because... Bo, this is going to be huge when it gets out."

"Can it not get out?" I plead.

"Depends what you want to do," he says, and that's when I know Spencer will do everything I ask, but it's up to me to make the decisions about this.

"I don't know, but she's my daughter, Spence. She's my *kid*." That hits me as hard as Tema's *he's my dad,* and my voice wavers. "I have a kid."

Spencer exhales noisily. "It'll be okay, Bo. I've got your back. We'll deal with it, whatever you want to do."

The thing is, deep down, I already know what I want to do.

11

Hettie

ABIGAIL'S PARENTS LIVE ON the hill on the way to the castle so it's not that long of a drive.

I wish it was longer.

The trees on either side of the road are still white with snow. Thanks to the proximity to the Arctic Circle, winter is cold in Laandia and lasts long into April.

There were already flowers breaking through the ground in Victoria when we left.

I sit on my hands to warm them. It also helps with the shaking.

Abigail talked to her parents and told them we had been invited to stay at the castle. I know she hasn't ever told them who Tema's father is, but it wouldn't be difficult to do the math and figure out it was Bo. The Lockes' have kept so many secrets for me over the years.

I need to tell them everything. They deserve it.

When Bo and I first got together in high school, we would hang out at Abigail's, usually with Spencer. Her brothers were younger, and always at hockey practice or tournaments, so we would have the place to ourselves.

Bo loved how the Lockes' treated him like just another friend of their daughters, not like he was part of the royal family. Mrs.

Locke made his favourite cookies, Mr. Locke always wanted to know what time he would bring us home—I stayed there most weekends—and there was always an open invitation for Taco Tuesday dinners.

The world has seen how some royal families are treated, and I'm glad it was never like that for Bo's family, but even a little extra attention was too much for him.

Bo might have felt like a Rapuzel-like character, but he was like Pinocchio to me—all he wanted was to be a regular boy.

But how can you be a regular boy when you grow up in a castle with a father—however cool and laid-back as he may be—as the king?

The only voices in the car during the drive to the castle are from Tema and Abigail in the backseat, and that's only because Tema comments on everything she sees, like usual.

Abigail is so good with her. Sometimes I think she's done a better job at mothering Tema, and then my little girl holds up her arms to me, and I then I know I'm her mother and my heart gets all warm.

I can't believe Bo knows about her. He knows, and the world didn't end like I always thought it would.

What did I think would happen? That Bo—quiet, solemn Bo—would overreact and try to snatch my baby away from me?

The thought actually did pop into my mind more than a few times over the years.

He's smart. Methodical. He thinks before he speaks.

He would call Spencer and get him to figure out how to get Tema away from me rather than do it himself.

It's not fair to Spencer for me to be afraid of him.

He was at the wedding, the only one of the family to be there. Bo had Spencer and I had Abigail as we stood under the trees and told the forest how much we loved each other. Spencer held the ring that Bo put on my finger before the justice of the peace proclaimed us husband and wife.

Spencer opened the champagne after it was over and hugged me and told me I was good for Bo. And then he and Abigail flew back to Battle Harbour and neither of them ever told a soul what they had witnessed.

Spencer might not be of royal blood, but the way he kept our secret made him as much of a brother to Bo as Kalle, Odin, and Gunnar are.

"Mrs. Theissen is making up rooms for you," Bo tells me. "I'll see that you're settled, but then I have to run back into town for a bit. Will you be okay? I'll be back for dinner."

"Can we have pizza?" Tema chirps from the backseat.

Bo glances at her in the rearview mirror. "I can do pizza."

"Your father..."

"Will be back tomorrow morning. I'll talk to him then."

"Okay."

He glances at me. "Really? Just okay?"

"I'd rather not say how freaked out I am in front of the back-seat," I say under my breath.

Tema bounces on the seat. "Can I meet the king?"

"Tomorrow," Bo promises, like it's no big deal.

I met King Magnus at the queen's funeral and I doubt he remembers me. He had just lost his wife and had five children plus a country to comfort. Bo introduced me as Hettie—no last name, no explanation. I wonder what would have happened if he had told the king I was his wife?

"What will he say?" I ask under my breath.

Bo shakes his head. "No clue. But it'll be okay."

"How can you know that?" I demand a little too loudly.

"He might be the king, but he's just my dad. And she's his..." Bo raises his eyebrows and mouths *granddaughter*. "Right?"

And that is the only hesitation Bo has shown about Tema. "Her birthday is July 8," I tell him. I can tell he's trying to do the math. "Wedding night," I mutter.

"Ah."

I shut down the memories of that night before they can explode and make this even messier than it already is.

I can only hope Bo is doing the same thing.

But it's so difficult when he pulls up in front of the castle, which looms above us, snow-covered and intimidating.

"You're really bringing me here," I say in a quiet voice, staring out the window.

"You're really letting me," Bo corrects.

"I don't have a choice."

"You always have a choice with me, Hettie. About everything."

Bo and I dated from when I was seventeen to when we married when I was twenty.

During those four years, we broke up six times. During the four years we were together, I only visited Bo's home a handful of times, and never to meet his parents.

The breakups were the reason for that, and since breaking up with Bo had been my decision every time, I only have myself to blame.

I loved Bo Erickson, the man, but I never thought I was good enough for Bowden Erickson, the prince of Laandia. Being the daughter of one of the most notorious families in Battle Harbour, if not all of Laandia will do that to you. But Bo is still a prince, so I wonder how I would have felt if my family hadn't been an issue. Would I have felt worthy then?

An older woman—somber in dress and appearance—greets us at the door. "Mrs. Theissen," Bo says to her, standing between her and me like he's offering himself as a shield. "These are my friends Hettie Crow and Abigail Locke, who are in town for a few days. I've invited them to stay here."

I don't miss the slight flaring of nostrils at the mention of my last name. "You are most welcome," Mrs. Theissen tells us, dark eyes taking in everything. "It's always nice to have friends of the prince to stay with us."

"I'm Tema," my daughter pipes up, as she often does when she thinks she's not getting enough attention.

"It's lovely to meet you, Miss Tema." That dark gaze flicks from Tema to me and over to Bo. "I'm Mrs. Theissen. You come and find me if you have any problems. Let me show you to your rooms."

As we climb the stairs, I blank out on the snippets of history Mrs. Theissen throws over her shoulder. Thankfully, Tema and Abigail are right behind her to take it all in.

"Do you often have friends stay here?" I ask Bo in a low voice. Yes, it's borderline petty; yes, I had a flare of jealousy at any female "friends" Bo might have invited here, but I blame the surge of exhaustion that washes over me. It's been a very long day, and it's still not over yet.

I'm going to have to talk to Bo about many things.

Bo studies me, his face expressionless. He was always very stoic when he was younger, but his face is like a blank canvas now. "No," he finally admits. "I have no idea what she's talking about."

A relieved giggle escapes and Bo gives me a lopsided smile.

We reach our rooms—Abigail gets the room across from ours—and Mrs. Theissen bustles through, pointing out things that we should be able to figure out for ourselves. "Please let me know if you have any concerns," she finishes. "I still use the castle intercom system, so let me know if you need anything. Dinner will be—"

"We're having pizza," Tema interrupts. "Bo said so."

"Well." The older woman sniffs. "I'll let His Royal Highness make those arrangements."

And then she's gone.

And I'm here. In the castle of the royal family of Laandia.

With Bo.

Abigail takes Tema with her to explore her room across the hall, leaving me alone with Bo. There's so much I want to say, so much I need to talk to him about.

"I have to go back into town," is the first thing that comes out of his mouth.

"Right now?" I hate that I sound nervous. Terrified, actually.

"I'm sorry." Bo reaches out to touch my arm, but pulls back with a grimace before contact. "It won't be for long. I'll be back—with pizza."

"You're leaving to get pizza? I'm sure they deliver anything you want here."

"It's not just that." He hunches those big shoulders and I take pity on him. I know this is a lot, and if he needs a bit of space, giving it to him is the least I can do. "I'm sorry, Hettie. I have to go."

And then *he* leaves. And I let him. At least he gives me an apologetic glance as he walks away, leaving me standing in my room.

My room in the castle. It actually can be called a suite, with a sitting room complete with couch and table by the window. There's a massive fireplace, already ablaze, and I can see into the bedroom through the fire.

There are shelves of books and a television, but nothing else for kids.

Not like there has been a lot of children running around the castle.

Tema is the first grandchild. She's the third in line to the throne, after Kalle and Bo. I knew all of this, but it sinks in that much more actually standing here in the castle of the king of Laandia.

I knew I married a prince, but I never expected Bo to be king. The thought of Tema being so close to so much power is terrifying.

And laughable. I'm a *Crow*. Tema's great-uncle publicly insults King Magnus every chance he gets. Two of my brothers are in jail. I haven't heard from my mother in over twenty years, and my father…

Has no idea I'm back in town. It's not any family one would want to be associated with, let alone the royal family.

"What am I supposed to do now?" I ask out loud.

"Want a tour of the place?" a voice in the doorway asks.

I whirl around. "Kate?" I ask with surprise.

There, in front of me, stands Kate McKibbon—yeah, one of *those* McKibbons, who might have a shot at second place in the worst families of Battle Harbour.

At least she has a brother in the police force now, according to Abigail's mother.

I remember Kate as one of Princess Lyra's friends, and a former love of Prince Gunnar. Gone is the gangly teenager; instead Kate is tall and poised, professional in her black pants and white shirt.

"Hey, Hettie." Kate gives me a welcoming smile. "Welcome home."

"It's not my home," I tell her.

"No, but—Bo asked if I would show you around."

"He did?"

"Well, he did through Spencer." Kate bows from the waist. "Personal secretary of the princes. They share me. I was brought in for Odin before he got married, but I didn't want to go with him and Lady Camille when they moved to Saint Pierre, so I stayed."

"Bo needs a secretary?" I blurt out.

"I help out when certain circumstances arise." She shrugs, and I take that to mean times when a wife no one knew about shows up with a child.

"So you know…"

"Spencer filled me in," she explain. "I need to know since I'll probably be the one making the announcement."

Announcement. I never thought—

It's everything Bo never wanted. "So you know about—"

Kate smiles. "I'd love to meet your daughter."

12

Bo

I KNOW I SHOULDN'T leave them at the castle, but as soon as I led them through the door, I felt the walls closing in on me, just like I always do.

Kate texted me that Spencer had asked her to show Hettie around, so I know Spencer has filled her in.

Between her, Spencer and Duncan, as well as Mrs. Theissen, they make sure all our stupids are covered up.

Maybe leaving Hettie at the castle moments after I finally bring her to stay is another stupid, but I do it anyway.

I jump in the truck and head straight back into town to The King's Hat. I know I'm supposed to take a security detail with me, but I don't hang around long enough to organize that.

I need to talk to my brothers.

And when I walk into Kalle's pub, there they are, standing at the bar, waiting for me.

"Dude." Gunnar, our youngest brother, greets me with a grin and a one-armed hug. "Didn't know you were coming in. Both you and Odin in town at once—it's like something is wrong."

I meet Odin's questioning gaze before he hugs me. "Is something wrong?" Kalle demands as he slaps my shoulder.

Obviously, Spencer didn't fill them in.

"I'm here to talk to Dad about... something," Odin offers.

"He's in London, he'll be back tomorrow morning," Kalle says.

I look at my big brother with surprise, remembering his hesitation about becoming king after Dad's health issues. Before then, he never knew what Dad was doing, where he was. He'd been a complete apathetic about how the country was ruled. And now, from this single sentence, I can tell how things have changed.

I'm glad because it means I'm off the hook, at least once Kalle and Edie get married and start having babies.

"What's going on with you?" Odin asks, pushing a foaming pint of beer in front of me. I pick it up, already tasting the first mouthful of frothy bitterness.

"Wait," Gunnar orders, holding out his glass for a refill. I stand still until my brothers each have a full glass, and then in unison, we drink.

Gunnar bows out first—his glass only half empty—and then Odin with a laugh. Spencer doesn't even try any more, but Kalle gives a good effort, giving up at three-quarters to take a breath.

I finish the pint and push it away for more. "I got married," I blurt out, swiping at my face.

Kalle's glass stops halfway to his mouth. Gunnar isn't as lucky, and a spew of beer flies out, most of it landing on Odin.

"That's one way to tell them," Spencer mutters.

"What?"

"When?"

"Who?"

"I got married," I repeat. "Eight years ago."

"To Hettie?" Gunnar cries. "But you helped her get out of town. *I* helped her get out of town."

I found out later that when Hettie left, she had wanted to do it quietly, without fuss. Without saying goodbye to me. Spencer had helped her, enlisting Gunnar to stop by her sister Mabel's place to pick up a few last-minute things.

I knew nothing about this, and when a picture of Gunnar at Mabel's late at night was shown to Kate, his girlfriend at the time, I believed the worst of him. I even reprimanded him about ruining things with Kate.

It wasn't until years later that I found out what really happened.

"Yeah," I say, bowing my head. Yet something else to feel guilty about. At least it worked out for the best—Gunnar moved on with Stella, and Kate forgave him, even before she knew the truth. Still, I hate that I was responsible for my little brother getting his heart broken.

Odin shakes his head. "I don't understand."

Kalle refills my glass, his expression serious as he pushes it toward me.

"No use trying, I've got more to tell you." I take another long mouthful of beer and set the glass down with a resolve I don't feel. "I married Hettie in a secret wedding that no one knew about except Abigail Locke and Spence."

They round on Spencer, who raises his hands in surrender. "Dude," Gunnar accuses.

"And then she left town," I continue.

"And now she's back." Kalle shrugs as all eyes turn to him. "I heard Mabel talking to Tyler."

Heads turn to where Mabel Crow, Hettie's older sister and Kalle's new manager, is watching us from across the room. She wiggles her fingers at us.

"She's back," I confirm in a tired voice. "And she brought her daughter. *Our* daughter."

"Shut the front door," Odin breathes. "Spence, you should have told us about that."

"That was news to me," Spencer says heavily.

"Did *you* know?" Gunnar asks me.

"I did not."

"What does this mean?" Odin demands. "For the line of succession."

"I don't really care about that. I've got a kid." I stare into my beer. "What am I supposed to do?"

"What do you want to do?" Kalle counters. "I mean about Hettie, for starters. She came back, so does that mean—"

I cut him off with a shake of my head. "She wants a divorce."

Gunnar grimaces. "You can't really blame her."

"Why did she leave in the first place?" Odin asks.

This is what I didn't want to get into. There's a lot of emotions around Mom's death and I know I'm not the only one who hasn't dealt with them.

"The wedding was two days before Mom died."

Three expressions of understanding face me. "Ah." Odin nods. Gunnar bows his head.

"You were a mess after that," Kalle reminds me.

"We all were," Odin adds.

"I wondered if that had something to do with it," Gunnar muses. "I mean, I didn't know about any wedding, but anyone who saw you and Hettie knew it was the real deal. You were just so—" He claps his hands together.

"Joined at the hip?" Odin offers.

"Yeah, but in a good way. You were tight—and happy. At least most of the time. It was... nice. When I heard she was leaving, I didn't get it. For days after, I thought you were about to take off as well," he adds, looking at me sadly. "I couldn't picture what you'd do without her."

Kalle quickly adds some levity to the somberness. "Look at all the compassion and insight from the young one." He reaches out and rubs Gunnar's head.

"At least I had a clue what was going on." Gunnar ducks away.

"Yeah, well, I didn't handle things well with Hettie after..." I trail off. I already said the words once and that was enough. "She got tired of me being a mess and took off."

"I think there was more than that," Spencer chides. "You were uncommunicative. No one could get through to you, not even Hettie."

They all look at me like I'm about to explain why I had been like that. Because yes, our mother's death was difficult for all of us, but at least they could function.

Because they weren't the reason that she died.

"I don't want to get into that now," I say with a shake of my head. "The point is, I have a child. A daughter. And I have no clue what to do about it."

"You do what you have to do—you be a father," Kalle snaps. His blue eyes—same shape as mine, but lighter—narrow as he says it, like I'm about to bail on Tema.

That is not an option. That has never been an option.

Already, I want Tema in my life with a ferocity that frightens me.

"But what if Hettie leaves again?" Just voicing my biggest fear makes it seem more real. Like it could really happen. "What then? How am I supposed to be a father here and Hettie is in British Columbia?"

"Make sure she doesn't leave," Gunnar says simply.

13

Hettie

IT'S SURPRISING HOW LITTLE there is to do in a castle.

At least for me. Kate gives Abigail and a very excited Tema a tour of the grounds while I text Timothy and tell him about what has happened.

It's strange that I haven't thought of him all day.

I met Timothy on a very bad day, during a very bad month. He worked in the office with me, as one of the agents, but we'd never spoken. He was handsome and successful; I sat behind the desk answering phones and wanting to disappear most days.

We met when Tema was in kindergarten, on a day I had been rushing to pick her up. It was a wet day, as it can be in Victoria, the rain coming down in sheets. A car rear-ended me a few blocks from the office.

There wasn't much damage save a dent and a broken taillight, but when I got out of the car into the rain, my phone slipped out of my hand and the screen smashed as it hit the street.

I was frantic to find someone to pick up Tema from school and was about to leave the scene of an accident when Timothy stopped. He had been driving by and somehow recognized me from the office. He lent me his phone to call Abigail, suggested a garage that he knew for repairs, and gave me a ride home after I dropped off the car.

He didn't say anything when I cried.

It had been a bad January; a bad case of Covid for all of us meant I was forced to take more than two weeks off work. Time off meant no money, and we were already struggling to make ends meet. My grandfather was in the hospital with chest pains and Mabel had visited us over Christmas which always made me miss home more. Now with car repairs and needing a new phone... it had been a very bad day.

The next day I showed up at the office ready to apologize to him but found a bouquet of flowers at my desk, as well as gift-bag. Timothy had bought me a new phone.

I told him I couldn't accept it, thanked him but tried to give it back, but he was persistent. There were reasons he was a good real estate agent. I ended up keeping the phone and agreeing to go for dinner with him the next night.

And the one after that.

It had been over five years since I left Laandia, and I was still sad. Lonely. I still felt connected to Bo, but I had seen pictures of him with his family. With other women. There was guilt that came with spending time with Timothy, but considering the distance between me and Bo, and the years that had gone by without any contact, I was able to push it aside.

Slowly, Timothy bumped into my life like a floatation belt thrown in to a rough ocean. I didn't need him; I made sure I never relied on him, but I had to admit, he was nice to have around.

He knew the truth about Tema. It took me over a year to tell him, but eventually I trusted him enough to tell him about Bo.

He told me all along that I should tell Bo about Tema.

He was the first man other than Bo that I'd been involved with, and yes, there's shame of betraying my wedding vows but Bo already did that years ago.

Bo telling me that getting married had been a mistake had torn a hole through my heart, so it was easy to justify my relationship with Timothy. I might have still been in love with Bo when I left Battle Harbour, but I didn't really consider myself married.

Or at least not to someone who loved me like I should be loved.

Timothy loves me. And *he* wants to be married to me.

With him, there's no baggage of who my family is. He couldn't care less about their reputation. Timothy belongs to a normal family, not royal, with both a mother and a father. I might have hesitated when he first talked about us getting married, but that was because of Bo. Because I knew I was going to have to finally end things.

When Bo proposed to me—the real proposal, not the many times he told me he wanted to marry me, or when we would make plans to live somewhere far away from Laandia, hiding from the world and Bo's responsibilities—I felt like a princess in a fairy tale. I was the kitchen servant, covered in dirt and ash, pulled out of her life of drudgery to marry Prince Charming. My family was... not well off. Not respected. I'd been looked down on my entire life because of the opinions of my uncle. The choices my father had made. The behaviour of my brothers, and the way my mother abandoned us.

People looked at me and saw just another Crow kid, one who wouldn't amount to anything.

They didn't see that I loved to read and do crafts. That I babysat the neighbourhood kids—when I could convince their parents that I was trustworthy and would never abandon them by running off in search of a good time like my mother did. That I visited my grandmother every Sunday, at whatever street corner she had parked herself on.

No one saw that I wasn't my brothers; that I was different from Mabel with her hard edges and sharp tongue that were her only defense against being taken advantage of.

But Bo saw me, and managed to push himself through my walls. The walls I had put up so I wouldn't get hurt.

When he told me he'd marry me that minute if I'd only say yes, I finally did. I had been protesting for months, trying to come up with another, final excuse for why we couldn't be together, and I was so tired of it. I wanted to be with Bo—wanted it more than anything. I was angry with my family for putting me in the position of not being able to have the one thing I wanted most.

So I said yes without thinking of the consequences.

And Bo married me days later.

And now, look at the consequences. I'm here, in the castle, and Bo is nowhere to be found. I have a child—we have a child that I refused to tell him about for some petty fear that Bo would take her from me.

He would never do that. I know that. I've always known that.

I didn't tell him because I was afraid he wouldn't want *me*.

A knock at the door brings my thoughts come to a screeching halt. *Bo.* Jumping to my feet, all I can think is that *he came back to me* as I get to the door in record time.

It is Bo, with an armload of pizza boxes, but also—

"Spencer," I say simply, and walk into his arms.

"Hettie Crow." Spencer sighs. "My favourite girl."

I can't stop the tears and his arms tighten as I sniffle into Spencer's coat.

His very nice coat. I always knew Spencer would be important, would make a difference, but seeing him like this—a smart, camel covered overcoat over a tailored suit—

I can't see if it's tailored, but I bet it is.

"It's so good to see you," I say into his lapel. My pain at leaving Bo had consumed me for so long and I had forgotten what else I missed from home.

Like Spencer.

"You too."

We stay like that for long moment until I finally pull back. "I've got a new favourite girl for you," I tell him, wiping under my eyes.

"I heard." Spencer hands me a handkerchief and I stifle my giggle into the soft cotton because who his age carries handkerchiefs? "I can't wait to meet her."

"Abigail's here, too," I say like I'm giving him a gift.

And he smiles like I've given him one. "I heard that too." He picks up the bag he had set down when I launched myself at him. "I brought wine. I thought we'd have a reunion."

"With pizza." Both Spencer and I turn to Bo with the mountain of pizza boxes in his arms.

"I didn't know what kind she likes," he says sheepishly. He also has a bag of juice boxes and three bags of cookies.

"Well, we're not going to go hungry."

Bo meets my gaze, returning my smile and... something happens to my heart. It clenches, like someone has given it a squeeze with their fist—a very warm fist because a warmth spreads through my chest.

It's strange and yet comforting. Because if I can feel it, then I know Bo can too. And that just relieves one of my fears.

The one that's afraid he no longer wants me.

It might be easier if he didn't, then I wouldn't have to choose. But the way my heart feels after a simple smile suggests the choice might not be as difficult as I thought.

Which is just wrong; I have a good man waiting in British Columbia who wants to marry me and take care of my little girl. Timothy supported my decision to come back here without a worry what seeing Bo again would do to me.

He didn't seem to worry at all.

Which seems wrong, because Bo is *Bo*. My first love. Plus, he's a prince; not only *a* prince but one of the sexiest in the world.

I still have a copy of the People's magazine to prove it.

I may have Timothy waiting for me, but here, in Laandia, I have a really good man who I'm still married to. It's all very complicated, made more so because Bo knows about Tema now, and I know he'll want to do the right thing.

Is that why I told him? To make something happen? To force his hand? To shock Bo into acting?

I'm not entirely sure.

"I brought food, but I wanted to…"

My heart squeezes at the expression on his face. Bo likes easy and safe and no drama or conflict. We always got along so well because that's what I wanted too.

It's still what I want, but I know I can handle difficult and drama and when things don't go my way.

Can Bo?

"I saw your sister." He puts the boxes on the table, filling the room with the aroma of melted cheese and pizza sauce.

"You went to The King's Hat." It's not a question. Neither is: "To see your brothers."

Bo shrugs. "Odin is in town."

"Did you tell them...?" I trail off. About Tema. About me.

Bo nods and I bite my lip. "What did they say?"

But before he can answer, the door bursts open. "I smell pizza," Tema cries.

14

Bo

W E EAT PIZZA AND open one of the bottles of wine Spencer brought.

It was his idea to avoid a serious conversation with Hettie tonight. "She'll be exhausted," he said as he drove me back to the castle. "She flew across Laandia twice today, and that's before she was kidnapped and taken to the castle."

"I didn't kidnap her," I muttered as the car pulled up to the door of the castle.

"Well, let's have a friendly catch-up before things get heavy so she won't think that. Besides, I haven't seen her in years. I miss her."

"I thought you were here to see Abigail."

Spencer shrugged. "Her too. I can't believe they just showed up without warning."

"They would have warned someone, just not us." While Spencer may have his finger on all things in Battle Harbour, it's clear secrets can be kept from him.

There would have been fewer secrets if I had given him the okay to check on Hettie all those years ago.

Yet another regret to add to the pile.

When Tema gets back into the room, I'm amazed how excited she is to see us. I may be her father, but she doesn't know me. And Spencer is a stranger.

But the little girl seems overjoyed at the company, which makes me wonder if Hettie keeps things quiet in Victoria. I know nothing of what their life is like—and I'd really like to find out.

But Spencer has never steered me wrong, so I take his advice and we keep it casual.

Though I'm not sure if Tema understands casual.

She peppers me with questions about living in a castle and the Viking ancestors, if there's a dungeon and what would be the best way to punish the prisoners. Apparently, Kate got a bit graphic on their tour earlier.

Tema demands all the demographic information about the town from Spencer, and wants to know many people in the country call my father the king.

Along with the questions, she tells us all about her friends from home, her baseball team, and the plot of her favourite book, all the while shoveling two slices of mushroom pizza into her mouth.

She's adorable, but exhausting.

Hettie takes it all in stride, distracting Tema when she gets too personal, making sure she has milk instead of juice, and eventually, settling her on the couch with her iPad and an episode of a kid show.

Within ten minutes, she's out cold.

"It's been a long day for her," Abigail says with an affectionate smile.

Once again, I realize how amazing mothers are because Hettie doesn't even struggle as she picks up the sleeping child without waking her. "I'll put her to bed."

"Wait," I say without thinking and stand up. "Let me. Please." At Hettie's nod, I reach out and take her into my arms.

She feels soft. Pliable. But she's also a dead weight, like one of the logs I have to prop on my shoulder to carry. I have no idea how Hettie lugs her around.

But it feels... nice. Like Tema belongs in my arms.

I rest my cheek on the top of her head as I carry her into the bedroom.

Hettie goes before me and pulls down the covers. "Just put her here," she instructs, patting the pillow.

"You don't have to change her? Or—I don't know—brush her teeth?"

"She'll be okay for one night. I don't want to wake her. I'm sure she'll be up early."

"Yeah." I gently set her down, pushing a tendril of hair off her cheek. Tema's eyes stay closed, even as I pull the blankets up to her chin. "She's really asleep."

"She's always been a good sleeper."

"Yeah." It's the only thing I can say because I have no idea what kind of sleeper Tema is, or when she sleeps. What does getting up early mean to her? Six a.m. or ten? I don't even know *where* she sleeps.

I watch as Hettie kisses her forehead and backs away from the bed.

"I'm sorry I never told you." Hettie's gaze is fixed on Tema so I'm not sure if she's apologizing to me or our daughter.

"Yeah." Because what else am I supposed to say?

"It's just that—"

"We don't need to talk about it now," I interrupt. The room—Hettie's bedroom—is dark and warm from the fire. The hiss from a white-noise machine masks the sound of Tema's breathing. She looks so tiny in the bed.

"I thought you'd want to know."

"I do. I want to know why, and how, and everything about her. I want to know it all. But not tonight. It's been... a lot."

"It's been a long day. I didn't really know what to expect, but I definitely didn't plan on ending up here." Hettie spreads her hands. "I thought you would have reacted... differently."

"Yeah, well..."

"Get advice from your brothers?" she asks with a smile.

I shrug. "And Spencer."

"I missed him." Her gaze meets mine as my heart gives a spasm of envy until— "And you, too," she confesses.

"Hettie..."

"No, I know." She shakes her head, The braids are gone and she's piled her hair in a bun on the top of her head. It wobbles with the motion. "We can talk about it later. I just... I wanted you to know."

Does that make it better or worse?

I'm not sure but, with a last glance at the sleeping Tema, I follow her into the other room, where Spencer and Abigail fall silent. It's obvious they were talking about us.

I'd be talking about us too.

Despite what I said, it takes all I've got not to demand answers of Hettie as I sit down and grab another slice of pizza. Spencer refills my glass of wine and opens another bottle. I follow Spencer's lead, letting him tell the girls all the latest town gossip, including the reunion he's had with his half-sisters. Abigail counters with news of her family.

I don't mention mine, nor does Hettie.

But I do talk about the lumberjack competitions I entered—and usually won.

"We watched you on TV," Abigail tells me, looking comfortable on the couch beside Spencer. The two of them aren't touching, but it looks like that would be easy to change. "I have to admit, I was very surprised when Hettie found out. The first couple times, we watched on YouTube—"

"You watched me compete?" Buck Marsden got me into the competitions when he was frustrated with, what he called my inability to get a life. It had been a year after Hettie left, and I knew I was floundering, only I didn't know what to do about it. My brothers tried, but they were grieving, themselves. I never told my father how bad it was for me, too ashamed that I had never told him I was responsible for my mother's death.

I've never admitted it, but Buck saved me; he and the competitions that let me unleash my anger and pain on helpless logs.

Because I stay in the background of my family, I sometimes forget that I'm a public figure, and for some reason, people find my life interesting. Even so, it feels strange to know that while I was missing her so much, Hettie was watching me chop and saw… and win.

I won quite a few of the competitions and eventually used my winnings and the money I earned from sponsors to open the first of my wildlife reserves. I set up one for bears about an hour outside

Wabush, and last year opened one for wolves on the edge of the National Park.

Taking care of animals helped as well.

"Why did you stop?" Hettie asks. "You were…"

"Incredible?" Abigail offers.

"You should see him in real life," Spencer says, looking more relaxed than I've seen him in a while. "Those chips really fly when he's got an ax in his hand."

"You and your brothers really like weapons," Abigail notes. "Odin and his sword-play, you and the axes; Kalle with his curling—"

I give a bark of laughter. "I would think a baseball bat would be a better weapon. Or a hockey stick."

"Are you kidding? Remember I curled when I was younger, and those rocks really pack a punch. If you could pick one up and throw it—"

"That's a big *if,*" Hettie reminds her. "You took me curling a few times and I could barely move the thing."

"Kalle could throw one," Abigail says with such certainty—and more than a little admiration—that Spencer leans back to look at her.

"It kind of sounds like you might have a thing for the man with a broom." He raises his eyebrow. "What aren't you telling me?"

"That I had a crush on Prince Kalle for most of my life?" Abigail replies. "Well—duh."

"You had a crush on Kalle?" Spencer cries, and Hettie shushes him while trying not to laugh too loudly.

"He was my celebrity crush." Abigail pats Spencer's knee, her hand lingering for a moment too long. "You were my real thing."

"I—really?"

I've never seen Spencer at such a loss for words and I laugh along with Hettie. The two of us would talk about how Abigail had a thing for Spencer and how oblivious Spencer was about it. It wasn't that he didn't have feelings for Abigail, but I know it was the shadow of my sister who kept pushing any other woman into the background.

"Just think of how much fun we could have had," Abigail says lightly.

"I had no clue," Spencer marvels with an expression of disappointment.

"You're a smart boy," Hettie begins.

"But so very stupid," Abigail finishes, and I get the feeling this isn't the first time the subject has come up between them.

I wonder what they said about me.

"So, is there anyone over there in Canada that you want to tell me about?" Spencer prompts. He shifts on the couch, throwing his arm along the back, his fingers only inches from Abigail's shoulder.

I glance at Hettie to see if she's watching, only to find her looking back at me.

It's like someone has flicked a lighter inside my chest.

Hettie is beautiful, even more now than when I married her. When I look at Tema, I see my sister, but now I notice how much Tema looks like her mother. The same heart-shaped face, delicate nose and chin. A mouth that curves up, always ready to smile.

I would very much like to kiss Hettie's mouth again.

Instead, I wrench my gaze away from her. Until we have a conversation, there will be none of that.

I flick my gaze back to her, to find her still watching me.

"No one worth mentioning," Abigail says to Spencer. "At least, no one who would keep me there."

"Keep you there?" My tone is sharp with eagerness as I turn back to Hettie. "Are you thinking of coming back here?"

Hettie looks at Abigail and it's like the two of them are having another silent conversation. I always hated when they did that. "I love British Columbia," Abigail finally says. "But sometimes I miss the snow of Laandia."

In unison, we all turn to the window where, outside, the snow has been softly falling for the entire evening.

"You're not planning on driving back into town tonight, are you, Spence?" she asks with a gleam in her eyes.

Despite everything that isn't said, it's still fun to be together. The four of us spent so much time together in our youth that being back with Hettie and Abigail feels good. It feels right.

It also feels like I should have my arm around her, or her hand resting on my thigh, but we don't touch.

It takes a lot not to touch her.

But there is someone else in the picture for her. Hettie came back to ask for a divorce, so it must be serious.

Hettie is serious with someone who isn't me.

It's really hard not to press her for more information.

Instead, I sit and listen and laugh, all the while racking my brain to come up with a way to get rid of this other guy.

In a nice way.

Because Gunnar is right—my best option for keeping Tema in my life is to make sure Hettie doesn't leave. And to do that, I need to give her a better reason to stay here with me than go back to what she might have waiting for her in Victoria.

I can do that.

15

Hettie

WE FINISH THE WINE. Eventually, they take pity on me and my constant yawns, and Bo clears the pizza boxes, stacking them outside the door, where, apparently, someone will remove them.

It was so nice to be able to spend time with Spencer and Bo again that I didn't want to be the one to end it, regardless of the exhaustion that weighs me down. It takes everything I have not to curl up with Bo in the comfortable-looking chair.

I could sit on his lap, throwing my legs over the side. He would put his arms around me, playing with my hair and I—

It's not fair for me to even think about it. It's not fair to Timothy or Bo, and I definitely don't need thoughts like that running through my mind.

I asked Bo for a divorce, and now I want to sit on his lap?

I'm so messed up.

Bo leaves with Spencer and Abigail, so I know he doesn't want to be alone with me. It's probably for the best. The more tired I get, the more my mind shifts back to how I felt in his arms this morning.

This morning, I was in his cabin across the country, and now I'm here as a guest in the castle. To say that things are moving fast is an understatement.

It's after eleven, but with the four-and-a-half-hour time difference, I decide to call Timothy before I go to bed. As I wait for him to pick up, I tell myself the sudden sadness I'm hit with is because I miss him—no other reason. "Hi, you," I say in a cheerful voice.

"I didn't expect to hear from you tonight. How's the castle?" Timothy asks without much emotion—no hint of worry, disappointment that I am so far away from him, not even a touch of jealousy—but that's how he always is.

When I met him, I'd been struck with how easy he was to be around. Calm, centered, relaxed. He was as good in a group as he was one-on-one. He enjoyed a drama-free life, he told me, and liked it like that.

"Most people have drama in their lives that they brought on themselves," Timothy would say. "I don't do that. Nothing really is worth getting upset over."

My life had been a jumble of emotions when I met him, and I appreciated his calmness. But lately, I've been wondering if Timothy thinks I'm worth getting upset over.

"The castle is... big. Beautiful."

"And your prince?"

"He's not my prince," I say quickly.

"I'm glad to hear that. Guess what I'm doing tonight?"

"Meeting Marcus for a drink?" It's Wednesday night, and on Wednesdays, Timothy meets his best friend for a beer, along with three of their friends that he's had since high school.

I envy Timothy his circle of friends. He tells me they're my friends too, but no one has been really that welcoming.

I don't know how I would have gotten through the last eight years without Abigail.

Abigail and *Spencer*, I remember and miss part of what Timothy is saying. "… and Thomas said he wouldn't dream of it." Timothy laughs and I join in, even though I have no idea what the joke was.

Not that his friend Thomas makes many jokes. They all share Timothy's even-ness, which comes across as a lack of personality in most of them.

How can I say that? At least I'm not marrying Timothy's friends—I'm marrying Timothy.

If I get the divorce from Bo.

That's the plan. That's why I'm here.

Maybe it's because I'm so exhausted, but it doesn't sound like a great plan right now.

I've never slept in a more comfortable bed.

And that's with a squirming Tema tucked in beside me, her little body as warm as a hot water bottle.

We sleep in later than usual because the curtains are so dark and thick and my body clock hasn't adjusted yet.

Flames still crackle in the fireplace, giving enough heat and light so I can see that Tema's eyes are still tightly closed. I wonder if someone came in to stoke it already this morning. Bo poked it last night before he left.

Bo.

It was comfortable with him last night, but then again, it had always been comfortable with him. He always made me feel safe.

He made me feel a lot of things—attractive. Wanted. Respected. Seen.

None of those have changed. He's the same Bo, albeit with thicker walls around his heart.

Or maybe they were always thick, but I had the key.

Tema stirs, rolling over in her sleep to throw an arm out, which hits me in the neck.

"Mommy," she says sleepily.

"Good morning," I murmur, reaching out to stroke her back. She curls into me.

"Why are you here?" Her eyes blink open. "Why am I in your bed? And I'm still in my clothes."

I drop a kiss on her forehead, breathing in her special Tema-smell.

Which is a bit riper than usual, since we missed both bathtime and teeth brushing last night. "You fell asleep and I didn't want to wake you to get you changed. We're in the castle, remember? Prince Bo's castle. We're staying here with him."

Tema rolls over and stretches like a cat. "My dad."

My heart skips a beat at the ease with which she says that. "Your father," I confirm.

She stares up at the dark ceiling. "It's very dark here. Is it always this dark in Laandia?"

"The sun gets up a little later because we're farther north than in Victoria. And remember I told you it will be a different time?"

"I remember." She yawns, showing the spots where she's already lost teeth. Four gone already, the adult teeth poking up from her gums. She lost her first tooth while eating an apple and didn't even notice. She was almost hysterical when she realized she'd swallowed it, and thought her stomach would grow a new tooth.

I calmed her down and Abigail helped her draft a note to the Tooth Fairy explaining what had happened and could she still have her money for the tooth even though there was no tooth?

We didn't have extra money for the Tooth Fairy, but I still found five loonies to leave under her pillow that night.

Money had always been tight even with Abigail's help. My sister sent money when she could, and when Tema turned three, I started getting strange deposits in my bank account once a month. Since Mabel and Abigail's parents had been the only ones to know about Tema, I suspected it was Mrs. Locke, but I never said anything, fearing that they would stop.

And I needed the money.

Every few months when things were especially tight, Abigail would make some comment about telling Bo, but I pretended to ignore her. Or I'd have some excuse ready.

"I think I may like Prince Bo as my father," Tema decides like she can read where my thoughts are headed.

"Because he lives in a castle?" Tema has taken to the idea of Bo as her father with the ease of being presented with a new toy, but it still feels strange to me.

Or maybe it's strange that Timothy brushed off my concern last night. I said that I didn't want her to become too attached yet until we figure things out, and he didn't even ask what we needed to figure out.

Their relationship, I wanted to snap, and how Bo can be a part of her life when we live so far away.

"But he doesn't live in the castle, at least not all the time," Tema argues with just enough certainty that I have to smile. "He told me he lives in a forest and he cuts trees. I asked if he was a woodcutter like Hansel and Gretel's father, and he said he didn't know their father was a woodcutter. How can he not know that?"

Tema likes dark fairy tales.

"Because we read all the fairy tales and Bo reads other books. I don't think he's the same kind of woodcutter." The air feels cold outside the covers, so I snuggle down. At home, Tema has her own room, leaving Abigail and me to share, and my favourite nights are when I fall asleep in Tema's bed when I'm reading her a story and we wake up together.

"I really hope not, because that father was horrible and abandoned his kids to die," Tema says vehemently. "Do you think Bo would do that? I don't think he would."

I do my best to stifle my laughter. "I don't either."

"Do you think he'll lock us in the castle and I'll have to grow my hair really long to escape?" Tema asks with the sweetest serious expression on her face.

"No, I don't think he'd do that either." I love her imagination.

"Is the king a good king?" is the next thing she wants to know.

"Yes, a very good king," I tell her with the patience of the mother of a seven-year-old. These are normal discussions with Tema.

"Have you met him?"

"Years ago."

"Before me."

"Before you."

It's difficult to remember what life was like before Tema. When I lived in Battle Harbour, when I was with Bo—it's all coated in a haze now. Almost like it happened in a dream.

Only sometimes, I'm hit with super sharp memories and have to wait until the haze coats it again.

It's easier that way.

"Mommy, if I'm a princess, does that mean I'll be different?" There's a note of concern in her voice that tugs at my heart.

"You, Tema-toot, will be the same as you've always been."

"I don't think you should call me Tema *-toot* if I'm a princess," she says in a haughty voice.

"Oh, that just means I'm going to call you that even more. Tema-toot, Tema-toot," I sing, rolling over to tickle her until she makes an adorable sound of passing gas and I laugh.

"You are a horrible mommy," Tema cries as she hops off the bed.

"Am I?"

She stands there, looking at me. "No, you're really not."

I hold open my arms and Tema jumps back onto the bed. "You're the best Mommy."

"And you're the best Tema."

"I'm the only Tema I know."

"There's got to be more of them out there."

"I don't want more. I like being the only one."

I hug her tight. "Are we going to stay here?" she whispers.

I honestly came back without a plan to stay in Laandia, but now that I'm here... now that Bo knows about Tema, things are very unclear.

But Timothy is waiting for me—waiting for an answer. "I haven't figured that out yet," I confess.

"But you will?"

"Of course I will," I tell her with more confidence than I feel. Because that's what a mother does: never let them see you sweat.

"Good." Tema burrows into my arms for a moment before wriggling free. "I," she declares with an undecipherable accent, "must use the loo. Does that sound princess-y?"

I laugh as she crawls over me to jump out of the bed. "Very regal. But keep your socks on, the floor will be cold."

"This whole place is an icicle. It's the coldest castle I've ever been in."

"And you've been in so many castles."

I laugh at the expression on her face. "Worst mommy ever," she sings over her shoulder as she skips to the bathroom.

"That's because I have a horrible daughter," I call after her. "But I love her lots."

"I love the worst mommy too."

My heart is full and I promise myself that I'll do the right thing for Tema.

16

Bo

THE NEXT MORNING, I'm up early waiting for my father to return.

"Miss Crow and her daughter haven't been down for breakfast yet," Mrs. Theissen informs me as I head to the dining room. "Your brother is in the fitness centre."

For a moment, I'm tempted to go find Odin, but it feels wrong to talk to him about this before I even tell Dad. And what would I ask Odin—help me make Hettie stay? Is that even the best thing for Tema? She has a life in Canada—school, friends. A life that I'm not part of.

"What time does Dad's flight get in?" I ask Mrs. Theissen.

"He took the first flight out of St. John's, so he'll be in his office for his nine o'clock phone meeting," she says, pouring me a cup of coffee.

"You don't have to serve me," I protest. Mrs. Theissen has been looking after the castle since before I was born, but that doesn't mean she looks after *us*. Our parents taught us early that, just because we're privileged, it doesn't mean we're entitled. Meals may be available for us, but we serve ourselves and we clear the table. And all of us make sure to thank the staff.

"You seem out of sorts," Mrs. Theissen says with uncharacter-istic sympathy.

I stare unseeing at the scrambled eggs in the warming dish. "I need to talk to Dad."

"I'll push back his nine o'clock. Will fifteen minutes be enough?"

It took me less time to tell my mother. "Does he have any meetings outside the castle today?"

"No, I don't believe so."

"Fifteen minutes should be fine. Thanks, Mrs. Theissen."

"Of course, Your Highness." She touches my shoulder. "It's nice to see Miss Crow back in town." I look at her strangely. "She was a good friend of yours, wasn't she?"

I have no doubt Mrs. Theissen knows exactly how good a friend Hettie was. I wouldn't be surprised if she even knew about the secret marriage.

Laandia doesn't have a spy organization, but if we did, I have no doubt Mrs. Theissen would be running it, with Spencer as her second-in-command.

"Yeah," I say, forcing myself to start filling my plate. "She was."

I eat breakfast alone, and then pace around the castle until it's time for me to talk to my father. But all too soon, I'm standing before the closed door of his office.

Nothing is going to happen to him, I repeat over and over again as I knock on the door.

It can't. Nothing can happen to him.

"Enter," Dad calls in his deep voice.

I take a final breath and push open the door. "Hey."

Dad's office looks more like a living room than a place of business, with all the comfortable furniture set up around the fireplace. There are pictures everywhere—family and paintings—as well as Dad's collection of gold records and Olympic medals.

One of his guitars hangs on the wall by the door, a new addition to the décor.

"Hey." Dad's face lights up with surprise when he sees me, and before I'm all the way in the room, he's come around from behind his desk to give me a hug.

It's been a while since I've been home, so I take the hug, and hold it a little longer than usual.

"I didn't know you were back." Dad grins and motions me to the chair in front of the desk. "Although I don't need to know things like that," he says, waving his hands around. "You are a grown adult with a life of your own and I don't need you to keep me informed of your plans to come home. I am your father, though. You *could* tell me things like that."

"Yeah, yeah." I settle into the chair and Dad leans against the desk. "Nice try at the guilt."

He shrugs. "I do my best. So, to what do I owe the pleasure?"

"Got a minute?" I ask.

"For you?" He checks the diary on his desk. "I have fifteen. How long are you in town for?"

"That depends." It sounds more ominous than I intended.

Dad frowns and reaches for the red Tim Hortons cup on his desk. "What's up?"

"Silas'll never forgive you for the Tim's addiction," I remind him, watching him take a sip.

"I know, I know," Dad groans. "And I like Silas, so I try. But it was right there in the airport." He looks longingly at the red cup. "The pods just don't cut it."

"You could buy local."

"Are you here to lecture me on my coffee preference?" He fixes me with his gaze, the one that always knows when something is wrong, whether it's with one of us or in the country.

He looks more kingly than he usually does this morning, in a navy jacket straining at his wide shoulders and flaming red tie and jeans, rather than beat-up sweatshirts and flannel shirts that he wears around the castle. He's broader than any of us, but other than Gunnar, we're all taller than him.

I'm not sure who I'd rather be facing—the king, or my father.

I had the same concern when I told Mom all those years ago.

"What's going on, Bo?" King Magnus of Laandia asks with a frown. "Because something clearly is."

I stare at the painting behind his desk. "I need to tell you something."

"I figured that out myself." He rubs his hands together. "Is someone gonna get in trouble?"

"Maybe."

His smile fades. "This sounds serious."

"Yeah." I swallow twice. Take a deep breath, but the words just won't come.

"Bo. What's going on?" Dad prompts. "Just say it."

"*I-got-married.*" The words come out extra fast and jumbled together incoherently and I try again. "I got married."

To his credit, my father doesn't show any reaction other than a quick widening of his blue eyes. "Married."

"Yeah."

He presses his lips together. "When was this? And why wasn't I invited?"

"It was eight years ago." He frowns. "Hettie. I married Hettie."

"Does that have anything to do with a little birdie telling me she's back in Battle Harbour and staying right here under my roof?" I shrug. "What does that mean?"

"I haven't figured that out yet," I admit.

"Have you been married this whole time?"

"It's complicated."

"I would think so." Dad has a perfect poker face, and I can't read his expression because there is no expression to read.

"There's more," I say heavily.

I can't tell if he's upset, angry, or slightly amused. "I would think there should be. Let me have it."

"Hettie has a daughter. *I*... have a daughter." This gets a blink. "I didn't know," I add quickly. "Spencer wants a paternity test, but she says it's mine and I believe her. She looks like Lyra."

"You have a daughter." He slowly walks around his desk and falls into his chair, still holding the coffee.

"I didn't know. Tema. She's seven. I just met her."

"Because you've been married for eight years."

"It happened... Hettie says... I didn't know." I don't think I'm making sense, just saying the first thing that comes to my mind.

"I would hope you didn't because, to quote my father, I'd tan your hide if you had a child and didn't take responsibility for her." Dad looks across his desk, looking more like an angry father than a king.

"I would never do that."

"Glad to hear that." He nods slowly. "I always thought I raised you boys right. But you did let your wife, who didn't know she was pregnant, I assume, leave the country. And as far as I know, you haven't seen her since then?"

"Yeah. She left... It was after Mom... A couple of weeks after."

He lets out a heavy sigh. "Ah."

"Yeah. So it wasn't a good time to get her to stay."

Dad makes a sound in the back of his throat. "No, it wasn't really a good time for much, was it?" He takes a deep breath and pastes a smile on his face. "So. What are you going to do about it?"

"I don't know. Hettie says she wants a divorce. I... don't know what I want." Is this the time to tell him I think I'm probably still in love with her, or does that make me look pathetic? Because I don't think I'm looking good in my father's eyes, and even at twenty-nine, that still stings.

"I see. Do you still love her?"

"I haven't seen much of her."

"That's not what I asked."

It doesn't matter if loving Hettie makes me pathetic. It is what it is. "I don't know. Maybe." Probably.

"Well, my advice—did you want my advice?"

"Kind of, yeah."

"Smart boy. My advice is to spend some time with her. Get to know present-day Hettie, and see how much she's changed from past Hettie. Because you might be still in love with past Hettie, but you don't know a thing about present-day Hettie."

That makes sense. "Yeah."

"Yeah. Because if you feel differently about this new Hettie, you've got to let her go."

"What if she takes Tema back to British Columbia?"

"You're a father now, and we'll figure that out. We are pretty fortunate that you can spend the time and money travelling back and forth. It's not the most convenient, but we'd make it work because that little girl is a princess of Laandia."

"Can you make her stay?" I ask hopefully, because that would make it so much easier.

But Dad laughs. "I can't even make my own children stay, so no, I won't do that. But we'll make it work somehow. Your priority is to figure yourself out. Why did she leave in the first place?"

"Mom... I was..." I can't bring myself to say anymore.

I can't tell him it's my fault.

"Broken-hearted," he offers. "Yeah. We all were. And young, and not mature enough to give Hettie what she needed. And I bet you didn't let her give you what you needed."

"Her family," I begin, not sure how to broach the sensitive topic.

"I know her family. But you don't marry a person's family."

"You kind of do. In our case you do."

"That is true. Why don't you decide what you want to do? Or let Hettie decide. This may be a moot point. Time has gone by and you might not feel the same about her."

I'm pretty sure I do.

17

Hettie

SPENCER ESCORTS US TO breakfast before he leaves for his office in town. I'm not sure if he lives in the castle or just stayed the night. And if he just stayed the night, exactly *where* he stayed.

Abigail certainly seems to be in a good mood this morning, but I don't ask for details. If there's something between her and Spencer—something more than the crush she confessed to him last night—then I will have to factor that in any decision I make about the future.

After we eat—after Tema inhales possibly more food than she's ever eaten at one time, because she insists on sampling everything in the dining room, including a tiny sip of Abigail's coffee—we go back to our room.

I want Tema to take some time to finish a few of the math activities that her teacher sent with her. She's on March break, but I wasn't sure how long we would be away. Tema loves school, loves her teacher, and homework has always proven to be a great way to keep her busy.

Especially while we're in the castle and I'm not sure what we're allowed to do or where we're allowed to go. And I don't want to leave this morning because Bo is talking to his father and I want to be around when he's finished.

Tema is at the table, the scratch of her pencil and her muttered comments loud in the quiet room, and I sit on the couch in front of the roaring fire. "It's a good room to have," Abigail surmises, flopping down beside me. "Spence said this is where Lady Camille stayed before she married Odin."

"It seems kind of surreal that I'm in the same room that a princess stayed in."

"It shouldn't be surreal at all," Abigail gives me a knowing look.

Yes, I am the mother of a princess now—or at least I assume Tema will be given a royal title, given how taken Bo seems to be with her—but I don't want to talk about that now because at this very moment, Bo is telling his father all about what we did eight years ago, and what I did nine months later. Abigail was supposed to distract me, which she is not doing well with her knowing looks.

I'd be better off finishing the bottle of wine Spencer left last night. Wouldn't that make it all better, me showing up to a meeting with the king with wine on my breath?

Will I even be meeting the king?

"Is Camille a princess? Because Odin isn't a prince anymore," I wonder. "Or still is a prince, but just can't be king?"

"I have no idea about the succession laws of Laandia, but *you* should." There's another of those looks.

"I'll find out soon enough," I say weakly.

Abigail drops her voice. "What do you think will happen?"

I glance at Tema at the table. She observes more than I can ever imagine, but at least second grade subtraction seems to be distracting her from our conversation. "I have no idea," I whisper.

"What do you want to happen?"

Abigail knows me better than anyone. I should be asking her what I want to happen because she'll have an opinion and a pretty good idea of where my head is at.

The problem is that my head and my heart may not want the same thing.

"I don't know that either." I rest my head on the back of the couch. "Did I totally mess things up by coming back?"

"I think you should define mess."

That's a good idea. Did I mess up my perfectly happy life in Victoria by coming here? I don't miss Timothy as much as I should, so what does that say about our relationship? And what have I done to Bo? I kept a *child* from him. Not only that, but I'm forcing him to deal with the guilt that he's held on to about his mother's death.

I'm forcing him to deal with me and what I want for the future. It's not fair if I haven't even figured it out yet.

"Last night was fun," Abigail says when it's obvious I'm too deep in my thoughts to respond. "It was good to see Spencer, to hang out with him and Bo again."

This is as good a distraction as second grade subtraction. "Why did you and he never hook up back in high school?" I wonder, tucking a cushion into my lap.

"Who said we didn't?"

My jaw drops. "Abigail! Why didn't you ever tell me?"

"There wasn't much to tell." She holds up three fingers. "The first time was during one of your breakups, and we met to try and figure out how to get you two back together. Second, was graduation—"

"When we crashed at Spencer's dad's place?"

"When he had a place. Spence says he lives here full time."

"Do not change the subject! When was the third?"

"The day after your wedding."

I think I would react differently if Tema wasn't at the table. If she weren't here, I would jump to my feet and demand to know about every single moment the two of them shared, moments that I had no clue happened. I tell Abigail every detail, whether or not she wants to hear it. How could I not know any of this?

But because Tema is there and moments might constitute something other than a G rating, I keep my lips pressed shut so my mouth doesn't flop open like a fish.

"How did I not know this? Three times?"

"What's three times?" Tema calls.

"I can't wait until you learn your three times tables," I manage. Motherhood has definitely made me more quick-witted.

"Why didn't you ever get together for real?" I hiss.

Abigail lowers her voice as well. "Because Spencer has been in love with Princess Lyra almost as long as you've been in love with Bo," she says ruefully. "Everyone knows. It's obvious."

"Ah. That." She does have a point. Bo never liked to talk about the connection between his best friend and his sister, but it was there for all to see. "I'm sorry, Abs."

"Oh, so am I. I thought maybe the third time was the charm, but then—" She cuts off abruptly.

"Then I left and you came with me," I finish sadly. "Why didn't you stay? And give it a try with him?"

"It was never an option," she says simply. "You're my ride or die, Het. Always have been."

"But Spencer..."

Abigail smiles but I can see the touch of sadness in her eyes. She's given up so much for me, and for what? "There was no choice. I will always pick your friendship."

"I wish I'd known. I wouldn't have let you come."

"Like I would ever pick a man over you! And I wouldn't have wanted anything different. I've been really happy in Victoria," she assures me. "I like our life there."

"So do I, but…"

"But this is home."

And the way Abigail says it, I know it's true for both of us. British Columbia may be beautiful, and living in Canada has been great, but Laandia is our home, whether we want it to be or not.

"I never thought I'd miss it," I admit. "Leaving was so easy—well, not leaving Bo, but the rest of it. Leaving my family—"

"You are not your family," she says sternly, just like every other time she's told me that.

"I know, but it's hard…"

"And anyone who knows you would never include you in their judgement of them. Which no one should do anyway."

"But people do."

"People do," she says with resignation. "And that's not fair to you."

We share a look of sadness. Abigail has witnessed first-hand what the people of Laandia think about my family. About me. And about her too—being my best friend has tarred Abigail with the same brush at times.

It's not fair. None of this is fair.

"Have you talked to Timothy?" she asks to change the subject.

"Last night." I wave my phone at her. "He says he's giving me space, but there's not a lot of texts from him. And he hasn't sent anything today. He doesn't say anything, but I don't think he's happy that Bo wants us to stay here."

Abigail snorts. "Not surprising."

There's something in her tone, something I've heard but never wanted to ask about. "Do you... do you even like Timothy?" It's something I've been wanting to ask her for a while, but it seemed too awkward in Victoria. Here, with the distance between me and the man I love—

Is Timothy the man I love?

"Of course I like him," Abigail says quickly. Too quickly. "He's kind and decent, and he'll make a great father figure for Tema. There's nothing not to like about Timothy."

"But..."

"But..." She chews on her lip and I know there's more.

"Be honest," I remind her. "That's what we do. Except for you keeping Spencer a secret from me."

"There was nothing to tell," she protests. "And yes, I like Timothy—but honestly, Het, I don't much like *you* when you're with him."

"Oh." I stare into the fire, because what do you say when you're best friend tells you something like that?

"It's nothing big," she assures me, grabbing my hand. "And I still love you. It's not like you turn into a mean person when you're with him, but you're not... There's something missing. You're not you. You're some version that you think is what Timothy wants. Have you ever really told him what you want?"

"I don't know what I want," I say helplessly. "I want a good life for Tema. I want my brothers to stay out of jail. I want Mabel to be happy."

"None of those are for you. What do *you* really want, Hettie?"

"I don't know."

"Yes, you do. You're just scared to admit it." She looks at me pointedly. "You left because you thought it would be easier on Bo. I know you never wanted to."

"I didn't," I admit in a low voice.

"You have to stop making decisions based on what other people think. We want you to be happy, but you have to figure out what you want first."

Is she right?

"And Tema will be fine, regardless of what you decide—Timothy or Bo? Or—neither."

"I don't think there's a Timothy or Bo decision to be made," I protest.

Abigail cocks her head and stares at me. "C'mon, Het. It's *Bo*. Are you trying to tell me you're not falling for him again?"

I think long and hard about her question, trying to do what she said, and think about what I want.

What I've always wanted.

"I don't know if I ever stopped," I finally confess.

18

Bo

I HEAD STRAIGHT TO Hettie's room after I talk to my father because I know she'll be waiting to hear from me. Nervously waiting, just like I was.

Now I'm filled with a giddy sense of relief. I didn't really know what my father was going to say, but I thought it would be much worse than this.

It wasn't all that bad, really. He didn't understand why I made him promise not to leave the castle today, but he seemed to understand everything else. At least he accepted that I was married and the father of a seven-year-old girl.

He took it better than I did, telling me to go get Tema and Hettie so he could meet them.

Tema—

Dad told me he remembers meeting Hettie at Mom's funeral. I knew she had been there but had blanked most of the day. The week. The month.

We were together for almost four years, and I never once introduced her to my parents. I tried, so many times, but Hettie sidestepped every invitation or outright refused my suggestions.

She broke up with me when I pushed too hard.

I could tell that while she loved her family, she hated them too. They were never a problem for me, but Hettie couldn't believe that. I would have been happy to have remained married to her, to see what I could do about getting her grandmother off the street. To help her brothers in some way.

But she wouldn't let me. And then I let her go.

I knock on the door to her room and Hettie answers almost immediately, like she'd been lurking by the door.

"Bo." My heart gives a thump when I see her. "How did it go?"

"He wants to meet Tema," I say without any preamble. "He wants to meet both of you."

She pushes me back and shuts the door behind her so we're out in the hall. "So you told him?" she whispers.

She's standing very close to me, close enough for me to smell the coconut of her shampoo. At least I think it's her shampoo.

She could have been drinking piña coladas all morning for all I know.

There's that giddiness. "That was the plan," I tell her. "Just came from his office."

She takes a deep breath. "And?" For a moment she looks terrified.

"And he wants to meet her. Like I said. And you, too. Again. He remembers meeting you years ago but wants to say hello."

"Is he mad?" she whispers.

"At you? Why would he be?"

"Because I kept—" She crushes her lips together.

Ah. The guilt.

"His grandchild from him? I don't think he's thrilled about that, but he's never been one to hold a grudge."

"Oh. Okay." She takes a deep breath. "We're going to meet the king. When?"

"Now, I guess." Hettie's anxiety must have been rubbing off on me because now I'm nervous about the whole thing.

And I shouldn't be. This is going to be fine. Great. It's all good.

Hettie gathers Tema, frets about what she's wearing, that she needs a haircut, tells her to behave six times, all on the five-minute walk to Dad's office.

I guess it's five minutes. It feels like forever. But finally, we're here, standing outside the closed door.

I glance over at Hettie with what I hope is a reassuring look and then I knock. "Enter," Dad calls.

"Ready?" I ask Hettie.

"Open the door," Tema orders, grabbing the doors' knobs and pushing both of them open.

"Well, hello there."

My father stands by the door, hand stretched out to open it. He's already shed his jacket and tie and cancelled his next meeting.

Tema stops and stares at him. And then: "Your Majesty," she says in a clear voice, dropping into a curtsy.

"No need to do that," Dad says, bending over to raise her up by the shoulders.

"But I practiced for years in case we ever came back and I could meet you. Of course, I didn't know you'd be my grandpa when we met," Tema tells him.

"Grandpa," Dad murmurs with a sheepish smile. "So you wanted to meet me?"

"You're the king of another country," Tema says with a touch of scorn. "Why wouldn't I want to meet you? I have another grandfather," she adds. "He has a boat. And a great-grandfather. He paints pictures."

"I know. I have one over here." Dad points at the picture on the wall.

"Hey! I know that one. He painted that when I was four."

"Do you remember when you were four?"

"No. But there's a picture because I got into Grandaddy's paints and made a big mess. If you look here—" Tema darts over to the painting and points up. "Here. That's my finger."

"Well, look at that." Dad peers at the watercolour of the trees, from the view of someone lying on the forest floor and looking up. "There's a finger print there."

"That's me."

"I like the painting even more now." He smiles down at her, and I can see the exact moment the king of Laandia falls in love with his granddaughter.

Hettle takes my hand.

19

Hettie

WE SPEND HALF AN hour with the king, with him giving Tema most of his attention. Even when Duncan, Spencer's father and the right hand of the king, shows up to tell King Magnus of his next meeting, we don't leave.

Duncan postpones the meeting for an hour and stays with us, talking to me and Bo as the king plays a game of Tema-checkers with my daughter.

Tema made up the game last year while I was doing my best to teach her how to play chess. It's a combination of the two, and she made up so many rules that it's impossible to figure it out, but the king does his best.

There's a lot of laughter.

But finally, the king—he told me to call him Magnus—stands and announces that he really needs to get some work done.

"But you're the king," Tema points out. "No one should tell you to go to work."

"I work for the people, like your mom. Like Lord Laz here, and Bo. They might not always tell me to get back to work when I'm goofing off, but I have a responsibility to them."

"Do you like to goof off?" she asks.

He winks at her. "It's my favourite thing to do. And I'd really like you to come back tomorrow and teach me more of that game. Does that sound like fun?"

"Yes." And then Tema leaps into the arms of the king of Laandia.

I clutch Bo's wrist so tight that he must feel the imprint of my nails. But the king only folds Tema into his arms and hangs on tight for a long moment.

With a sigh, he finally sets her down. "Will you do me a big favour?" he asks her.

"Of course."

"Will you go with your—with Bo there, and go to the kitchen and see if you can convince the cook to make me a sandwich?"

"I can make you one!"

"I'd like that a lot, but the cook might not. You can him tell what to put in it, though."

"I'll do that." Tema runs to Bo and grabs his hand. "Let's go, Bo Daddy."

I think Bo's heart melts at her words, at the ease of her touch. I know I do. Seeing them together...

And then there's that guilt.

"Hettie, if you wouldn't mind hanging back for a moment," the king says in a low voice.

"Of course, Your Majesty." I watch, wide-eyed, as Tema pulls Bo from the room. Duncan nods and follows them, leaving me alone with the king.

Magnus smiles at me as he leans against his desk. "Magnus," he reminds me. "I am still your father-in-law."

I laugh nervously.

"She's a little firecracker," he adds. "We haven't had that kind of energy in here for a long time."

"She is. But she's a good girl. Smart and funny…"

"You've done a great job with her. On your own." There might be a hint of reproach in his voice, or I may be imagining it.

"About that…" I begin.

"Bo said you had your reasons."

"I did. For leaving, and for not telling him."

I would have never imagined the king of a country to look so sympathetic. "I expect you were afraid we'd take her from you," he says in a gentle voice.

My mouth literally drops open. "I—I did think that," I admit.

"Understandable. I am a king, after all."

"You're not that kind of king," I point out.

"Thank you for thinking so highly of me."

I flush. "She's everything to me. I couldn't take the risk."

"She's a special little girl. Why did you leave in the first place? If you don't mind me asking."

It's not like I'm being questioned by a king. Or even interrogated by my husband's father. King Magnus seems like he really wants to know about me.

Or he's very good at pretending.

"We were very young," I begin. "And maybe we shouldn't have taken that big of a step and gotten married, but we were in love."

"I don't question that. I'm surprised that I didn't hear anything about it. I like to think I'm close to my children."

"He told Queen Selene."

The king clears his throat. "He did? I never heard—"

"Just before the accident. The same day. I didn't know this until Bo told me yesterday, but it explains a lot of things."

The king sits down behind his desk. There's a heaviness to his shoulders that wasn't there a moment before. "Why don't you explain it to me?"

I take the seat opposite him, tucking my hands between my legs. I don't think King Magnus is the type of king I need to be careful of what I say in front of but there's always been a wariness when I talk about Bo to anyone.

"Bo thinks he was the cause of the queen's accident," I say simply.

Magnus sucks in his breath. "There's no way he could have been. There was a storm, the bridge was icy…"

"You need to tell Bo that," I urge, leaning forward. "He's convinced that the queen was so upset to find out about our wedding that she shouldn't have been driving, and it caused her to lose control of the car."

Magnus covers his mouth with his hand. "No."

"I told him it wasn't his fault, but Bo has spent the last eight years thinking it is. And once he told me, it explained everything. The days after the accident, he shut down. He wouldn't talk to me. He didn't want to see me. For four days, I didn't know where he was. I was frantic. I couldn't get hold of Spencer and no one else knew about us—"

Even after so long, my eyes are damp just thinking about those days. How worried I had been about Bo. The entire country was in mourning, but all I cared about was one man who seemed to have disappeared.

"They went out on a boat," Magnus says quietly. "Bo, and Spencer, Kalle and Gunnar. They were gone for three days. I thought it was a good idea, but I didn't know. Odin stayed with me, and Lyra..." He takes another deep breath. "It wasn't a good time for any of us."

"I can only imagine."

"But he came back." He gestures for me to continue.

"He was different. It was like he was frozen. He wouldn't talk to me, didn't want to see me. I couldn't... I couldn't." I bite my lip. "Finally, he called, wanted to talk to me. We met at the high school, and he said—"

I don't want to repeat what Bo said. The words have been burned into my mind, but it still hurts too much to say them out loud. "He said we made a mistake. That we never should have gotten married."

Magnus makes a noise in his throat I take as sympathy, so I continue. "I didn't know how to get through to him. He was a wall."

"He is very wall-like."

"I was hurt. I was twenty years old and newly married to a man who wanted nothing to do with me. I left because it hurt too much to be around him. And I thought it would be easier for him."

"I saw my son at that time, and nothing was easy for him. You certainly went far enough. Why British Columbia?"

"My grandfather was there. He took us in, helped us out."

"I'm happy to hear that."

"I didn't feel like I had a choice, but looking back, I shouldn't have run."

"What did your family say about it all?"

I choke back a laugh. "They don't know anything about it. You know my family. They're not the sort you want as in-laws. I'm sure they would have been over the moon to hear I married a real-life prince. And had his baby." I shake my head. "My mother might have come back for that."

"When is the last time you saw her?"

"I was seven."

Magnus nods as he stands, moves out from behind his desk. "Hettie, I can't pretend to be happy about just finding out about all of this now. The press..." He chuckles. "It's going to be fun. Not."

"Do we have to tell anyone?" I ask cautiously.

"I guess that's up to you, and what you plan to do. You haven't figured that out yet?"

"I need to talk to Bo."

"I suggest you do that. But, Hettie, you need to know that I consider you part of my family now. You not only married my son, as unorthodox and unexpected hearing about that is, but you made him smile. It's like he woke up from a very long nap."

My eyes start to sting a bit hearing that.

He motions me to stand up. "And not only that, but you brought us that little girl. I think that's a pretty big deal. I understand there's some conflicted feelings about your own family, but do know that we're your family now."

I've never felt unconditional acceptance from anyone before and I blink before the sting in my eyes becomes embarrassing. "Thank you, Your Majesty."

"Magnus," he reminds me. And then he reaches out and the king of Laandia hugs me.

20

Bo

TEMA INSISTS ON DELIVERING the sandwich back to Dad's office but Hettie is already gone.

"Turkey and salami with cucumbers and spinach," Tema tells Dad as I set the tray onto his desk. She let me carry the tray, only because she thought the king needed a glass of milk and wasn't sure she could manage.

"Sounds delicious," Dad says with a grin. "Now, get out of here so I can get some work done. Family dinner tonight?" he asks me. "Everyone is invited."

I nod, already sensing Tema's excitement. I escort Tema back up to their rooms, wanting to talk to Hettie. Needing to talk to Hettie.

But she's not there.

"How did it go?" Abigail asks.

I'm still processing. "We're having dinner tonight," I manage. "Family dinner. But that includes you," I add.

"I'm already terrified," Abigail says with a grin as Tema dances into the room. "Back to your math sheets. We can play after lunch."

"It's just dinner with the family," I tell her.

"The *royal* family," she reminds me. "You forget that not everyone is used to that."

"I guess."

Abigail glances through the fireplace into the bedroom. "My bet is Hettie is wandering around, trying to get back here, so maybe you should go track her down." She gives me a knowing glance. "It might be a good idea to talk a little as well."

"That was my plan."

"Good boy. I'll keep the child occupied for as long as you need."

I head for the door, pausing before I leave. "Abigail?"

"Bo?"

"Is she happy there? In Canada?"

Abigail opens her mouth as if to speak, then shuts it, pressing her lips tight together. "As much as I want to interfere, I really can't," she admits. "I have to leave it up to the two of you to figure it out."

"I was hoping you'd... maybe you'd let me know..." It sounds so childish to finish the thought. "Never mind."

"I can't tell you if you have a shot because I don't know if you're ready for that shot," Abigail says, reading my mind like our friendship hasn't been stretched by time and distance. "And if you're not ready, there's no point, because it's not just the two of you that would get hurt." She takes a step toward me, close enough to poke her finger into my chest. "I will *destroy* anyone who hurts that little girl," she hisses.

Abigail is pretty short, so I have to smile to see her threaten me.

"Do not smile, Bowden Erickson. I know where all the bodies are hidden. I remember you are afraid of zombies—"

"Zombies?" Tema calls out. "Like the Walking Dead?"

"It was a mistake to let you watch that and you promised never to mention it," Abigail throws over her shoulder. "One time," she says to me. "Ten minutes."

"I have lost all respect for your parenting abilities," I tell her with mock sadness. "How could you let her near that show?"

"Just because you can't handle it, big boy," she teases.

I snort and then reach out to pull Abigail into a hug. "I missed having you around," I tell her in a gruff voice.

"Of course you did." But the way her arms tighten around me suggests she might have missed me too. "Now go find your girl."

My girl.

I find Hettie wandering the hall with the family pictures, from the most recent family shots of Odin's wedding to a painting of my great-grandfather, the first king of Laandia.

From the look on her face, I can tell she has no idea how to get back to her room.

"You lost?" Her face lights up when she sees me, but then the light dies right away, like she doesn't want to let herself be happy to see me. I'm not sure what to think about that. She asked for a divorce. There's someone else, someone important enough to try and make a clean break with me. It will never be a clean break. Even without Tema in the picture—and she is the whole picture now—my heart has always told me that Hettie belongs to me. She has my entire heart and that won't change regardless of our marital status.

"You'll figure out your way around soon enough," I tell her.

"I might not be here long enough for that."

The thought of her leaving again makes my stomach clench, but I do my best to hide any reaction. Instead, I point to the painting of Leif Erickson. "It's all his fault, you know."

"What is?" She moves down the hall toward me, like we're a set of magnets drawn to each other.

At least that's how it is with me. Even with Hettie all the way on the west coast of Canada, I've always felt the pull. There's always been a tug with a little voice constantly in my head: "*Go get her.*"

I've managed to ignore it because I've been more afraid of what I'd find if I went to get her.

"He's the one who wanted to be king," I tell her, staring at my great-grandfather. There's some resemblance to Dad, with the shaggy red-gold hair streaked with white, and Odin, with the serious expression. "I've always wondered if it would have been better if he'd left it alone."

"Better not to have helped save Canada from Germany invading?" Hettie asks with a frown.

"Better not to have asked for a country in return."

"I'm not sure if anyone else would think that. You look like him, you know. Different hair, but the eyes are the same."

"He was a soldier. A warrior."

"And you're not?"

"I've never fought for anything in my life," I admit with a sinking of my shoulders. "Including you."

"No. You didn't." Her voice is flat but not accusing.

I hate that she thinks that, but I deserve it. "How do you think it went with Dad?" I change the subject.

"He loves her." Hettie's expression softens like it does whenever she mentions Tema.

"I don't think it's that hard."

"No. She's amazing," Hettie says with a mother's pride.

"Yeah. Will you go for a walk with me?" I ask. "Outside?"

She nods, the softness changing to wariness. "I need to get my coat."

"The one you have isn't warm enough. You can use some of Lyra's things."

She follows me down to the closet on the main floor where we keep our ski and snowmobile gear, and I find her a jacket and boots. They're a little big but much warmer than what she brought with her.

We leave through the side door. Even in March, the snow is piled in drifts but at least the paths are clear. "Odin told me a funny story of when Camille first came here," I say as we walk around to the back of the castle." Apparently, he found her outside whipping snowballs at this group at the gate. You remember the Odinites? The group that wanted Kalle to abdicate so Odin could be king?"

Hettie nods. "They must have been devastated when it was Odin who stepped down."

"I don't think anyone from the castle really cares what they think," I say drily.

"That's not very royal of you," Hettie teases.

"Maybe not, but they riled up the people, and Kalle couldn't have appreciated it. Although he wasn't really into the king stuff until a few months ago," I muse, leading Hettie to the back garden. It's still covered in snow and no one has bothered to shovel the paths out here since it snowed last night, but I know the layout.

This is one of my favourite areas—how the gardens and lush green lawns disappear into the forest on one side and up to the cliff edge on the other.

I feel like I'm on top of the world out here. The only place better is on the battlements, looking out to the ocean. It's quiet and cold up there, but it's a great place to think when I can't chop something.

"Did it bother Kalle?" Hettie wants to know.

"I never asked him. Probably should have. Camille was upset enough for everyone. They insulted her—and her dog, which is the very worst thing you can do to Camille. Odin said she's got a wicked throw."

Hettie laughs. "I think I'd like Camille."

"I think you would, too. It's too bad she didn't come with Odin."

"I can't believe he's married. And Kalle will be this summer. Any news about Gunnar?"

"Haven't heard anything. Stella will make him wait, make him grow up a bit." Talking about my brothers being married is strange like—

It shouldn't feel so strange, since *I'm* married too.

For now.

Outside, it's fresh and crisp and very cold. I breathe deep, my lungs filling with Arctic air, and Hettie hunches her shoulders. "How is Lyra?" she asks politely, burrowing hands into pockets.

"Good. I guess." I keep in touch with my sister through infrequent texts and Instagram reels that she keeps sending me. "She's in Chicago."

"I'd ask what she's been doing, but I'd rather talk about you. Tell me what you've been doing," she invites.

I tamp down the feeling of awkwardness. This is Hettie.

This is *Hettie*. Spencer was right: it was easier when it was the four of us. It was easier to push down what I was feeling.

Or maybe I didn't have to push it down as much when we were pretending to be friends. In all the years I've known her, I've never felt simple friendship for Hettie. It was always so much more.

"I live in Wabush," I tell her. "I set up nature reserves in the north part of the country. But you know all that." All that is information that can be found on the family's Wikipedia page.

"Are you there alone?" she asks.

"The Marsdens still live next door."

"I meant, *alone?*"

I stare ahead into the trees that are fast approaching. I want nothing more than to grab my ax and make short work of the first dead maple I can find.

But no; here I am making small talk with my wife who I haven't seen in years.

What do I tell her? What am I allowed to say? "Yeah."

"Just...'yeah'?" There's a note of frustration in her tone and I can't blame her. There are things—years of things and people and places—we need to find out about, so I might as well put on my big boy pants and get going.

"Yeah," I repeat. "I'm not going to tell you I've lived like a monk, but there's nobody in my life. Never anyone serious since you left."

There's so much history between us, and now so much uncertainty, so there's no point beating around the bush with Hettie. If I know something, I might as well tell her. And if I don't, I'll tell her that too.

"That sounds lonely," she offers.

I shrug, unwilling to get into just how lonely I've been. I like being alone, enjoy my own company, but loneliness is a whole other beast. "Tell me about this guy."

"You're not wasting any time."

"Too much time has been wasted," I counter. "You're here for a reason, so let's hear about it."

Hettie's exhale comes out as a cloud of steam. "Timothy. He's a real estate agent."

I snort. I can't help it. Hettie loved the beach, the forests like me. She was happy with animals, with books. I can't see her with someone who spends his time pushing houses onto other people.

"He's nice," she protests. "He's a good man. Decent."

"And he wants to raise Tema?" Because as a father, I need to know that. My feelings for Hettie aside, the main issue here is Tema. What's best for her.

It's a shock how quickly my way of thinking has veered off to focus on her.

She's my daughter. I *should* be thinking of her.

My question hangs between us. "He cares about her," she says carefully.

That doesn't say much. "Does he love her?"

"Everyone loves Tema." Hettie's smile is full of pride, full of love, and I get that. I've only known about Tema for less than a day, and already it feels like my heart has expanded so that Tema could crawl inside of it.

How is that possible? I've never given much consideration to being a father but now it's all I can think about. And I have a feeling that this isn't going to change when the shock wears off. "Yeah, I—she looks like Lyra."

"I know." Hettie gives a rueful laugh. "We have to make sure we don't have any magazines or anything with her picture in the house."

"Might be tough," I mutter, thinking how often Lyra seems to find the spotlight. She's like Gunnar in that way—loves the attention—only Lyra's questionable choices often land her on the tabloid covers.

Hettie glances behind us at the castle growing a little smaller with every step. "The world does love the Laandian royal family."

"Has Abigail been with you the whole time?" I ask, as usual wanting to get off the topic of my family.

"She wouldn't let me go on my own, and when I found out about Tema, she wouldn't leave me. I couldn't have done it without her."

"I wish you didn't have to. I wish you told me." The sudden pain has me catching my breath.

"I'm sorry," she says, and she sounds sincere. "I wanted to, so many times, but..."

"Why didn't you? You find out you're pregnant and—" A horrible thought occurs and my gut twists.

"There was no doubt that she was yours," Hettie says firmly.

"But you still didn't want to tell me."

Hettie sighs. The only sounds are the crunch of snow beneath our boots, the caw of a crow in a nearby tree. "The day I found out I was pregnant, my grandfather came home with a magazine. We lived with him for the first two years, and he was a huge help, but he couldn't understand—he thought I should have forgotten about you the moment we flew out of Laandian airspace. Clearly, he didn't understand the concept of love much."

"Probably hated seeing you hurting. If you were," I add, clearly fishing for information.

And Hettie knows it. "I was," she says softly. "And you're defending the man who told me to get over you." I shrug and Hettie watches me for a long moment before continuing. "He brought home the magazine because it had a picture of you. You were with a group of girls from high school. Crystal. Amy."

"Ah." I'm beginning to see where this is going. "You never liked them."

"They never liked me much either. You were holding hands with Sophie Laz."

Spencer's youngest sister. I have a vague memory of when it was that Hettie might be talking about. "When was this?"

"About three months after I left. I told myself that the missed periods were because my body was adjusting, but when I started throwing up every day, Abigail made me take a test. It was positive. Obviously. We talked about it all night, and I was going to call you. I didn't know what I was going to say, but I planned on telling you. And then I saw the picture and you had moved on—"

"Hettie, no. That night—" I blow out my own cloud of steam. "I barely remember that night. It was Sophie Laz's eighteenth birthday and she was at Kalle's celebrating with some friends. Neither Kalle or Edie were there, and I was drunk. Stupid drunk. So drunk that I let Crystal and those girls do shots with me. So many shots. The rest is blurry, but I remember one of your brothers was there, and said something to me about you. I got in his face, demanded to know where you went."

"Which brother?" she asks.

"I think it was Reggie, before he—" I cut myself off.

"Went back to jail," she finishes coolly. "You can say it. Reggie is the second of my brothers who went to jail. My lovely, rule-abiding family."

I'm not about to get into that with her. "Yeah, well, the girls were being stupid, and Sophie left her own party and dragged me out of there by the hand before I got into a fight. There must have been someone outside with a camera. After Mom died, there were always reporters in town taking pictures of how we were doing. Obviously, that one showed that I wasn't doing well."

"No."

"I went back to Wabush after that. Nothing happened with anyone from here." Which may imply that something happened with someone not from here. "I mean—"

"I thought..." She heaves a sigh. "I thought a lot of things."

"Yeah. Like what?"

We walk for long minutes and I let Hattie take her time to find the right words. The castle grows smaller in the distance, and I start to breathe again.

There's something about being here that makes everything tight. Everything harder, even breathing. I love my family, but I don't love who we are.

I never have.

"I thought about telling you every day," Hettie finally admits. "I'd plan out conversations with you—ones where you were mad, and others when you were happy. But it was the little voice in my head that kept telling me that you'd want Tema but not me." Her voice catches, and if her hands weren't stuffed in her pockets, I would take one of them in mine. "I thought if I told you about her, you'd want her to come back here, live in the castle, but you wouldn't want me." I stop walking, fixated by the raw vulnerability in her voice, her face. "I thought when I left, you stopped loving me. And I couldn't take the chance of you taking away my baby."

"I would never do that," I vow.

"Yeah, well, you tell yourself lots of stupid things when you're missing someone."

"Hettie." I fight the urge to pull her into my arms, to show her how wrong she was. "I told you before, there has never been a day go by where I didn't want you."

"Then why didn't you come and get me?"

21

Hettie

B O STEPS AWAY FROM me. "I..."

"I thought..." I hesitate because I've never told anyone this, not even Abigail. "I thought if I left, you'd come after me. I thought you'd come find me, that we'd be okay."

I don't realize I'm crying until my cheeks start to get very cold.

"But you didn't," I manage. "Leaving you was the hardest thing I've ever done." I'm here, standing in front of Bo after so long and there's no room for secrets. "I didn't *want* to go. It was the last, the very last thing I wanted, but you shut down after the queen died. You weren't my Bo anymore, and I didn't know what to do to get you back. It hurt too much to watch you collapse on yourself. That might make me selfish—"

"No, you're right," Bo admits. He swallows, his gaze fixed on a point over my head. "I wasn't... me. I couldn't... I wouldn't have been able to come and bring you home, even if I'd thought you wanted me to."

"I did." Bo shuts his eyes at my whispered admission. "But I thought..."

"And I thought..." He shakes his head, his blue eyes focused on me again. "We made a mess of this, didn't we?"

I nod sadly. "Maybe. But we were young."

"Stupid?"

"Do you think it was stupid to get married?"

"No," Bo says quickly. "Marrying you was my dream and those two days together were the happiest of my life."

My heart does one of those squeezes again. "And then it went wrong. Losing your mother…"

Bo closes up. I can see it happen—his face tightens and his entire body stiffens like he's put up a wall between us. And that was why I left in the first place. After the funeral, he barely spoke. Wouldn't look at me. Spent all of his time in the forest.

His family let him go because they were grieving on their own, everyone concerned with how Lyra was handling it because she had been in the car with her mother.

No one knew about Bo's guilt, how he blamed himself.

My heart breaks for him, but I'm not letting this wall stand. "Talk to me," I say, trying for gentle and stern. "It wasn't your fault. You need to believe that."

"Haven't been able to yet. And look what happened."

"Things can change."

He shrugs and turns back to the castle. "But I've already lost you."

The desolation in his voice stops me from following him. I let him go because I can't tell him I still love him, that maybe I never stopped.

I don't know what to do.

The specter of Timothy hovers to the side, reminding me I gave a promise to a good man, and I will only hurt Bo if I give him false hope.

Even if I tell him I still have feelings for him, what good will that do? What would it change? My life has moved to Victoria—far away from my family.

That was the reason we got married without telling anyone. I had two brothers in prison, and a third who was a constant fixture in the town bars until they would throw him out for fighting. On paper, Hank looked legitimate, but Mabel had long ago relayed the rumours—that his garage was both a chop shop for stolen cars and a front for drug dealing.

Even in a country as small and beautiful as Laandia, there is crime, and my brothers seem to be always part of it.

My *family*—a few of my cousins are career criminals and I had an aunt who killed her husband with a cleaver. My grandmother lived on the street.

Even if I told Bo I still loved him, why would he want *me* when I come from that?

I stay outside as long as I can feel my toes, walking along the edge of the trees to the cliffs overlooking the sea. There's a bench, so clearly, this is a good thinking spot.

With all of my thinking, I don't seem to be able to make any decisions. I just come up with more questions.

It is a relief that Bo didn't replace me as soon as I left. That the love we shared didn't vanish—might still be there.

But then I circle back to my family and what the king must think of them. He said I was now a member of his family, but what does that mean?

It means my daughter will be seen as a princess, as soon as Bo admits his paternity.

Things will change when that happens.

I've no doubt Bo will want to do that as soon as he drums up the courage to face a reporter. He always hated talking to the press.

Tema will have to do that now for the rest of her life. The Laandian royal family has never been hounded like other monarchies, but there has always been interest because of King Magnus's popularity.

Prince Bo and his love child.

Secret marriage kept from the world.

Prince Bo's new family wants to overthrow the Laandian monarchy.

I can picture the headlines now.

Maybe it would be best to take Tema and go back to Victoria, pretending we never made the trip. I can convince Bo to give me a divorce—maybe he could visit once a year to stay in Tema's life.

That would be better for Tema. For the royal family not to have to deal with *my* family. Bo wouldn't have to deal with the press, the constant questions and finding the right words. That would be best for him.

But what would be the best for me?

22

Bo

"Bo," Dad calls as I head up the stairs to collect Hettie for dinner.

I may have left her outside alone, but I won't leave her to face my family by herself. And I did stop midway back to the castle and saw her walking to the bench.

And then inside, I checked out the window and saw her sitting on the bench.

I wait for Dad and Duncan to join me on the landing. "It's good to see you back," Duncan says as he gives me a one-armed hug. Duncan has been a constant at the castle my entire life and to see him without Dad would be strange.

"Hettie excited about dinner?" Dad asks.

"Would you be?" I counter.

He considers that. "Maybe not," he admits, which I don't believe. My father is the most outgoing person I've ever met. "But it'll be fun. And I can't wait for more of that little girl."

"She'll definitely shake things up around here," Duncan agrees, and after a nod at Dad, he keeps walking.

Dad puts a hand on my shoulder. "I want to talk to you."

"That doesn't sound good." Not that I can blame him—I've dumped a lot on this family today.

"Hettie said something to me that I didn't agree with." His face loses his customary grin. "Something about how you feel responsible for your mother's death."

My stomach twists painfully and I search for the right thing to say. "Yeah," I come up with.

"Is that true?"

I shrug.

"Bo—you can't be serious."

I can't meet his gaze. "I told her about Hettie," I mutter, staring at the wall behind his head. "She left to pick up Lyra and never made it home." I drag my gaze to him, so afraid of what I'll find in his expression. "What would you think?"

"I wouldn't think anything like that." He grips my shoulder, his expression earnest, like he's begging me to believe him. "Son, it was the weather. It was a storm in October that surprised everyone. Ice on the roads. And really, bad luck. It was an accident."

"She was upset," I say doggedly, like I'm a broken record skipping on the lyrics.

"You don't know that."

"She was when she left."

"But you have no idea what she was like in the car. Your mother was rarely upset, unless it was at me. She loved you, so so much, and I can't imagine her ever being as upset as you think she was."

I shrug because there's nothing I can say. There's nothing my father can say. I've felt this way for eight years and I'm not about to change just because he says *no, it ain't so.*

Dad stands and watches me for a moment. He's a tall man but I still have an inch or so over him.

His beard is mostly white now, with more in his hair as well. It's a new thing and I can chalk that up to his recent bout of appendicitis, the stress of running a country, and Lyra.

"I'm not going to convince you that you don't need to blame yourself, am I?" he asks ruefully.

"Probably not."

Dad nods. "Have it your way. I made an appointment with you tomorrow with a Dr. Patel."

I take a step back with surprise. "I don't need a doctor."

"She's a psychologist. I want you to talk to her. I think it'll help."

"I—what? You want me to see a shrink?"

That's the last thing I expected him to say.

"I should have made you go years ago," Dad continues. "Gunnar and Lyra have both talked to someone. Odin too. I should have made it mandatory for you all to go."

"I don't want to talk to anyone," I say with more heat than I need to.

"I know." He squeezes my shoulder. "But you're going to."

Doesn't sound like I have a choice.

I turn and walk—stomp—away. It's difficult for me to talk to people on a regular basis but delving into emotional terrain isn't my idea of a good time. What am I supposed to say? How am I supposed to bring things up? Am I even allowed to talk about royal stuff?

All this flies around my mind with warp speed, distracting me enough that I don't realize I'm outside Hettie's door. And my hand is raised to knock before I can stop my whirling thoughts.

Hettie opens the door just as a squeal of Tema's laughter drifts out. "She's almost ready," Hettie begins, but I cut her off.

"You talked to my father," I blurt.

Her mouth opens with surprise. "I—yes, I did." She steps back to allow me to come in. I know it's not because I'm welcome, but she had always hated confrontations where other people could hear. She spent years hiding her family issues even before we got together, and any disagreements—not that there were many—would happen in private.

Not in the hallway of my family home, but behind closed doors.

Spencer asked me once if we ever fought because he had never seen any evidence of it.

I step in and firmly shut the door behind me before I face Hettie. She crosses her arms. "About me," I add, just to clarify.

She lifts her chin. "I did," she repeats without an ounce of apology. "I thought he should know that you blame yourself. I thought he might be able to help."

"I don't need help."

The words slip out automatically and the expression on Hettie's face tells me I'm so very wrong.

"Is that Bo?" comes Abigail's voice from the other room. "She's almost ready."

"I don't want to eat dinner," wails Tema.

"Is everything okay?" I demand.

"It's fine. Tema is just being Tema. You lost me once." She lowers her voice. "Are you willing to risk that again?" Now it's my mouth that drops open. "You should talk to your father."

More voices from the bedroom, and suddenly Tema laughs. The sound does something strange to my heart.

"She's fine," Hettie adds. "Abigail's got her."

I don't want Abigail to get Tema. I want to be the one who makes everything better for her.

For my daughter.

But just looking at Hettie, I know there's no chance of me getting that opportunity unless I— "He wants me to talk to a therapist," I admit. I might be welcome in Tema's life, but already I know I want more.

I want to be able to get her, to make her laugh like Abigail does. To comfort and console and help her with her homework—

I'm jealous of Abigail and that's a horrible way to feel about my friend.

Hettie looks thoughtful and clearly doesn't have a clue about what's going on in my mind. "That might be better."

"I've never—I don't know—"

She reaches out and squeezes my arm, her hand lingering on my forearm for an extra moment. "There's a first time for every-thing."

"Hettie..." And then I look at her—really look at her—and I forget what I'm about to say.

Her hair is long and straight and... glossy. The light hits the top of her head and gives her a glow. She's wearing makeup—not a lot but enough for me, who vividly remembers every freckle and birthmark on her body—and a dress.

At least I think it's a dress; it's black, short sleeved and looks like an over-sized T-shirt that hits at her knees. Tights.

Yes, I check out her legs. "You changed," I say stupidly because my mind flashes back to another Hettie—twenty-years old and impossibly beautiful in a pink dress with flowers in her hair. Walking toward me on a warm autumn day with a smile brighter than the sun.

Why did I ever make her leave?

"I'm about to dine with royalty." She tries for casual, but there's a note in her voice that I suspect is fear. I'm glad I didn't make her go down alone.

"It's my family," I counter, my own voice sounding strained.

"What's wrong?"

"You—the dress." I motion to her legs, which probably isn't a good thing. "Made me think of you in your wedding dress."

"Oh." Her hand slides off my arm.

"You looked so beautiful then, and your hair." I swallow, fighting the urge to touch her hair. "You look even more so now."

Her voice catches and the way she looks at me... "Thank you," she whispers.

I'm not one to believe in second chances but the way Hettie looks at me... maybe.

Just maybe.

23

Hettie

BO SAID I LOOK beautiful.

It's been a long time since someone told me that, other than Tema. Timothy is a good man, but he's not free with affection or compliments. But Bo, even with his reserve and quiet stoicism, never hesitated in telling me that I looked pretty, or catching me in a hug.

I'm not without affection, and it's not that Timothy never touches me, but it's one thing I missed about Bo.

One of many.

When Tema emerges, followed by a harried Abigail, it's obvious what the problem was. Her dark red hair is a frizzled nest from Abigail's failed attempts at making it look presentable for a royal dinner.

"You want to try?" Abigail asks. At least she managed to keep Tema from pulling the dress off. My daughter is at the stage where she hates wearing anything but her favourite pair of purple velour leggings when forced to dress up.

"You look pretty," Bo says and Tema's face lights up.

"We can go now," she says to me. "Prince Daddy says I look pretty."

I look at Abigail and then at Bo. His expression is bemused and I can tell Tema has got him wrapped tight around her finger. I shrug. "Let's go then."

"Sorry about the hair," Abigail says.

I laugh. "You do a better job than I do. At least you kept her away from the scissors."

Tema leads the way to the staircase, dancing in front of Bo. It is going to take a while for me to find my way about this place.

And for the first time, I allow the little thought of *maybe I should stay* take root.

"Are you the oldest?" Tema demands of Bo as we start down the stairs. I'm torn between looking around at the variety of weapons in this place and their conversation.

"No, Kalle is, and then Odin."

She peers up at him from beneath bangs that need a trim. "You mean there's princes bigger than you?"

Bo chuckles and my heart gives a funny squeeze at the sound. "Just Kalle, but he can't swing an ax like I can."

"You have an ax?"

Bo nods. "Odin has a sword."

Tema clutches her hands together. "Do you think he'll let me play with it?"

"Absolutely not," I cut in. "No weapons allowed."

Bo glances over his shoulder at me. "He's got training ones too. Camille got pretty good at sparring with him when she was here."

"That's Lady Camille; the one who runs a country?" Tema demands.

"She's been using Google," Abigail offers.

"That's never a good thing," I mutter.

"Tell me about Prince Gunnar, who used to race cars. Do you think he'll teach me to drive fast like him?"

Tema has always wanted a brother, always been intrigued by big families. I've told her the bare minimum about mine, and luckily out of sight means out of mind for her because she's never wanted to know more.

She wants to know everything about the royal family.

"Nope," Bo announces. "I'll teach you to drive."

"Really?" And she takes his hand. The expression on Tema's face as she looks up at him...

It kind of breaks my heart. It's amazing to see the connection already forged between them, but the fact I denied them both any relationship weighs heavy.

Almost as heavy as the knowledge that, in a few moments, I'm going to be face-to-face with the princes that Tema is demanding to know so much about.

And I doubt they'll be happy with me. King Magnus was kind and welcoming, but he's had years of practice being polite and diplomatic with his enemies.

Does Laandia have enemies?

I can only imagine Kalle, Odin and Gunnar will see me as an enemy because of what I've done to Bo.

My chest tightens with every step. I got past the king un-scathed, but these are Bo's brothers, and I know how close they've always been.

Gunnar lost the love of his life because he helped me leave. He might have found happiness with someone else, but I'm sure he blames me for that.

They all must blame me.

This is going to be brutal.

"When can we start?" Tema demands.

Bo laughs aloud. It's been so long since I've heard him laugh that I've forgotten the sound. It's big and booming, kind of like a sudden fireworks display, and very infectious since it's the total opposite of his personality. "When you're sixteen," he says, and Tema chortles along with him.

She keeps hold of his hand, walking carefully beside him rather than skipping down the stairs like she does at home. We reach the main floor, the double doors where we first came in.

I can picture the princes and Lyra running through the halls, sliding down the banister. Playing in the secret passages and down in the dungeon.

I imagined growing up in a castle—every kid in Battle Harbour did—but now there's a chance that my daughter might have that opportunity.

The castle is grand and beautiful and incredibly intimidating, but there's also kind of a homey feeling to it.

"Good evening." Mrs. Theissen steps around the corner.

Except for her—homey houses don't have housekeepers stepping out of the shadows.

"The others are in the small dining room," she says to Bo. "Even His Majesty is already there."

Does that mean we're late? "Thanks, Mrs. Theissen," Bo says.

She nods. "Is there anything you need in your rooms?" she asks me and Abigail.

"Everything is fine, thank—" I begin.

"Lego," Tema decides. "Do you have any Lego around here?"

"Tema," I hiss.

Mrs. Theissen nods with a hint of a smile. "There may still be some in storage. I'll see what I can find for you."

Tema mimics her movement. "That would be lovely, thank you," she says in a grave voice.

I can only shake my head.

Bo leads us to the dining room and pauses for a moment, glancing down at me with an encouraging smile. Abigail knows how nervous I am, even without me saying a word, and gives my hand a squeeze before drifting behind me.

She's always got my back. "*Small* dining room?" she murmurs.

Bo clears his throat and steps through the doors. "Hey."

Heads turn and my stomach actually clenches with fright.

The princes of Laandia—Kalle, Odin, and Gunnar—are big and broad and, quite frankly, beautiful. The pictures online don't do them justice. It's been years since I've seen them in person and they look the same, only different. Better, like they've grown into their height, their shoulders, and their smiles.

Only no one is smiling at me.

And why would they? I am Hettie Crow, daughter of a fisherman, part of the Crow family whose reputations are a part of the lore of the town, like how Leif Erickson helped fight off a German attack during World War II. This is the Laandian royal family, and I didn't tell Bo that he had a child.

That might be actually treason. They have dungeons in the castle. Abigail needs to—

Bo touches the small of my back like he knows I'm about to bolt. His hand is strong and warm and sends a shiver through me that isn't a bad one.

It's the first time he's touched me since that hug.

"There she is," calls King Magnus from beside the massive fireplace, the sleeves of his flannel shirt rolled up because of the heat of the fire. "C'mon over here, little one."

And my daughter dances over to the king of Laandia, who crouches as he holds open his arms to her. She gives a high-pitched squeal of laughter as Magnus swoops her off her feet, carrying her over to Duncan Laz.

The king of Laandia just picked up my daughter.

His granddaughter.

"Looks like she made a friend," Abigail murmurs.

Bo chuckles as he presses me forward. I take a step, feeling like I'm facing a firing squad.

The princes of Laandia never come across as very royal, but there's no denying each of them has a presence. Kalle—oldest, biggest, and broadest—wears his confidence like a shroud. He still looks like the athlete he was, but there's a maturity that he's gained in the last eight years, like he's grown up.

Or maybe it's because of Edie.

Everyone in Battle Harbour knows Edie England, saw her friendship with Kalle as the first step to their inevitable love story. It's nice to see them finally together, and the two of them standing there—like a perfect royal couple.

"Hettie." Edie is the first to speak. Her smile is friendly like the king's, but there's a hint of grace to her steps as she comes toward me. I can totally imagine her as a queen someday. "It's good to see you."

"Thank you for giving Mabel the job," I tell her instead of the polite greeting I should have practiced. "She really likes working at the pub."

"She's doing us a favour," Edie assures me, pressing my arm. "Plus, she's a lot of fun once you get to know her."

Odin is right behind her and I'm amazed when he stoops to brush an awkward kiss on my cheek. "It's good to see you, Hettie," he says, sounding like he actually means it.

"You, too," I stammer. "Congratulations on your marriage." My cheeks flush.

"We could say the same to you." Gunnar shoulders aside his big brother. "I always knew Bo had his secrets, but this one is a biggie."

And then he hugs me.

"I'm... sorry?" I manage, too astonished to return the hug.

"It should be Bo apologizing," Kalle snorts, heading for the carafe of wine on the table. "Haven't heard anything from him about why he kept this so quiet."

They didn't know. And they have no idea why Bo never told them.

I never really believed Bo didn't tell his brothers about our wedding. I knew how close they were and while I thought he'd be able to keep it from his father, I expected Bo to confess to the princes.

I assumed he would, and when there was still no word over the years... well, I didn't feel all that friendly toward the family. But if they didn't know, if he really didn't tell anyone...

Bo stands solid at my side as they greet Abigail, Kalle handing us glasses of wine filled almost to the brim. They are just as friendly to her and she responds with casual reverence.

"You didn't tell them?" I ask Bo in a low voice.

"No," he says out of the corner of his mouth.

"I thought you would have."

"No." His gaze meets mine, still a little wary. "I wanted to do it together, but after you left..." He shrugs.

There was no point, I finish silently.

Edie takes the lead, asking me questions that could be polite conversation if the situation were different.

They want to know everything about me, including why I left, and what's going to happen now that I'm back.

I'd like to know that too.

Magnus joins us with Duncan, still carrying Tema. The two men both have hearts in their eyes when they look at Tema, who must already know the power she has over them. "These are your uncles," Magnus tells her.

"Prince Kalle, Prince Odin, and Gunnar," Tema recites like she's learned their names in school.

"I'm a prince too," Gunnar points out.

"Can you still be a prince if you race cars?" Tema asks him.

"You can be anything you want if you're a prince," he says with a grin.

Kalle snorts again. "She reminds me of Lyra," he says to Bo.

"I see Mabel," Edie corrects, smiling at Tema.

"I remind me of me," Tema tells them.

"Tema," I hiss. King Magnus chuckles.

"I don't know these people so I have no idea if I'm like them or not," Tema says without an ounce of apology in her voice.

"They're your aunties," Magnus says.

"Aunties," Gunnar guffaws. I know what he means—Mabel would hate to be called auntie.

"You remember when Aunt Mabel came to visit. I mean," I stammer, not knowing if I should admit that. "You were pretty young."

"I still don't know them," Tema says.

"We'll change that," Bo promises. "You hungry?"

24

Bo

FAMILY DINNERS ARE THE one time we can all relax within the castle walls. It's just family, no foreign leaders or celebrity friends. And now that we've opened it to include Edie and Stella, Gunnar's girlfriend—who rushes in with Spencer just before the meal is served—it's even a little more comfortable. There's the usual teasing and roasting, but the competitiveness that inevitably comes when the four of us are together subsides. Unless, of course, Lyra is home, and then we all have to pay homage to her. She likes to think we're all her minions.

Hettie seems to relax when Stella arrives. Stella is Duncan's daughter and grew up with us until Duncan divorced her mother and moved into the castle full-time with Spencer. She's only two years younger than Hettie, and the two of them, along with Abigail, spend most of dinner talking about people from high school.

That is when Abigail isn't laughing with Spencer.

"I thought Spencer and Lyra—" I overhear Stella say to Gunnar.

"Spencer," Gunnar corrects under his breath. "Never been sure about Lyra."

"You don't know that," Edie says from beside me.

"No one knows anything about what Lyra thinks." Kalle shakes his head.

"And whose fault is that?" Edie chides. "She's your sister."

My sister is the one topic Spencer and I have never talked about, mainly because she's my sister and, as much as I love her, she's high-maintenance. Plus, I've seen Spencer with Abigail, and I've always liked what I've seen. It's easy with the two of them. Comfortable. And, selfishly, it works with Hettie and me.

When there was a Hettie and me.

Tema sits on the left side of Dad and basically holds court at the end of the table. She's smart and quick and so funny. Polite, but speaks her mind, whatever might come into it. I've never really spent much time with children, and neither have my brothers, and all of us seem to watch the little girl with a sense of awe.

For me, there's a new feeling of pride toward her, at how she gets Duncan Laz not only to talk about his time in the rock band Kraftiig, but to also give a demonstration of air guitar.

I thought Stella was going to spit wine all over the table when he did that.

Hettie asks Edie about her wedding plans. Stella grabs Tema's attention when she tells her about her animal rescue in town, and the two plan a visit. Gunnar and I talk planes.

It's like a normal family sharing a meal together.

No mention is made of the fact Hettie has been gone for eight years.

Not until the end of the meal.

The plates have been cleared and Kalle refills the wine glasses. Tema is wide awake and still has both Dad and Duncan completely under her spell. I like the way Hettie manages to keep watch over her as well as focus on the conversation.

"So, Hettie," Kalle begins with a sideways glance at Odin. "Now that you're back, what does that mean for the two of you?"

"That's none of your business," I jump in quickly.

"Oh, I think it is," Kalle says mildly. "The whole monarchy thing makes it my business."

"We're not talking about it now. Or here."

"When do you propose we talk about it then? When she disappears for another eight years, taking the third in line to the throne with her?"

"Kalle—" I growl, but Hettie holds up her hand.

"It's okay, Bo. Kalle is right—we do need to have this conversation but I would appreciate doing so when my daughter isn't within earshot. Her listening skills are very well developed, especially when the topic is something she shouldn't be hearing."

"What shouldn't I hear?" Tema calls from her seat at the other end of the table.

"Fair enough," Kalle has the grace to look mollified.

"And I do realize your responsibility to the throne, but I'd like Bo and me to be able to talk first, if that's all right. All this has been rather sudden—"

"Eight years," Gunnar coughs into his hand, and I glare at him. "Sorry, Hettie."

"It's complicated," I say through gritted teeth. Yesterday, I told them what I know. There hasn't been time for anything to have changed.

That's not entirely true; what hasn't changed is the fact that I still might be completely in love with Hettie Crow, only I'm determined not to mess it up like I did before.

"Kalle shouldn't have said anything," I say as I walk Hettie back to her room after dinner. Tema has Abigail by the hand and is skipping down the long hall.

I've never seen anyone skip in the castle. Not even when we were kids. We ran, wrestled, and raced. Not even Lyra skipped.

"He wasn't wrong," Hettie says. "We do need to talk about it."

"About what, exactly?"

"What's going to happen. The future? Tema's future."

"The fact you want a divorce," I can't help but add. "I didn't think that was appropriate dinner conversation."

Hettie doesn't confirm or deny.

Abigail and Tema disappear into the room and I linger in the hall with Hettie. All my positive feelings about how perfectly Hettie fit in with my family, and how well Tema did at dinner, are overshadowed by one word.

Divorce.

We haven't had much of a marriage to speak of, but still—part of me knew that Hettie was still mine. At least I hoped she was. If we are to make the split legal, that means she's gone forever. Maybe not Tema, but Hettie.

The thought knots up my insides.

"Do you want to talk about it?" Hettie asks. Her lips press together and she looks... I'm not sure if it's wishful thinking, or I'm transferring my thoughts on her, but Hettie looks sad.

"Not really," I admit. "But yeah."

"I have to give Tema a bath. If you don't mind waiting—"

"Can I help?" Hettie looks surprised. "I mean, it's not like I've ever given a kid a bath before, but I figure it's something I need to know how to do, right?"

"Let's give it a try then."

Bathtime consists of filling the tub with a mountain of bubbles and letting Tema play in them. Hettie brought a collection of ducks and boats and a Slurpee cup she uses to rinse the shampoo from Tema's hair.

"Always wash her hair first," Hettie instructs. "And leave the conditioner on for a while because she's got the worst tangles."

"It's not the worst. Abigail has curlier hair than I do unless she makes it straight," Tema says, not looking up from her naval battle—boats against ducks.

Abigail went back to her room as soon as I stepped up to help with bathtime. Not that I do much to help. Hettie gives a play-by-play as she does things and I'm okay with that. Tema looks slippery and there's a lot of bubbles. I wouldn't want to deal with soap in the eyes.

But even though I sit on the toilet and watch, it's surprisingly nice to be involved.

Hair care has been finished and Tema is still mid-battle when Hettie's phone rings from the other room.

"That might be..." she stammers. "I need to check."

Him. It must be him. "Go take it. I've got this," I tell her, trying for casual and coming up with mildly miserable.

"I can call him back," she insists.

"Go take your call. How hard can this be?" I wink at Tema. "I know how to give myself a bath."

Hettie bites her lip. "I'll be right in the next room. Behave yourself, please," she says to Tema.

"We're good." I wave her away. "Do you normally not behave?" I ask Tema, moving closer to bob one of the ducks on top of the bubbles. Every time it lands, bubbles fly everywhere, making Tema laugh.

"I always behave," she announces.

"Do you always tell the truth?"

Tema grins. "Of course. Princesses always tell the truth."

I'm not sure that's always the case, but I'm not about to correct her. Not when I've got an opportunity right before me. "Do you know who your mom is talking to?" This time I nail the casual.

"Probably Timothy." She makes motorboat sounds as she moves a boat over a mountain of bubbles, much like a fishing boat in the middle of the Atlantic.

I wonder how much bubble bath Hettie dumped in the water. Any time I've had a bubble bath, they've never lasted this long.

"This Timothy—what's he like?" Part of me is straining to hear any of Hettie's conversation, but she's taken the call in the living room. I wonder what she's telling him. Things about my family? Things about me?

"He makes waffles," Tema reports.

"Like, for a living?"

"No, for supper. He can only make waffles."

"I can make more than waffles," I can't help but tell her.

"It's not a competition," she says with an expression older than her seven years.

"I know it's not."

"That's what Mommy always says when I complain about something my friend Mikey can do that I can't," she explains. "She tells me all the things that I *can* do. You're a prince. Timothy sells houses. There's lots of things you can do that he can't."

I squint at Tema. "Are you sure you're only seven? You're not some small old person in a kid body?"

"No!" She laughs and scoops a handful of bubbles and blows it at me.

"I wouldn't start that," I warn her, taking my own handful of bubbles. "I'm very good in a bubble fight."

"Not as good as me." She leans out of the tub to smear bubbles on my beard.

"It's not a competition," I remind her with a laugh, dumping my handful on her head.

"It's *on*," Tema cries.

I've never had so much fun playing in the bubbles. Of course, the bathroom is a disaster when Hettie comes back.

"What are you doing?" she demands.

I look at Tema and Tema looks at me. "Get her!" Tema throws the first handful of bubbles at Hettie and I'm quick to follow with a laugh that echoes around the bathroom.

25

Hettie

I DID NOT EXPECT bath time to become a water fight. Bo surprised me.

It's not the first time since I've been back.

He helps me put Tema to bed, cleaning up the water damage in the bathroom while I brush the tangles out of her hair. He sits on the edge of the bed while I read her a chapter of Harry Potter.

He drops a kiss on her forehead when he says good night.

I take a minute with Tema, but the excitement from the bath has worn off, and the lavender bubbles do their trick like they always do. Her eyes are heavy and with one last kiss, I back out of the room.

"Mommy?"

"Yes, Tema-toot?"

"I like it here. I wish we'd come sooner."

The sigh escapes before I can stop it. "Me too, baby. Me too."

Bo is poking the fire and I wonder if he heard our comments. Not that it matters; I do wish we'd come sooner. Seeing Bo with our daughter, it's not difficult to feel the regret of not telling him.

If I had told him I was pregnant, things would be so different. But I didn't, and here we are.

"Thank you," I tell him as I sink onto the couch.

He frowns. "I'm not sure exactly what you're thanking me for, but you're welcome. I had fun." He points through the fire. "With her."

"Thank you for not being upset about me not telling you. You had every right to be angry."

"Ah." He sets down the poker and comes to sit beside me. Not too close, but less than a cushion distance apart this time.

I make note of how close he is, and how I wouldn't be opposed to having him a little closer.

Not that I should suggest, or hope for it.

"Getting upset wasn't really an option." Bo shifts, resting his arm on the back of the couch as he looks at me. "If I was mad, it would have gotten in the way of me getting to know her." He points to the bedroom. "But you never know what the therapist is going to tell me to do."

I smile, realizing he's joking. "You're going to talk to someone?"

"I don't really have a choice there either," he says ruefully.

"Like you told me, you always have a choice."

The blue in his eyes is intense. "Do I?"

I don't think he's asking about the therapist. "I think it'll be good for you," I say instead.

"Have you ever?"

I shake my head. "It probably would have helped when I was growing up, but no. Anyway, I have Abigail. There's no keeping secrets from her, and she's always quite open with her opinions."

"What do you think is going on with her and Spencer?" Bo frowns again, and just the slight movement in his forehead makes him look more like his father.

The king.

I have to remember that this isn't just Bo sitting here in the warmth of the fire with me, but a man who has a duty to his own family, as well as a country.

"Nothing. Yet." Because Abigail might give in to whatever she feels for Spencer, but she won't consider anything longer than a few days until she knows what I'm going to do. And it's not just me that will keep Abigail at my side. She loves Tema almost as much as I do.

"Depends on this, then." Bo motions between the two of us. "Maybe."

The fire cracks and sparks flare as a log catches fire.

There are still sparks between us, but we need more than that. We need... I'm not sure.

Forgiveness? For ourselves as well as each other? It would be a start but would it be enough. We have eight years to get through.

We need more than one conversation for that.

"Maybe we should figure it out. For their sake." Bo's fingers stretch out to rest on my shoulder. The touch sends a jolt through me and I shift without realizing it.

Bo drops his arm.

"I don't know if it's that easy," I admit.

"It could be. You tell me how you're feeling, and then I'll tell you how I feel."

A smile tugs at my lips. "Why do I have to go first?"

"Because you're braver than I am."

"I don't know, I've seen you climb pretty big trees."

"You've had a baby. Alone." He shifts again but his arm doesn't move. "What was it like?"

"Having a baby?" I laugh. "It hurt."

He grins and it's so nice to see him open and... happy. There have been a lot of emotions crossing Bo's face, but I haven't seen a lot of happiness since I've been here.

Except when he's with Tema.

"I think I could have figured that out," he says. "Tell me about it."

"For the most part, it was easy. I was pretty sick for the first six months, and I didn't get that big. I managed to hide it until around then, if I was careful to wear baggy clothes. I might have a picture." I reach for my phone, reminded of the brief conversation with Timothy earlier.

He had asked what we had for dinner. Nothing about how it felt sharing a meal with the royal family. Nothing about what was said.

He spent more time telling me about his latest condo deal than asking how I was.

I push thoughts of Timothy out of my mind and scroll through my photos. There are so many of Tema and I show them to Bo.

He moves closer so we can look at the screen together, close enough for me to smell the spiciness of his cologne, almost masked by the soapy lavender scent of Tema's bubble bath.

"Here. This is me a few days before I went into labour."

Bo takes a long time to study the picture, even touching the screen with his finger. "You're beautiful," he says roughly. "You always have been, but seeing you like this... I wish I'd been there."

I nod. *Me too*. But I can't tell him that. Not yet.

"Were you with anyone?" he asks. "When you went into labour?"

"Abigail. We were watching The Suitor."

Bo makes a disgusted sound in his throat. "Do you still watch that?"

"Yes, and I have yet to ask Odin what he was thinking going on the show."

He tips his head back and laughs quietly. "I think we all asked him that. Craziest thing he's ever done, but at least it got him Camille."

"In a roundabout way. Tell me about—"

"No," he interrupts. "You first."

So I tell him what the contractions felt like, how scared I had been, but that Abigail had been as tough and strong as she always is. How my grandfather had been painting in his studio and we couldn't get him to hurry, so we left without him, taking a taxi through the streets of Victoria because I was terrified I wouldn't get to the hospital in time.

"Abigail kept complaining how we were missing a good part of the show to distract me. It was the overnights episode, and we kept talking about what we thought would happen, until the contractions got too severe and I couldn't really talk anymore. Things moved pretty fast—I was seven centimeters dilated when we got there, and about two hours later, I had Tema."

"Just like that?"

I snort-laugh. "No. No, it wasn't just like that, but that's what it feels like now. There were a few scary minutes because she was in distress, but I was pretty out of it. Abigail says it still haunts her."

"I guess I'm glad she was with you." He smiles ruefully, bitterness coating his tone like syrup on a spoon.

"I wanted to call you." I drop my gaze, unable to watch how he reacts. "I probably shouldn't tell you—"

"You should."

"We'd been talking about it for days. The entire pregnancy. Abigail would never give her opinion because she said it was up to me, but when I told her to get the phone, that I wanted you there—" Bo makes a noise in the back of his throat and my own tightens. "—she got it for me. She was ready to dial... and then I had to push because we needed to get her out. It wasn't until after that she said anything about it, but I... I didn't think it was fair."

Bo gets to his feet and begins to paces in front of the fire, his long strides eating up the room. It hurts to watch him.

"No," he mutters, hands pulling at his hair. "It wasn't fair. I missed *everything*—"

"Because I was afraid," I finish. "You're right, Bo. We did make a mess out of this."

"What do we do now?"

I get to my feet and walk over to him, my steps slow and measured so I don't give in to the urge to run.

Run to him, not away.

And I want to go to him, want to throw myself in his arms, apologizing for everything and showing him how much I missed him.

But not yet. And maybe not ever.

I stand before him and touch his arm. My fingers barely brush the flannel of his shirt when he makes a low groaning noise and brings his hand to cup my face. I lean into his palm, and the moment lengthens.

The fire cracks loudly in the quiet room, but neither of us moves. I study his face like it's the last time I'm going to see him.

Blue eyes the colour of the sky on a summer day. Dark blond hair that needs a cut. He'll get wrinkles early because of the furrow on his brow when he's deep in thought.

The reddish-blond beard tries to hide the mouth...

I trap his fingers between my cheek and my shoulder because I want him to keep touching me. It's difficult to pull my gaze away from his mouth. The mouth that gave me so many different kisses over the years. My first kiss had been from Bo.

I always thought he'd get my last one.

The room is warm, warmer still being so close to Bo. What would happen if I leaned in, tilted up? Because of the height difference, I'd have to go up on my tiptoes unless he lifted me up. I'd wrap my legs around his waist...

"Hettie." Bo's voice is low and pleading and I sway closer.

Tema coughs in the next room.

The sound is like a bucket of cold water and I jerk my chin, Bo's hand falling from my face. "Timothy." The expression of horror on Bo's face— "Not that I'm calling you Timothy," I quickly add. "It's just... I have... he's..." I glance over to my phone like Timothy were sitting there with it. "Bo. I made a commitment to Timothy."

"Yeah." The word is so gruff it's a growl.

"But I made a promise to you, all those years ago."

He stares at me, blue eyes darkening, and I raise a hand to his chest, resting it over his heart.

How can you tell if you break a heart? Does the beat change? Does it stutter when it cracks in half? Is there a physical reaction to hurting someone that bad?

Can I break Bo's heart?

"I need to decide what's best for me, and for Tema," I whisper. "I have to think of her. She has a life in Victoria. School. Friends. She's happy there."

"I know." It's almost a groan and his hands slide to my waist, resting on my hips. It's a gentle touch but it burns through to my insides. His head droops and he looks so sad. "It's just…"

"I know," I breathe.

Bo's head jerks up. "Do you? It's not just me?"

I meet his gaze and there's no hiding when he looks at me like that. "It's taking everything I've got not to be in your arms right now."

"Then *why*? Why are we doing this to ourselves? If you want to be with me—"

I do…

The words hang between us, and in that moment, it would be so easy to forget Timothy, to forget my life and let Bo be Bo. Let him convince me to stay.

Because in this moment, it would be so easy.

I draw in a shaky breath. There's more to us than this moment. There's eight years to repair, and while Bo could convince me, I need him to convince himself.

"When you told me that it had been a mistake to marry me, that broke me," I tell him in a low voice. Even the memory of it feels like a punch to the stomach. "And now when I find out it was because you felt guilty—"

"Why are you bringing this up? It was my fault."

"No." I plead with him with my gaze. "It wasn't. But only you can convince yourself to believe that. Going to talk to the therapist is a good start. Let's see what they say, and then..."

I can't even say *maybe,* although the word is right there, waiting like a conversation you don't want to have. Because before I can even think it, there are conversations I *need* to have.

"You said something earlier," I remind him. "About not losing me again."

"So if I don't see this doctor..."

"I don't think I can," I finish. I mean to step away from him, but I can't bring myself to break the connection. "But it's not just you. I have to deal with my guilt, because it's not going away. And my family. This isn't just about how we feel about each other."

"It's important," Bo insists.

"Yes, but we've never had a problem with how we feel about each other."

Feel. Not felt. And because of how I feel at this moment, how I've always felt about Bo, I let him pull me closer and rest his chin on the top of my head. His arms go around me and I wrap mine around his waist.

It feels so good to have him hold me that I let it go on for long minutes.

Probably longer than I should.

26

Bo

I ALMOST KISSED HETTIE last night.

Holding her in my arms after so long almost broke me. The way she looked at me, how soft her skin was against the roughness of my palm...

I've never felt a physical pain from wanting someone so much. But I've never wanted anyone like Hettie.

I didn't give in to the want. Hettie hasn't said how she feels about me, despite the way she might look at me. And there's still Timothy in the picture.

Timothy.

However much I dislike the thought of another man sharing her life, I respect Hettie too much to put her in that situation.

Even though I didn't kiss her, she haunted my dreams after I finally went to sleep. It was our wedding and Hettie walked through the trees toward me. It's not the first time I've dreamt of that day, but it was different this time.

Tema was there.

Tema danced beside her, with flowers in her hair and a huge smile on her face like she was the happiest she'd ever been.

I wake up, still full of emotion. Heck, my cheeks are even wet. There's love and pride, and so much gratitude, and all I want is to go to them. Go to Hettie and tell her I'll do whatever she needs me to do.

But I don't. I give her space, and I take some for myself.

It's good to know it's not just me, that there are feelings for both of us going on, but it's not as easy as it should be.

Eight years apart, and everything that's gone on in that time makes things complicated.

And because of that, I tell myself not to rush Hettie, for fear of her making the wrong decision. Or one she'll regret.

After a quick breakfast and a much-needed cup of coffee, I head to the fitness centre to blow off some steam. Years ago, Dad suggested I not take my ax into the forest around the castle in case any environmentalists catch wind and take offense.

It has happened in the past. Actually, I think it might have been Hettie's uncle who caused a fuss when I was sixteen, penning an editorial for the newspaper announcing how the king and his family don't care about the land and their carbon footprint. All because someone took a picture of me cutting down a tree.

It was a dead tree, but that was left out of the article, which got picked up by the American press.

I start with weights. When Kalle was ten, he was already big into sports and asked for a set of weights for Christmas. Dad did one better: he took out the large space where the Viking lords used to hold court and made it into a fitness centre for us. There's a weight room, bikes and treadmills, as well as an empty room for Odin to spar, or Lyra to dance.

It's one of the few things I miss about living in the castle when I'm in Wabush.

There may be more—like my brothers and Lyra—but the duty of being a prince weighs too heavy on me to give anything else much thought.

Odin finds me when I'm halfway through my second set. "Brother," he calls, startling me out of my thoughts. "You're up early."

"I'm always up early." I set the bar down and wipe my hands. "I thought you were heading back to Camille today."

"Not until later. I've got a couple of meetings. I wanted to check on how you thought dinner went last night."

"Other than Kalle going after Hettie?" I snort. "It was great up to then."

Odin waves away my concern. "You got to give him credit. He's new to this *I'm the next king* stuff, and for you to show up with a ready-made princess—"

"Is he threatened by a seven-year-old?"

"Maybe. I don't always know what goes on in Kalle's head. I do know he has to work on his diplomacy."

I laugh at that. "Just a little."

"So do you."

My laughter stops at the seriousness in Odin's tone.

"Bo, this is going to be a storm when it comes out, and you can't go around shouting at everyone who looks sideways at Hettie. I'm sure she's got her reasons, but the truth is that she left her husband and didn't tell him about their child. There's going to be many out there who won't believe Tema is yours, too."

My hands fist. "What are you trying to say?"

"That the next few weeks aren't going to be easy, and you both need to be ready for it. If she's planning on staying."

I pick up a dumbbell and start bicep curls. "I don't know what's going to happen. She wants me to talk to someone first."

"I think that's a great idea." He nods as I switch hands. "Finish up and come spar with me. It's been a while."

If I can't swing an ax, then a sword is the next best thing. I set down the weight and follow Odin to the training room.

Because Lyra's dancing days are long past, the space has Odin written all over it. He's taken a few of his swords to his new place in Saint Pierre—he'd definitely have to fly private for that—but most of his training weapons hang on the wall, from light to heaviest.

We both pick up the big ones.

"Dad set up an appointment for me this morning," I tell Odin after we picked our swords and agreed on rules. "With a therapist."

Odin chuckles as we touch blades before backing away. "That's got to be fun for you."

"Yeah."

Odin feints left and skips back as I take a swing. It's been a while since I've wielded a sword, and it feels clumsy in my hand. He parries my second thrust and then swings for my throat. I manage to block just in time.

"So how do you really feel about Hettie being back?" he asks over the clashing of metal. The blades may be for training—without a point and with dull edges—but they're real steel and heavier than they look.

"I've agreed to talk to this doctor, not you."

Odin blocks my reckless swing with a grin. "You can practice with me. It'll do you good."

"Always such a know-it-all," I grumble.

"Always. So? Happy? Sad?" He punctuates each word with a swing, forcing me back a step.

I give myself a shake. I used to be pretty good at swordplay, but Odin has continued to work at this, and it shows. "Confused. It's complicated."

"Must be, especially when you're not talking about why she left in the first place."

I miss my block and Odin's sword brushes against my bicep. "Gotcha."

"Once. And you're distracting me. Go again."

"Why did she leave?"

"Is this your way to find out stuff? Maybe *you* should work on your diplomacy."

Odin laughs and feints left again before coming at me with a forward thrust so strong that I almost end up on my butt on the floor.

"I got a second chance with Camille, remember?" Odin pauses to let me find my balance again. "I'm rooting for you."

"Glad someone is."

We spar for a while. Odin has a better technique but I have strength on my side, so I like to think we might be evenly matched. Until Odin calls it and throws me a towel. I'm dripping with perspiration whereas my big brother doesn't seem to have broken a sweat.

"Good match. You need a little practice to get back to where you were," he points out with a grin.

"It's not fair when you try to talk to me," I grumble.

"I did want to ask you about Tema. Don't get all uptight," he warns when I start to bristle. "It's just..." I wait until he collects his thoughts. "You're a *father*."

"Yeah," I say in a heavy voice.

"That's... wow. You're the first of us. Camille and I are talking, but she wants to wait a year or so. And Kalle—"

"My money is on Edie being pregnant within the year."

"Has he said something?"

"No, but I can tell. He's not going to waste any time."

Odin hefts his sword to rest it on his shoulder. "You really didn't know that Hettie was pregnant?" he demands.

"I had no clue."

"I have to ask because you seem to have jumped into the idea with both feet. I think it would have taken me some time to process. Not to mention get used to the idea. It took me long enough to find my footing when I saw Camille again."

My brother's second chance worked out for him. Am I an idiot to think it might for me as well?

She's happy there.

I wipe down the blade and hang it up. "I didn't really have a choice," I admit. "If I got angry about her not telling me, it would take away my time with her. I know she had her reasons. And I don't know how much time I've got with them."

Odin puts his sword on the rack. "You really think Hettie will leave with her?"

"I don't know. I get why she didn't tell me—I don't like it, but I get it. Things weren't good between us when she left, and that was on me."

"What happened, Bo?" Odin faces me, his expression one of concern.

Odin has always had his life together. Even when he abdicated his position as second in line to the throne, he ended up smelling like roses with Camille, running things in in Saint Pierre while the rest of us scrambled. We're close, but I've never had much in common with him. We both like books and weapons with sharp edges; he's able to communicate, and I have problems with that. But when I need to talk to someone, Odin is always one of the first on my list.

"I know I didn't know about the wedding, but anyone who saw the two of you together could tell how much you loved her," Odin continues.

"I'm the reason Mom died." I don't mean to tell him. The words just popped out and now I can't take them back.

Odin whirls around. "What?"

"I'm the reason Mom died." I don't need a deep breath of courage; I just say it. After keeping the secret for so long, it's surprisingly easy to confess. It's like I want people to know. To blame me so I have more of a reason to feel guilty.

"No, you're not." Odin shakes his head. "It was an accident. You weren't even there. There was that freak storm and the bridge was slippery and she—"

"I told her I married Hettie and then she left to pick up Lyra. She was upset. She shouldn't have been driving."

"Why would she be upset?" Odin's expression of concern is gone; now he's only confused.

"Because I'm a prince and I got married without telling any-one." Odin shrugs. "She was *upset*," I say loudly. "I got married and no one knew about it."

"Maybe?" I can tell Odin isn't convinced. "But Bo, I can't see her being that upset to make her lose control of the car. This is the woman who taught our brother to race cars, remember?"

"I—"

I *did* forget. I forgot all about the fact that it was *Mom* who taught us all to drive. Duncan and one of the drivers did most of it, but Mom would take us out on the back roads behind the castle, laughing as the speedometer went higher and higher. She taught us what to do when we swerved, how to drive in the snow.

She took us to deserted parking lots and let us do donuts until we were dizzy. She could be going eighty and pull the parking brake; a sweet move that would have her going in the opposite direction before you'd know what was happening.

Our mother had liked speed, had liked to drive fast, and she was really good at it.

How could I have forgotten that?

"She was ready for one of us to meet someone and get mar-ried," Odin continues, unaware of the flurry of my thoughts. "Maybe she was mad that you didn't tell her, but she would have been happy if you were happy. It's stupid to blame yourself. If talking to a therapist has taught me anything, it's that it was an accident. It's no one's fault."

For the first time, the words start to sink in.

27

Hettie

I DON'T SEE BO the next morning. When I make my way down to the dining room with Tema and Abigail, Mrs. Theissen tells me he's already eaten breakfast.

I'm not comfortable asking the housekeeper where he might be or to start wandering around the castle in search of him.

And after last night, I need a little space, anyway.

That moment in my room—I thought Bo was going to kiss me. And the worst thing was that I *wanted* him to.

This only adds to my guilt.

It's not fair to Timothy for me to want to kiss someone else, and I need a little space to figure things out.

Timothy has been... not Timothy since I've been gone. Or maybe this is the real Timothy and I've been too close to see what he's truly like until now. It's not that he's *bad*, just... lacking. Maybe he's always lacked and I never thought I deserved more? Or it's not until I've come back here, sharing the same space as Bo and seeing just how much I mean to him, that I take a closer look at my relationship with Timothy.

And to be honest, I'm kind of finding it... lacking.

No one would be able to tell we are on the cusp of getting engaged by the way he talks to me on the phone. There's no affectionate banter, no loving comments, or sexy innuendoes about missing me.

Even when we're FaceTiming and his face fills the screen, there's nothing in his expression that suggests that I am the most important thing in the world to him.

Now, when I see the way Bo watches me...

The look his eyes, the way he touches me. The way he *doesn't* touch me.

When we were together, I never thought I deserved his love, but these days...

I deserve to be the most important person to a man. Except for Tema, of course. She will always take precedence over me, and if the man doesn't show me that he realizes how special she is, how lucky he may be to have her in his life—

Like Bo does.

It must be difficult to date a woman with a child, but Timothy never seems to struggle... but he doesn't make much of an effort either.

Am I seeing him through Bo-fogged glasses or is this really how things are with Timothy and me?

I don't know.

"These are the best waffles ever," Tema announces mid-way through breakfast. She pierces one and waves it in the air. Maple syrup drips onto her plate.

"Then eat them and stop playing," I tell her.

"Do you think the castle makes better waffles than Timothy?" It's not my imagination; there's a hint of mischief in Abigail's voice.

"Yes," Tema exclaims, then, "Sorry, Mommy, but these are *royal* waffles. I could eat them every day, but I don't think I can do that with Timothy's."

"It's okay," I concede with a sideways glance at Abigail, who's giving her plate a little too much attention. "They are really good."

Abigail is Team Bo all the way.

"Are you ready, Mommy?" Tema demands a short while later. She has stacked her plate after eating every bite of her waffles.

I can get used to having breakfast made for me. Abigail does most of the cooking because she enjoys it more, but even she gets tired of the monotony.

She stayed at the castle last night and she was as excited as Tema for the waffles. Abigail also didn't have any qualms to ask Mrs. Theissen if Spencer had left for work.

He had, which started Tema off about us going into town.

Today's plan is to drop Abigail and Tema off at Abigail's parents', while I track down my sister in town.

"Let me finish my tea," I tell her with a laugh.

"We need to stop at Coffee for the Sole," Abigail says. "I've been dreaming of their coffee since we left."

"You don't drink coffee anymore," I protest.

"Because I love Silas's coffee so much." She pretends to swoon. "It's like he adds something to it."

"It's made with love," I say in my own dreamy voice.

"I was thinking more like a drug."

"Can I try some?" Tema wants to know.

"Coffee? No," I tell her. "Drugs? Even bigger no."

"Drugs are stupid," my little girl says. "Everyone knows that."

"I don't know about everyone else, but I'm glad you do." Abigail grins at her.

"Are you ready *now*?" Tema demands.

I take a last sip of my tea. "Yes. I just need to find us a ride into town."

Mrs. Theissen magically appears, like she's been listening outside the door. "I can arrange to have someone drive you into town," she says, all business-like. Maybe eavesdropping is part of her job description. "And pick you up when you're ready."

"That... I think..." I stammer. It feels awkward, like we're a burden.

"Thank you, Mrs. Theissen, that would be lovely. I'll see if I can borrow a car to get us back," Abigail says for me.

"No need. We have vehicles and people to drive them. His Majesty may want you to have a detail as well."

"A detail?"

"Security detail. Every member of the family should have one. Prince Bo seems to avoid it if at all possible."

My mind flies back to Bo in high school. "Has it always been like that?"

"No, it's been fairly recent. Since Lady Camille had a few incidents, His Majesty decided all those in the castle need to have someone assigned to them."

Abigail raises an eyebrow. "I'm sure Bo loves that."

"It's probably a big reason why he doesn't stay here very often," I agree.

"I'm sure it is," Mrs. Theissen says. "Now, when would you like to leave?"

"Now," Tema cries, and the older woman deigns to smile at her enthusiasm.

"I'll have someone waiting for you outside when you're ready," she promises and glides off.

"I think I'd like her if she didn't scare me so much," Abigail says under her breath.

True to her word, there is a car and warmed and waiting to take us into Battle Harbour.

During the drive down the hill, I look around more than when Bo brought us to the castle. Then, I had been frantic with worry about everything—Tema, Bo, what the king would say. I'm still concerned about the future, but a lot of the worry is gone.

There's more uncertainty now, but that sickening ball churning in the pit of my stomach seems to have disappeared.

Bo is a big reason for that. Also, the fact that the king didn't arrest me for treason for not telling him he had a granddaughter.

The snowfall of the first night is piled on either side of the road but the tree branches are bare. It's warmer than when we arrived, maybe just a few degrees but enough to start the melt and make people feel like spring might actually be on the way.

While we drive through town, Abigail points out things to an excited Tema. I notice that there's been a few changes in the town, but it looks mainly the same.

Candy store hasn't changed; Ye Olde Fish Shoppe is still here. The King's Hat stands as proud as Kalle at the far side of the town square.

"Are we going to see the puppies?" Tema demands as we get out of the black SUV in front of Coffee for the Sole.

"After we go see Nana and Papa Locke," Abigail tells her. "We'll pack up some toys and books if you're going to be staying at the castle."

"Am I?" Tema turns to me with a hopeful expression.

"Do you want to?"

Tema screws up her face. "I like staying with Nana and Papa but... it's a *castle*."

I glance at Abigail. "I think they understand."

"Maybe they can come stay there, too!"

"I think they're happy at their house." Abigail laughs as she holds open the door for Tema.

Inside, Coffee for the Sole has changed. Little things: new tables and chairs, mugs and the art on the wall have been updated, but it smells the same. I may be a tea drinker, but there's always been something about the scent of coffee that makes me want to give it another try.

"Well, isn't it Abigail Locke," Silas Bell, owner of the premier coffeeshop in Laandia calls as we approach the counter. We spent a lot of time in here during high school. "And Hettie Crow. And a small person I don't know." He grins at us, but his gaze fixes on Tema.

"I'm Princess Tema," my daughter announces.

I catch my breath. Bo and I haven't talked about going public with the fact that Bo is Tema's father, so Tema telling the entire coffee shop is...

I don't know what it is.

Silas laughs, not fazed in the slightest by her announcement. "Nice to meet you, Your Highness. What would you like to drink?"

"Abigail says you have unicorns." Tema rushes to the counter and props her elbows on it. Abigail gives me a wide-eyed glance and follows her.

"Unicorn *froth*," Silas corrects. "Unfortunately, unicorns like to stay out of the snow. Hot chocolate?" he asks me as I stand behind Tema with my hand on her shoulder.

"Yes, please. Look at that fish on the wall!" Tema darts to the corner of the shop where the plastic fish flops against the wall when a person walks by.

"I didn't hear you two were back in town," Silas says after he takes our order and instructs one of the baristas to start on them. The shop is full, with nearly all the tables occupied, but there is no one in line.

"We're keeping it quiet," I tell him. "It might not be for long."

"I take it Princess Tema is yours? She's adorable." I hold my breath in case Silas starts with how much Tema resembles Princess Lyra, but after a last, long look at her, he turns his attention back to us.

"Thanks."

"It's strange I haven't even seen you around. Did you just get in?"

"We've been staying at the castle," I admit.

"Oh." Silas's eyebrows shoot up, disappearing into the dark hair that flops over his forehead. He takes another glance at Tema. "*Oh!*"

"We're keeping things quiet," I say again. It's not a warning, but it should be because Silas knows everyone, with his radar tuned to everything going on around here.

"Ah. I get it."

Does he? I think he really might and I'm not sure how I feel about that.

It won't be just one person who knows about Tema—the news will spread until some reporters hears and comes to make Bo's life miserable.

My life, too, but I can leave if I need to.

I could run away, but it's a lot more difficult for Bo.

Abigail chats with Silas while all this races through my mind. I pull myself back into the conversation in time for Silas to ask if we have plans tonight.

"You should come into town." He points to the far wall. "Next door. My, ah, my girlfriend opened a club."

"Girlfriend?" Abigail and I say in unison. Silas is older than us, but most of the girls in town have had a crush on him at one time or another. He might be the nicest guy I know.

"Fiancée," he admits, his cheeks reddening. "It's a recent thing."

"Who is she?" I eagerly demand.

"She's not from around here. Fenella Carrington," he says. "She's—"

"You're marrying Fenella Carrington!" Abigail's voice rises above the clatter of the shop. "Fenella Carrington, the influencer?

She's a model, too. Do you remember that ad for a purse a few years ago?" she asks me.

"I know who she is," I say. "I don't follow her, but I know who she is. Wow." I widen my eyes. "Congratulations. When's the big day?"

"Not until the fall, to give her time to plan."

"That'll be a good wedding."

"If you're here, you're both invited."

Abigail nudges me. "There's incentive to stay."

Silas passes us our cups. "On the house, as a welcome home to Battle Harbour. Hope to see more of you."

Abigail takes Tema's hot chocolate. "As long as we're here, we'll be back. I told Hettie I've been dreaming of your coffee." She takes a sip and closes her eyes. "Just like I remembered."

"Enjoy. And think about coming tonight. Thursday nights are fun."

"Definitely," Abigail agrees before I can say anything. "See you tonight."

We gather Tema where she's still darting back and forth in front of the fish to make it flop, and head back to the waiting SUV. Abigail is taking Tema to her parents' while I go see my sister. "Are you sure you don't want to take her to meet Mabel?" Abigail asks in a low voice as Tema climbs into the car.

I shake my head. "Next time."

"I can't say I'm not glad. She's the only grandchild they're going to get for a while," she says ruefully. "Not that she's mine..."

"She's yours," I tell her. "In every way that matters. I couldn't have handled the last eight years without you."

"You would have handled it just fine, regardless of whether I was there or not. But I wasn't letting you have all the fun by yourself." And she winks as she climbs in after Tema.

I wave as they drive away before walking across the square to The King's Hat.

28

Bo

DAD SETS THE THERAPIST up in one of the unused offices on the second floor. This one was supposed to be used by Gunnar and me—as if it were possible for Gunnar to share a room with anyone.

He would take it over with framed pictures of himself with famous women and evidence of his racing exploits. Although, seeing him at dinner last night with Stella suggests she would be front and centre of pictures he'd want to show off now.

I like them together. But I wouldn't want them to be staring me in the face all day because then I'd have to think about what I'm missing.

Hettie.

I wipe my hands on my jeans and finally look at the therapist. I've been looking at everything else in the room, and there's not much here. There's not even a window from where I can plot my escape.

The second floor isn't that high and there's still snowdrifts to break my fall.

Dr. Louise Patel is a woman in her thirties with a faint English accent. Which is surprising because I never would have expected the British to put much faith in therapy.

I'm not sure I do, but Dad suggested it. And Hettie is on board, so I really don't have a choice. She didn't say that there's no second chance with us if I don't do this, but I got that vibe.

What am I supposed to say to this doctor?

It's been five minutes since I came in and shook Dr. Patel's hand, taking the uncomfortable wing chair across from her.

If this was my office, I would definitely get better furniture.

I haven't managed to say anything, mainly because I don't have a clue what to say. Do I blurt out some of the lowlights of my life, like losing Mom? Losing Hettie? And then we could start the discussion about how it's all my fault.

That doesn't sound productive. Or fun. Plus, I've already stepped up to take the blame. What's going to change there?

I give her a weak smile and she takes that as encouragement.

"How are you, Bo?" Dr. Patel breaks the silence and my spiral of thoughts. "Or should I call you Your Highness?"

"Bo. Just Bo."

She glances at the notebook she's holding. "Prince Bowden Eugene Jerome Leif Erickson. That's quite the handle."

"Just Bo," I repeat. I've always wondered how my parents came up with our names. As far as I know there's no one on either side of the family with the name Eugene. Did they just decide on random names? Pick a letter—let's do Jerome for J.

"I would say you're more than 'Just Bo.'" D. Patel flips through the notebook. "You've been quite successful in the lumberjack world. I'm afraid I don't know much about the sport, but I saw videos of you. It's quite exciting—very impressive."

I shift in the chair. "Thanks. I don't really do that anymore."

"No? Championships three years running and suddenly you retire? Were you injured?"

"No."

"Too much attention put on you. You don't like the spotlight, do you?" Her brown-eyed gaze holds me and suddenly, it's like I'm stripped naked and sitting here, shivering in the chill of the castle. "Is that true? Your brothers and Princess Lyra have always seemed to seek the spotlight, but not you. You tend to stay in the background. Why is that?"

I lift a shoulder. How am I supposed to answer that? "The—the others," I stammer. "They're better at it. The people and the pictures and the questions. I've never been good at it."

"And does that mean you're less important? That you're not a full committed member of the royal family because you don't like talking to reporters?"

"Jeez." I rub the back of my head. "You don't beat around the bush, do you?"

Dr. Patel chuckles. "I don't see any reason to wait until you're more comfortable with me or this process because I doubt you will be."

"Got that right," I mutter.

"And, Bo, there's nothing wrong with feeling that way. Being put on the spot? Forced to share personal things with complete strangers? That's never easy for anyone, so if you think your siblings are better at it, it's just because they're able to develop a persona that can deal with it."

"A persona?"

She nods. "We'll get into that. But I just need you to understand you're not alone with being uncomfortable dealing with the press."

"Okay." I'm totally confused now.

"Have you ever spoken to your siblings about how they feel about being a member of the royal family?" she asks.

Have I...? There's always been comments about this reporter or that, complaints about being forced into suits and ties to attend an event or a meeting that will inevitably put me to sleep. But has anyone asked? Have we ever really talked about what being part of this family means?

"I guess not," I admit. "I know Kalle doesn't love it, but he can handle things."

"I get the sense that you don't think you'd be an effective ruler. Is this solely because you don't like talking to the press?" she prompts.

That question feels like she's kicked my shin to get my attention. "It sounds stupid when you say it like that," I protest. She cocks her head at me, and I feel my face flame. I rub the back of my head like the answers are going to be found there. "It is stupid."

"It's not at all stupid. You're an introvert, Bo. Possibly shy. Definitely reserved, and you prefer to limit communication until you're comfortable. None of these traits mean you would not be a successful king of Laandia, if it ever came to that."

"It won't."

"It could," she corrects. "I think that's the problem. You were born the third son. Middle children always get a bad rap, but that's not the problem here. You were born into a family who has a responsibility to govern a country and its people. You didn't ask for this; none of you did. But as a third son, you never expected to take over after your father. No one expected it, and therefore you have lived your life never imagining it."

"That's my problem? I have no imagination?"

"Not at all. You grew up knowing your brothers would take over. And then your mother's death—"

"That was my fault," I blurt out.

Dr. Patel pauses. "Why is that?"

"Because I told her I married Hettie, and then she left and got into an accident. She must have been so mad at me, and then..." I squeeze my knees tightly, welcoming the pinch of my fingers as punishment.

"Why do you think she was mad at you?" Dr. Patel asks in a quiet voice.

"Because I got married without telling her." I sound like a broken record. I said the same thing to Hettie, to Odin. To Dad. And they all care about me, so of course they would protest and try to change my mind, but there's no point. If I hadn't married Hettie—

If I had never married Hettie, there would be no Tema.

"What's going through your mind, Bo?" Dr. Patel urges. "You've just realized something."

"Are you a mind-reader?" I mutter.

"No, but your posture just changed. You can tell me if you like. Or not."

"Or not." But then she doesn't say anything, just sits there with a tiny smile on her face like she's waiting for me to break.

I last about thirty seconds.

"I've always felt like I needed to regret marrying Hettie like that because if we hadn't, then Mom wouldn't have died. But if we never got married, then there would be no Tema," I relent.

Another glance at her notebook, and I wonder if there's a full dossier on me in there. "Ah. Tema, the daughter you didn't know about until a few days ago."

"Yeah."

"How do you feel about suddenly being a father?"

"Surprised."

Dr. Patel chuckles. "I'm sure that's an understatement. What I meant is, are you happy about it? Angry?"

"Why would I be angry? Tema is an amazing kid. I'm lucky to have her as mine."

"Yes, she is yours, but Hettie kept her a secret. How do you feel about that? Take your time."

There's that smile again. With a huff of resentment, I think back to when Hettie appeared out of nowhere and showed me the picture of our daughter. How did I feel at that moment?

Shock... rage that she never told me. Wonder that we created such a perfect little human. Grudging respect for Hettie because why would she have told me when I pushed her out of my life?

Relief that I wasn't the only one who did something wrong in this relationship.

"I was glad that I wasn't the only bad guy," I tell her finally. "She should have told me. It's inexcusable that she never contacted me. But it's also inexcusable that I forced her to leave. I didn't give her any other option."

"It kind of makes you even, you mean?"

"Sort of."

"Interesting way of looking at it," she muses.

"Does that mean it's bad?" I demand.

"Not at all. None of your opinions or thoughts are either good or bad. They're just yours. Now, back to your mother."

I exhale, frustrated. Here comes the attempt to get me to change my mind.

"I can see how your mother might be disappointed that she wasn't at your wedding," she begins. "I don't have children, but if I did, and one of them got married without telling me? I'd be annoyed. And maybe some anger, but not enough to cause an accident. Was there something about your relationship that she didn't approve of? Did she not like Hettie?"

"No, but her family—Hettie's family..."

"How do you feel about her family?"

"They don't deserve her. No one is good enough for Hettie. Her mother abandoned her, her brothers don't care, neither does her father—"

"It sounds like you're angry with them, not your mother."

"I... She deserves better. She's so good, and smart and sweet, and they're... not."

"It's understandable for you to be upset when someone you care about is hurt. But that doesn't mean you can assume you know what your mother was feeling. And that's what you're doing. Assuming," she adds.

I don't say a word.

"You can't know what your mother was thinking that day," she reprimands gently. "But there is someone who might have some insight."

"Who?"

"Your sister was in the car with her. Have you ever talked to Lyra about this?"

29

Hettie

"T EMA WANTS TO MEET you. Again." I sit at the bar at The King's Hat. It's slowly filling up with the lunch crowd and it's surprising how many of the townsfolk wave when they see me.

Mabel is behind the bar. One by one, she picks up the glasses, holding them to the light to check for water marks before rubbing the glass. "The place looks great," I tell her.

She frowns. "It's getting there. Edie has been great," she relents. "She's busy with royal stuff and Kalle is hardly ever around, so it's been... kind of fun," she finishes with a ghost of a smile.

My sister has never been what you'd call upbeat. Or positive. Or happy. She took on a lot when she stuck around to help raise my brothers and me, and I think she decided that everything in the world is as difficult as that.

Or maybe she's just unhappy. I really hope not.

"I'm glad. Last night at dinner, Edie said—"

"What are you doing staying at the castle with them?" she demands. "I should have started with that."

I lean back, surprised at the abrupt change of tone and topic. "Where else should I be staying?"

"At home? Or with me?"

"Hard no. And you have a one-bedroom apartment. Tema would drive you crazy within a minute."

"She wouldn't."

"Trust me. Besides, I owe it to Bo—"

"You don't owe him anything," she bursts. She gives a quick glance around to make sure no one is within earshot and she lowers her voice. "He made you leave, Hettie. You didn't really have a marriage, so don't you think that it makes you owe him anything."

"But I do. We have a child together," I remind her in a whisper. Maybe this isn't the best place to talk. "Plus, Tema likes it there."

"What does she think about being the third in line for the throne of Laandia?" Mabel snorts. "Or did you forget to tell her about that, too?"

"I didn't forget to tell her about Bo. It was a conscious decision. And I apologized for that."

"And?"

"And what?"

"Did he forgive you?"

I bite my lip. "I think so. At least I hope so."

Mabel cocks her head. "You left your husband, didn't tell him you had his baby, and he forgave you?" She shakes her head. "The boy has got it bad."

"I don't know for a fact that he's forgiven me," I admit. "But he's been pretty good about everything."

"And have you got it bad?"

I'm not answering that. Mabel is black and white. She doesn't give much credence to emotions or feelings, and as far as I know, she's never been in love.

Probably because she's never let herself be that vulnerable. She's never let herself fall that far, or that deep.

I'm in deep with Bo. I fell really far with him and now…

"Timothy wants to marry me," I tell her.

"So you say, but has he proposed?"

"We talked about it. It would be good for Tema."

"And for you?" Mabel has always been blunt and to the point. "In my experience, a man wants to marry you, he just asks. There's no talking. And if a woman wants to marry him, she doesn't dither about, *oh he asked me, what should I do.* She says *yes.*" Mabel looks pointedly at me. "Have you said yes?"

"I'm still married." I keep my voice down just in case someone can overhear, although those who have come in for lunch seem to steer clear of my sister.

"For like a day. It doesn't count. If you wanted this Tim-guy, you'd march right up to the castle and make Bo give you a divorce. Don't let the past keep you hostage."

"We have a history," I protest. "A child," I mouth.

"Was it even a good one? The history. I never saw you together. It was *Bo, Bo, Bo* with hearts in your eyes, or *Bo!* with tears."

I stare at my empty cup from Coffee for the Sole, squeezing it until it's flat. Mabel eventually takes it from me.

"You've always made things too hard for yourself," she complains. "You married a prince, for God's sake. How can that be easy?"

"You think I should get the divorce and go back to Victoria with Tema?" I ask.

"Of course not!" She laughs. "You're an idiot to think about leaving." Mabel snorts. "Look around and see what you could have here."

"What was all that *marrying a prince is hard* stuff about then?"

"Well, it is," she says. "And you need to realize that. People love Edie because she's one of us, but Camille had a tough time at first. When people find out—" She shakes her head. "It's not going to be pretty."

"I can handle it."

"Can Bo? He didn't do too well before. And Tema?"

I bow my head. I hate the thought of the press going after my little girl, but then I remember the story Bo told me about Lady Camille and the snowballs. "She's seven," I point out. "I'll shield her for as long as I can, but I think she can handle herself when she's older."

"Of course she can; she's my niece."

"And I had no part in this?"

"Maybe Abigal did," she says grudgingly and I laugh. Sometimes Mabel's no-nonsense way is hard to take, but it's still one of the many things I love about her.

When my laughter fades, I look my sister straight in the eye. "Why would he want me?"

And she gets it. Mabel knows exactly what I'm asking.

"He doesn't want our family, Hettie," she says in a surprisingly gentle voice. "He wants *you*. That much is obvious, if he's got his head on straight."

"Do you think I should stay?" That's the reason I wanted to talk to her. Not to fill her in on Tema or find out the latest on our family; I want to know what my big sister thinks I should do.

I always have.

"Of course I want you to stay. I want my sister back. But I'm not about to tell you what to do."

"Why not?" I demand. "You always did when we were younger."

"That's because you were my baby sister. You still are, but you've grown up, Hettie. You've grown up into a woman who makes her own choices and knows her own mind. You know what you should do, you're just too scared to do it."

I shrug. "Tema does like it here. She's excited to have all this family now."

Mabel sighs. "I should probably tell you before you bump into him on the street," she says with reluctance.

"Oh no," I breathe.

"If Tema's so excited to have family, she's got another one if she wants it," Mabel says. "Reggie is back in town."

30

Bo

I FaceTime Lyra as soon as I get back to my room.

Since Mom died, I've felt that I was moving in a fog, with little that broke through. Thoughts of Hettie made it worse, so I pushed everything aside and tried to get through one day at a time.

I fell into the lumberjack competitions; I didn't really enjoy it, but I was good at it, and cutting through a two-foot log in record time did help with the anger.

I never realized just how angry I have been.

Angry. Invisible. Grieving—for Mom and Hettie both.

I might have a new appreciation for talking about feelings now.

Maybe. Just a little bit.

I sit back against my head board, iPad propped against my knees, and listen to the musical interlude of the call connecting to my sister. I think she's in Chicago; I'm not really sure.

That's bad.

I should have told her about Hettie and Tema when I told the others, but I've never felt as connected with Lyra. She's my little sister and I love her, but there hasn't been a lot of one-on-one time for us since Mom died.

Before that? Lyra used to follow me around, more than the others. She and Gunnar are the closest in age and shared friends and experiences, but it was me Lyra came to when she was upset. I'd take her into the forest and show her a squirrel's nest or we would look for the snowy owl that lived there.

She held my hand when we played in the dark tunnels under the castle.

I may not understand her life or have much in common with her these days, but at one point in our lives, Lyra liked being with me.

I never realized how me being responsible for Mom's accident, the accident Lyra was in, has pulled us apart.

Lyra's face appears on the screen, her hair more red than blonde and pulled up onto the top of her head. "*What* is going on?" she demands in lieu of a greeting.

"Hello, to you too."

"You never FaceTime me," she accuses. "You hardly even text. What happened?"

But she doesn't seem upset. She almost seems... happy.

And Tema definitely takes after her aunt. It's not just the smile, but the way her nose turns up at the end is the same. And the tilt of her chin. It's the direct way she looks at me.

Lyra is an aunt. That's going to blow her mind.

"Everything's okay," I assure her. "There's a few things I needed to talk to you about."

"Is Dad okay?" Ever since his attack of appendicitis in the summer, we've needed more frequent updates about him.

"He's fine. He's good. He's—it's about me," I begin awkwardly. "Hettie's back in town."

I've done a lot of talking today, and for a moment, I wish I could save this for another day. Spread it out a bit.

But no. This needs to be sorted out now. Explained. I need to know things, but before that, Lyra deserves to know what's going on.

"Hettie? As in Hettie Crow, former love of your life, who broke your heart when she skipped town?" Lyra's eyes darken, and for a moment she looks scarily like Dad when he has to give someone bad news. "That Hettie? Can't wait to catch up with her."

"Don't be like that."

"Don't be protective of my big brother? Jeez, I wonder who taught me to be like that?"

I laugh, suddenly remembering fourteen-year-old Lyra getting her heart broken by Michael Murphy and me pushing the poor kid up against the wall, Kalle right behind me.

He might have soiled his pants and definitely he never spoke to Lyra again.

She was very angry at us for that.

"Fair enough, but there's more going on," I relent.

"Please tell me you didn't welcome her back with open arms? Bo, don't be a doofus. She broke your heart right after Mom died. Who does that?"

"My wife?"

On screen, Lyra rears back. "Excuse me? What did you just say?"

"I married her—"

"No one tells me anything!" Lyra cries.

"No body knew," I say quickly. "Except Spencer and Abigail Locke—"

"*Spencer* knew?" Those eyes darken again. Lyra holds the screen far enough away so I can see her torso, and the way she fists her hand on her hip makes me think Spencer might be on the receiving end of her anger more than me.

I definitely need to warn him after this.

"Let me just say it, and then you can freak out," I plead. "Please? This was years ago. I married Hettie two days before the accident."

"The accident..."

"Mom dying. That one. We got married, Mom died, and Hettie left because I couldn't deal. With any of it."

"Okay..." She frowns. "That time is still a bit hazy for me, but she shouldn't have left."

"I think it's my fault that Mom died."

Lyra stares at me. And then she laughs.

"It's not funny," I protest.

"It's kind of funny," she retorts. "Everyone in this family thinks it was their fault that Mom died. Kalle thinks it was because he wouldn't quit sports and settle down with a nice girl, and Gunnar was all mopey because he was off racing in Europe and wasn't around, and even O thinks it had something to do with a conversation they had three weeks earlier. If anyone should feel guilty, it's me. She came to pick me up because I was too selfish and didn't want a castle car to come get me. The guilt is mine, Bo. Don't try to take it from me."

"It's not your fault. None of us liked having the castle car pick us up."

Lyra lifts a shoulder. "You all have to give me this."

"No, I don't. I told Mom I married Hettie just before she left to pick you up. She was upset."

"She wasn't upset," Lyra says.

"She... What?" And just like that, things shift. I'm glad I'm sitting down because it's like the room rocks just like that one time an earthquake was felt in Laandia back when I was six. "No. She was mad because I told her I got married to Hettie."

"*No*, she wasn't. She was in a great mood. We were singing, just before—ABBA, because we were going to see Mamma Mia in London. She was going to take me, so I downloaded the soundtrack for her, and she was playing it. We were singing." Lyra's expression softens and she stares at a point above her phone so, I know she's remembering.

I hate that I made her remember.

"We were having fun," she says softly. "She was never upset when she picked me up. And that day there was no mad, no being upset."

"You said you don't remember..."

"I remember enough." Grief washes over her features and a tear rolls down her cheek. My heart clenches because Lyra isn't one to cry.

None of us are.

"Don't," I urge.

"Don't what? It's gotten easier to talk about." She takes a deep breath and all I can think about is how brave my little sister is. "We got to the bridge and it was snowing, kind of sleeting. It was hard to see but she was still singing. Then the lights of the other car were right there... She stopped singing and we—" She blows out a shaky inhale. "I don't remember anything after that. I don't *want* to remember anything else."

I have to swallow a few times before I can say anything. "Lyra..."

"I do know that she was not upset about anything." Lyra's voice is husky but insistent. "She was *happy*. Happy to see me. She asked about what I'd done. She—I remember—she told me you were home, that we'd have a family dinner that night. She was *happy*, Bo. She wasn't mad or upset or anything."

The weight that had been pressing down on my shoulders like a pile of snow on the branches of a pine tree is suddenly gone. Lifted. Vanished.

Happy. She wasn't upset.

She still could have been angry when she left the castle, but it was obvious she'd gotten over it by the time she got to Lyra. We could always tell when Mom was upset. There was never any hiding it. Dad could wear the mask, but it was always clear how our mother was feeling, even when she shouldn't have been showing it.

She wasn't angry with me. She wanted to see me.

I didn't do it.

It wasn't my fault.

It's like the words are a billboard right in front of my face, and I'm reeling.

I don't know how to deal with it.

"I have to go," I mutter, finger stabbing the screen looking to disconnect the call. Lyra will never know what she just did for me, but there is no way I'm going to let her see me cry.

"Bo!" Her voice sharpens. "Do *not* hang up on me. It's bad enough that you ran away to the other side of the country when I needed all my family together. You sit right there and tell me just what the hell is going on."

I nod but can't speak. I focus on taking deep breaths, pushing the sob of relief down deep. I take a minute, and then another. Lyra waits.

"Hettie left because I thought it was my fault," I finally manage. "I pushed her away. She didn't have a choice. I thought marrying her was a big mistake because Mom died after I told her about it."

Lyra nods. "That's a messed-up way of looking at it."

"So is thinking it's your fault because she picked you up. Mom told me once that she really liked giving us rides to practice or someone's house because she could have us all to herself."

She blinks frantically and I know she's as close to tears as I am. "She said that?"

"It was a storm, Lyra. The bridge was slippery. If she was happy—it's no one's fault."

"I keep trying to tell myself that," she pleads. "Somedays it's still so hard."

"Keep trying, little sis. Because, trust me, when you realize that it wasn't your fault?" I draw a shaky breath. "It feels pretty good."

"You've been living with that for all these years." Lyra's voice is gentle. "Bo..."

"Yeah."

Lyra takes a deep breath, and then another. "And this is why Hettie left?" I nod. "Why did she come back? Are you back together?"

"She wants a divorce."

"You're still married? It's been years."

"For now. But there's more—"

She snorts. "Of course there is."

"Hettie has a kid." The words tumble over each other to get out. "A little girl. *My* little girl."

I've never seen my sister speechless, and it's kind of funny. "She has a baby?"

"Tema is seven."

I see her do the math. "And she's yours?"

I give a shaky laugh. "She looks like you at that age."

Lyra stares, open-mouthed. "This I have to see," she finally manages. "I'll catch the first flight back."

And then she hangs up.

31

Hettie

After I leave Mabel, I go for a walk along the pier before I call for a car to take me back to the castle, just like Bo and Spencer told me to.

It might take a while to get used to that.

But it doesn't take long at all for me to feel the old dread and frustration when I think of my family.

Eight years of not worrying about them, of not being hurt by their actions. Of not meeting people and wondering if they're judging me because of my brothers. If they think I'm just like them, only in a prettier package.

If I stayed in Battle Harbour, I could see Mabel all the time.

If I stayed, I'd have to deal with my brother Reggie.

Not that I ever had much to do with him. Mabel kept the worst of it from me. I know he burnt down the McKibbons' barn, and set fire to a dumpster outside the high school.

There was a rumour about him stealing from Clay Whiskey, one of the fishermen that my father knows. Bar fights, street fights. I think he tried to steal a car once, but I blame my brother Hank for that.

Mabel says I don't make it easy on myself, but I learned that from my family. Reggie had opportunities, as much as the rest of us did, and he chose crime. Same as my brother Lloyd, who let his temper get the best of him. I'm sure there are other reasons to kill a man, but Lloyd did it because he was mad and drunk.

Mabel kept herself out of trouble—for the most part. Same as Earl. Tommy got out and Hank… Hank probably has a finger in most of the criminal activity between here and Mary's Harbour but at least he keeps it quiet.

Reggie was smart and funny, always teasing and cracking jokes. He had options and wasted them all.

And I have to pay for it.

I wouldn't if I went back to Victoria.

My life in Victoria is many things: difficult, lonely, freeing, fun at times. It would have been a very different story if Abigail hadn't come with me; it also would have been very different if I hadn't discovered I was pregnant six weeks later.

Having my grandfather there was a lifesaver since we lived with him for the first two years, but he's an introverted artist preoccupied with colours and landscapes from Laandia. He helped financially but didn't do anything for a social life.

I've loved being away from the shadow of my family, but is that worth being away from my home? And keeping Abigail from her family? I told her so many times that Tema and I would be fine, but either she doesn't believe me or the ties that keep us together are as strong for her as they are for me.

If Abigail had moved home, I might have followed her.

But I would only be running away, same as before. Then, I thought it would be too hard to keep seeing Bo, so I left. And now? Will it be too difficult to deal with Reggie and his eventual troubles? Should I leave again?

I don't think so. Maybe that was me eight years ago, but I'm different now. I've changed, and there's no sense hiding from my family or the press—or how I feel about Bo.

Because I do feel about Bo. I feel a lot.

He lights up something inside of me, like a pilot light that's been dormant for years. He sees me, sees all of me. All the good and all the bad. Bo always said he loves me and doesn't care about my family, and he proved it by marrying me.

What would happen if I finally believed that?

Or if I stopped caring what anyone else thought about them? Because I am not my family. I'm not my brothers, or my mother, or my uncle who can't keep his mouth shut even when he doesn't have a clue what he's talking about.

I am me—a mother. The mother of a princess, the third in line to the throne of Laandia.

I'm a wife. And because of that, I'm a princess in my own right.

I'm a lot of other things, but they are the most important at this moment.

I walk the length of the pier twice before I pull out my phone.

But I don't call Abigail to check how things are going.

"Hey!" Timothy smiles as soon as he sees me on the screen. "It looks cold there."

The wind skips across the water, creating waves that crash into the pier. Occasionally I get splashed, but I keep walking. I'm wearing Lyra's jacket that is much warmer than the one I brought with me, and I pulled on a toque when I got to the water.

"It's March, so it's still pretty cold, but today, you can kind of feel that spring is coming."

Timothy frowns. "Your nose is really red, so it doesn't look like there's much spring there yet. We've already got flowers out here."

"I know." British Columbia is a beautiful place to live. It has the water and the mountains, and Victoria has a small-town vibe despite being the capital. It's been a good place to run to, but—

"You're just the person I was thinking about," Timothy says.

"Yeah?" For a moment, my heart gives a squeeze and I wonder if I'm doing the right thing.

"Yeah. I got a new listing and I think it's perfect for you. A two-bedroom condo in West Van overlooking the water. There's a school nearby—"

"Vancouver?" The squeezing of my heart stops abruptly. "I don't want to move to Vancouver."

"We talked about how it would be better for my career to get off the island," he reminds me.

"*You* talked."

Timothy's eyes flash with surprise. I've never disagreed with him.

Why not? I was happy with Bo and I argued with him all the time. Maybe Abigail's right about what I'm like with Timothy.

"I like Victoria," I continue before he can say anything. "Abigail is so close to the school she works at and Tema has her friends. I have friends there."

I have two—an older woman who works in the office that I take breaks with and another mother I met through Tema's school.

"You can make more friends," Timothy points out. "It would be so much better for me in Vancouver. And Abigail isn't planning on living with us after we get married, is she?" Timothy laughs like it's all a joke. Like separating from my best friend would be an easy thing to do.

He laughs like I want to move in with him. Like I want to marry him.

A huge wave crashes against the pier, splashing icy cold water against my jeans, and the front of Lyra's jacket. I jump back.

That might have been the wake-up call that I needed.

Because I don't think I ever have wanted to marry Timothy. Not really.

If I did, this wouldn't be so difficult—I would have showed up with divorce papers and a custody arrangement for Bo. I wouldn't be dithering about if I still had feelings for Bo. If I wanted to truly have a life with Timothy, I would be having it already.

Bo would be part of my past, and I wouldn't be wondering where he fits into my future.

Another wave crashes, but it misses me.

"Hettie?" Timothy finally realizes I'm not laughing. "Abigail's *not* going to live with us, is she? I mean, I like her and everything, but after we get married, I'd like some time for the two of us. But maybe she can stay close by, watch Tema for us so we can do newly married people stuff. Doesn't that sound nice? Give you a bit of a break."

"Timothy…"

"What? You have to admit…" He continues on with the reasons we would need our privacy, but I tune him out because all I hear is Timothy planning things *without* Tema.

He said he'd take care of her, but he never said he wanted to.

Timothy has never given Tema a bath or asked to help put her to bed. And while not all men are hands-on fathers, he has never once asked about my daughter since I've been gone.

"I don't think I want to marry you," I whisper.

But Timothy doesn't hear me and keeps going on about the benefits of making a move.

I have to agree with him there because maybe I was just looking for an excuse to come back. And Timothy gave me a great excuse.

"Timothy," I interrupt. "I need to say something."

"Yes, but this place—" Something in my expression finally manages to silence him, and he heaves a sigh. "Really?"

"I think maybe—"

"You're staying with the prince, aren't you?"

The fact that he doesn't even let me say it really irks. "I don't know if I'm staying with Bo, but I think it's best that I stay *here*. In Laandia. With my family."

"You hate your family," he counters.

"Well, maybe it's time that I stop feeling that way."

"You tell me you're staying for your family while the prince is putting you up in a castle? Don't tell me that's not the reason." For the first time since I've met him, Timothy sounds angry.

And for a moment, I want him to be angry because it's a sign that he cares.

But the anger is quick to fade from his eyes, leaving resignation, and it happens too fast for my liking. "Listen, Hettie, you figure things out. You need to do what's best for you, and I'll do the same. I thought we would be good for each other—I could help you with your career and you can help with my business—but I can see that's not going to be enough for you."

"It's not enough for anyone," I burst out. "Do you even love me?"

"Of course I love you."

"Are you in love with me? Because there's a difference."

"No, there's not."

"And that's the reason right there why I'm not going to marry you. And I'm definitely not moving to West Vancouver. I'm staying right here in Battle Harbour."

"Good luck, then." And Timothy hangs up.

He didn't even bother to fight for me. That stings.

But not enough.

32

Bo

M Y MOTHER WAS *HAPPY.* She was *singing.*

I can't seem to process it, so I do what I always do when I have something to think about: I take an ax out to the woods.

This time I make sure the tree is good and dead and already on the ground before I bury my ax in it. I also check that nothing is living in it. I'm sure I'd upset someone if it turned out there was a family of bunnies living in the trunk, but there's nothing there.

She was happy before the accident. Is it too much of a stretch to assume she was pleased about what I told her? Could it be possible that she was *happy* that I was married?

I just don't know.

Don't assume. Dr. Patel told me that several times today and for a moment, I wish I were back in her office to talk this over.

That's a big switch. Me, who can go for days without talking to anyone, wants to talk to someone about my feelings? What's going on?

What if I just take what Lyra said and go with it? What if I let myself believe that Mom wasn't angry when she got behind the wheel? It may be the complete opposite of what I've told myself for the last eight years, but what if?

For a moment, I let myself go there.

By the time the trunk of the tree is neatly cut in chunks that would be perfect for a buddy of mine to make into chairs, the thought has eased into my mind quicker than I would have thought possible.

It's there. It's swimming around. It likes it there.

Eight years is a long time to wholeheartedly believe something, so I know it won't stick around forever.

But I might be able to invite it back. The thought that my mother wasn't angry and therefore I can't be blamed for the accident.

With every lap around my mind, the thought helps lift the heavy weight off my shoulders.

I cut away the thicker branches and chop them into manageable logs, leaving the shrub in a pile. And then I stack what I can.

By the time I'm finished, my coat is off and sweat makes my shirt stick to my back. And all I want is for Hettie to come back so I can tell her.

33

Hettie

TEMA FALLS ASLEEP ON the drive home and the driver/security assigned to us offers to carry her in for me.

"I've got her, thanks," I tell him, throwing my bag over my arm before I gather her up.

After I picked up Tema from Abigail's parents, the car dropped Abigail off at Spencer's office.

They're meeting for a drink.

"What's going on with you two?" I asked before she jumped out of the SUV in the centre of town.

"What's going on with you?" she countered with a wink.

We talked about everything while Tema played with Mr. Locke—the pros and cons of returning to Victoria, the benefits of staying here. I did my best to leave Bo out of the equation—I left Bo and me out of the equation. Moving forward, I know he'll want to play a part in Tema's life, but he can do that from a distance.

It's not like the castle can't afford a few plane tickets.

But it would be best for Tema not to be spread between the west coast of Canada and the east coast of Laandia.

And now that I don't have Timothy waiting for me back in Victoria, the truth is there's not a lot waiting for me there. The same goes with Abigail.

We don't make a decision, but it's understood that we'll do this together, like we've done everything so far.

I'm a little excited but I need to talk to Bo first. I meant it when I told him he needed to work on himself, but if the first session with the therapist went well, there might be others.

If he was off to a good start at forgiving himself, then maybe…

I'm excited about the maybe.

The castle door opens for me, and I'm surprised to see Bo there. "Did someone tell you I was back?" I ask suspiciously.

"I sensed you." It takes a moment for me to realize Bo is joking and by that time, he's taken a sleeping Tema from me.

"I can manage," I tell him.

"I know, but I can help."

I follow him up to our room, unable to stop myself from watching the way he walks up the stairs.

Watching how one particular part of him moves.

Two parts—the way he holds Tema pulls his flannel shirt tight across his back, which is also nice to look at.

Bo is a beautiful man. That's undeniable. The royal family of Laandia is a very attractive family. But what people don't realize is that Bo is beautiful inside as well—and gentle and tender and kind and generous. There is a softness inside his strong, oh-so muscular exterior. And it's not that he's weak.

Bo may be one of the strongest people I know. He believed in something so whole-heartedly for so many years that he let it destroy something he loved. And now he's trying to fix that.

That takes strength and courage.

I open the door of my room and Bo takes Tema straight through to the bedroom and lays her on the bed.

Such a simple action makes my heart flutter. What if this was something he did all the time? What if we could have a real marriage—a real relationship with love and trust? Without guilt?

What if we could love each other and our daughter? Could it be as simple as that?

"Will she be okay by herself?" Bo asks as he follows me to the other room. He doesn't have a clue what's going on in my head.

How happy I am just to be here with him.

"For five minutes," I say with a grin. "If I leave her for six, I'm not sure." Bo looks at me strangely. "That was a joke."

"I know. You just... We didn't joke before."

I frown. "No, I guess we didn't. I never realized we weren't funny."

"It's not that we weren't funny... Weren't we funny?" He begins to pace, his long strides taking him from one side of the room to the other in record time.

"Maybe not." I do know we weren't lighthearted. We had deep thoughts on issues. Our lives revolved around family, and neither of them were very funny. "But things change," I decide. "And from the looks of you, something has really changed."

For maybe the first time ever, Bo looks ready to burst. I can tell he's got something important to say to me.

He pauses for a moment. "I talked to the therapist."

"And?" I hold up a hand. "It's personal. You don't have to tell me anything."

"I think I want to." He shakes his head with a shy grin. "It's exhausting, talking about myself."

"That's because you never do it."

"I didn't really have a choice this time. She got me talking about my brothers. Lyra. We didn't even get to my mother."

I hold my breath. "Is that for next time?"

Bo nods. "Tomorrow. She said we could wait for next week, but I didn't want to. If this works, I don't want to wait."

"What do you want to work?" I ask. "What are you hoping to get out of this, Bo?"

"I want to forgive myself. To...to love myself, so I can love you. Properly." His blue eyes meet mine and hold. "The way you deserve."

I press my lips together so he can't see my smile. I really hope he can't tell that I'm about to melt right now, melt straight into a gooey pile on the rug because Bo is soft and sweet and...

And he loves me.

It's there on his face and in his eyes, and in every move of his body.

He loves me.

"Tell me how it went," I prompt when all I want to do it rush into his arms.

He starts to pace again. "It was... good." He looks surprised to admit it, maybe as much as I am. "She made me feel like a selfish idiot about some things, but I needed to hear it."

"That's great. Not that you felt like an idiot but—"

"I know. But there's something even better. I talked to Lyra." He grips the back of his neck as he looks at me. "About the accident. She said—she remembered Mom was happy."

"She was happy?"

"She wasn't upset about anything. She told Lyra that I was home, that we would have dinner that night. They were singing."

"Bo." My hand covers my mouth and relief washes over me, leaving my arms and legs tingling.

He turns to the window, hunching his shoulders. "She wasn't upset with me," he says and it's like he's finally believing it. I want to clap my hands. I want to dance with joy. I want—

I want to hug him.

"It wasn't my fault," he continues, talking to the window as much as he is to me. "She might have been... maybe she was happy about us."

Three steps and I have him, winding my arms around his waist, pressing my cheek against his back. Bo turns around and then my cheek is pressed against his chest and that is so much better.

His hands slide up my back, stroking like he's touching me for the first time.

It feels like it.

It feels like the first time Bo kissed me in the parking lot of the high school before class. The snow was falling, his hand was warm on my face, and then he leaned in to kiss me.

Just like he's about to do now—

"Wait." With a shaking breath, I step back. "Wait."

"Do you love him?"

There's a raw, vulnerable look in Bo's eyes, and it makes my heart stutter with alarm. I stopped Bo from kissing me because I need to tell him about Timothy, but what do I tell him? And can I honestly say I don't love him?

I loved the idea of Timothy in Victoria—the thought of having a good man, handsome and funny, in my life. It's not that I need someone to take care of me, but I won't deny the thought of having a man around, a parent to share the workload, was tempting.

But does that mean I'm in love with him? Like I used to be in love with Bo? Like I'm—

I don't know how to describe how I feel about Bo.

And I didn't take the time to figure that out before I got on that plane with Tema and Abigail. I flew home without giving much thought to whether there are strong enough feelings for Bo to give it a try.

To fight for him. "I—"

"Because if you do," Bo says without giving me a chance to sort my thoughts. "If you love him more than you love me, I'll let you go. I'll give you the divorce, but I want to be in Tema's life. On your terms, whatever works for you. It's the least I can do for you. I never fought for you."

"No..."

"But I didn't fight for myself either. I let myself drift. But now..." He rubs his big hands down my arms, sending shivers racing through me. "If I had known... if I had thought it through—if I had talked to Lyra sooner and known my mom wasn't angry with me, then—" Bo gazes down at me with regret.

There's a wetness in his eyes, but as soon as I catch my breath, he turns away, swiping a hand across his cheek.

"We wasted so much time," he says, stalking across the room, his hand fisted on the back of his head. "And it's all my fault. If only—"

"You can't think like that," I stop him. "You don't know what would have happened if I had stayed. We were so young, Bo. Maybe we should have waited." He turns with an incredulous expression and I move to him again, like he's a magnet and I'm a helpless piece of metal. I rest a hand on his chest, feeling the comforting beat of his heart. "Maybe we needed to grow up first. It was so intense with you. We might have burnt out."

Bo shakes his head. "No."

"You don't know that. We can't go back and relive the past. We just take what we learned and what we've become and move on."

"And do you really want to move on without me?"

I raise a hand, tracing his strong jaw, hidden by his beard. I only have a vague memory of Bo without a beard, with hair curling around his ears in need of a haircut.

But the memory of how he looks at me—how he's always looked at me—has stayed firm in my mind. Maybe I didn't figure out my feelings for him before I came back because I didn't need to. I knew all along what would happen when I came back and saw him. Spent time with him.

"Bo," I begin but a knock on the door interrupts.

34

Bo

G*O AWAY.*

It's not possible to say go away when you're part of a royal family. But it's really tempting because Hettie was about to say—

I have no idea what she was about to tell me. And when she went to open the door, Abigail and Spencer were there with twin expressions on their faces.

I haven't seen that expression in years.

When were younger, it was always Abigail who would come up with plans—to go to a party, to skinny-dip in her neighbour's pond, to do the polar plunge on New Year's Day. She would come up with the idea and Spencer would agree and the two of them would gang up to get me and Hettie to agree.

Still, in all the years I've known Spencer, I've never been so annoyed to see him. Even when they burst out with some idea of us going into town tonight.

"No." It's always been my go-to response to the option of a social evening.

"Yes," Abigail says, always her response to my negativity. "It'll be fun. Silas told us about the new bar that *Fenella Carrington* opened!"

"So?' Fenella was one of Gunnar's ex-girlfriends, the line of them after Kate and before Stella merging together in a blur of names and faces.

If I had a list of ex-girlfriends like Gunnar did, would I have gotten over Hettie by now?

Because I'm not over her. Not in the slightest.

I watch her and Abigail talking about Fenella's new place—I checked it out when I was home last time and it's pretty cool. Definitely more of a girlie place than one I would frequent, but it's become popular in town. I look at Hettie's excited expression and wish we'd had time for her to say what she was about to say.

Because now she seems to have forgotten all about it as the three of them chatter excitedly about who might be there tonight.

I guess we're going.

I guess she's not going to tell me.

Maybe I don't want to know because if she doesn't tell me she wants to move on without me in her life, then I can go through hours without the pain of losing her.

I can pretend there's hope. That I have a chance.

"Okay," I agree and jaws drop.

"Really?" Hettie asks.

"Are you serious?" Abigail demands. "That has to be the quickest you've ever agreed to do anything."

"It'll be fun," Spencer promises.

"But what about Tema? Because I can stay here with her and you three can check it out," I offer. I don't think before I say it, but I have to realize it's a great idea to get out of being social.

Spencer lifts a finger. "I've got a plan for that."

"I like it," Dad says in a hearty voice, one that shows no fear of the unknown of looking after Tema for an evening.

I have fear of looking after Tema by myself. I offered, but I still have a healthy fear.

That's called bravery. Courage. Of offering to do something you're afraid of.

Or maybe it should be called idiotic because I don't have a clue what to do with a kid on my own. Still, I pushed for me to stay behind as Spencer explained how he talked to Dad and Duncan about babysitting tonight.

"Are you *sure*?" Hettie asks for the eleventh time. After Tema woke up from her nap, we headed down to the dining room for a quick meal.

It's only the five of us and Odin, along with Dad and Duncan.

"Because Tema is—"

"I'm a great babysittee," Tema cuts in. "I'll tell them what to do."

"That's what I'm afraid of," Hettie mutters. I can tell she's unsure about this, not because she doesn't want to leave Tema, but because *The king of Laandia is going to watch my kid?*

Those are her words, and she said them quite a few times while we discussed it in her room.

"Mrs. Theissen will be here," Spencer says to reassure her. "And it's a castle—if Tema acts up, they can throw her in the dungeon for the night." He ruffles Tema's hair as she cheers.

"No dungeon," I say quickly.

"No Mrs. Theissen," Dad says just as quickly. "We don't need her."

"We might need her," Duncan argues, looking intrigued at the thought. "I'll go see where she'll be hiding tonight."

Duncan runs off and Spencer grins. "You know he's got a crush on her, don't you?" he asks Dad.

"I do. And if it keeps him away from playing matchmaker for me, I'm happy about it. Now." He looks down the table at Tema, pretending to be serious but with a gleam in his eyes that should make Hettie very nervous. "What are we going to get up to tonight?"

Tema giggles, and the sound does something to my heart. "I think the question is, King Grandpa, is what *aren't* we going to get up to tonight?"

King Grandpa, I mouth to Hettie, and she smiles.

"Are all kids that resilient?" I ask in the car as Etienne drives us into town. I refuse security when I'm at my place in Wabush, knowing my neighbours and friends would look after me just as much as a hired a security team, but Dad insists I have someone when I'm home.

Etienne is the head of the team and I like him better than the rest of them.

"I think so," Hettie says. "At least Tema seems to be taking all of this in stride."

"She's a special kid," Abigail agrees. "But yeah, she took to this princess life pretty well."

"Who wouldn't want to be a princess?" Spencer wonders and I lift my hand. "You'd make a horrible princess," he scoffs. "You don't have the legs for it."

"What's wrong with my legs?"

"Have you seen the size of them? And way too hairy?"

"Are you saying that princess material is judged by the size and hairlessness of one's legs?" Abigail asks archly.

"I'm saying I remember Bo in a dress one Halloween, and it was truly scary," he counters and Hettie laughs.

"I remember that. I think it was one of Mabel's dresses."

Being with the three of them like this does something to my heart as well. I'm content living alone in Wabush. I've told myself I didn't need constant companionship, that I was better off by myself than dealing with personalities and opinions, but now that I'm with them, have spent the last two days with them, I can admit that I might be a bit lonely on my own.

That gets me wondering what it's going to be like if I go back there on my own, knowing what it could be like with Hettie and Tema and not being able to have it all.

But until she tells me differently, I'm going to hope I might have a chance to have it all. Somehow.

And because of this, by the time we pull up in front of Hela's, Fenella's club, I'm almost excited about the evening's events.

35

Hettie

"I**T'S SO PINK**," I gasp, staring around the bar.

"And starry," Abigail adds.

Having a child so young means that I missed out on the club years and going to bars and dance clubs. I can count on one hand the number of times I've been to a nightclub in Victoria.

Not that I'm upset about that—having Tema is the best thing I've ever done.

But even if I went to all the clubs Victoria has to offer, I'd still be excited to be here tonight. Abigail found us dresses somewhere—probably with Spencer's help—and I straightened my hair and put on makeup and a pair of shoes that is going to make my feet hurt tomorrow.

It'll be worth it. I'm here with Bo and Abigail and Spencer and it feels like old times. The way Bo looks at me in this dress sends shivers through me and I can't wait to finish our conversation from earlier.

It feels like tonight is the beginning of something. Maybe because I want it to be. But it feels like something is about to happen and I'm ready to go with it.

Plus, Fenella Carrington owns this place and she's—well, she's a lot of things. And she was standing with Silas when we walked in the door, so I got to meet her right away.

Abigail was tongue-tied because she spends more time on social media than I do. Not that I manage to say much.

Luckily, Fenella has to deal with a problem at the bar so we don't look too silly trying not to fangirl over her.

I don't bother trying to hide my admiration for the bar though.

The furniture and the glasses and most of the drinks have a pink hue but the ceiling is dark blue and the colour travels down the walls to end in a pinkish-lavender near the floor.

The ceiling and the upper walls are also covered with glittering silver stars.

"The night sky," Bo says staring up.

"Sophie did this." I love the pride in Spencer's voice. There were so many years where he didn't have a relationship with his sisters, and I'm so glad that has changed. "Isn't it amazing?"

"Tema would love it," Abigail agrees, her eyes wide with delight and turning in circles to drink it in.

"Does she like pink?" Bo asks awkwardly.

I nod. "And stars," I tell him. I think it's sweet how he's trying to find out everything he can about her, as quickly as he can. Even during the drive down the hill into town, he kept asking if Tema got into trouble a lot, some of the things she's done and how we respond if she's bad.

I'm glad he used the word *we* because the only thing that would make Abigail more of a mother to Tema is if she'd actually given birth to her.

I need to talk to her about what I should do. Her choices aren't dependent on mine, but she loves Tema and won't want to be very far away from her.

Tomorrow, I decide. I'll figure it all out tomorrow. Tonight, I'm just going to have fun.

With my best friends.

I don't get to go out with Abigail very often since one of us is usually watching Tema. Once in a while, we'll leave her with Granddad, but he gets so caught up with his painting that it's not always a good idea.

Especially when Tema is so interested in what he's working on that she wants to copy it. Once, she set up her own easel, got out her own paints.

She was five at the time, and paint was everywhere when she finally decided she was finished, and all the while, Granddad kept happily painting.

Spencer gets drinks for us while Bo secures a table. Abigail and I head to the dance floor.

It takes two songs for us to be noticed and another to gather a crowd.

"Well, Hettie Crow." Crystal Hansen still manages to look down at me while being at least two inches shorter. "Never thought I'd see you back here."

"Well, Crystal," Abigail says with fake brightness in her voice. "That almost seems like you missed us."

"Of course I have. Things haven't been the same since you left." She touches my arm. "I did my best to comfort Bo."

"I'm sure you did." I try to keep the snarl from my voice. Crystal was the epitome of a mean girl when we were in high school, and it seems like nothing has changed. She's still surrounded by her group of sycophants—fewer now than eight years ago, but still a considerable number.

"What brings you back?" Amy McKibbon asks. The question sounds sincere but I'm sure Amy's digging for gossip.

I know these girls. They made my life miserable for years, with their snide comments and gift of making trouble. Abigail had more problems than me, probably because she stuck by my side and refused to let them bully me.

"Bo," I say. "And Spencer. I wanted to visit my friends." And then I turn my back on them, doing my best to throw myself into the music.

"Not your family?" Crystal asks loudly. "I see that your sister has wiggled her way into a job for Kalle. I wonder what benefits she gets." She smiles slyly. "Or gives."

Abigail stops dancing. "You didn't just say that."

I hold up my hand to stop Abigail, because I've finally learned to fight my own family's battles. "You might want to rethink making comments about my sister and the future king of Laandia. I do have an in with the family, don't forget."

"You're going to tell on me?" Crystal sneers. "Really? Go cry to Kalle?"

"That's Prince Kalle to you," I correct. "But no, I wouldn't tell Kalle." I lean closer. "I'd tell Edie."

Crystal clamps her lips closed.

"I'm really surprised you're not over there now," Amy says.

"Maybe she knew there would be more excitement here tonight." Penny Black motions to a group by the bar. Two men are gesturing wildly but Fenella shakes her head.

One of the men... His back is to me, but there's something about him. I glance at Abigail and when she grimaces, I head over.

"You can't refuse to serve me," the man says loudly. "It's not right. It's not done here in Battle Harbour, which you don't know nothing about."

"'Cuz you're from some fancypants place, thinking you know more than us here. Well, you don't—don't know anything," the second one shouts. He's slurring his words more than the first, but both look like they've been overserved somewhere.

"Thinks she does," the first man says and there's something about his voice. And then Fenella Carrington glances at me and my blood freezes, because I know.

It's Reggie.

And like he knows I'm watching, my brother turns around. "What are you staring at?" he demands. It takes a moment but I can tell when recognition sets in. "Hettie?"

"Reggie," I manage even though every instinct is telling me to run.

"What the hell are you doing back here?" He glances between me and Fenella. "You friends with her? She won't give me another beer."

"I don't think you need another beer, Reggie. Why don't we go outside and catch up." I grab his arm, but he shakes me off.

"Not going anywhere with you—unless you got money? Help a brother out, Hettie."

"Let's go outside and I'll give you some. You can go over to Sailors Salon."

"They'll serve me," Reggie grouses, letting me lead him outside, his friend following. I don't recognize him but that's not surprising, since I barely recognize Reggie. He's thin and pale, and the laughing brother I used to know is nowhere to be found in his face.

It's sad but I don't let the disappointment dissuade me and push through the crowd.

I refuse to meet anyone's gaze as I get Reggie and his friend to the door, but Bo's face swims before me.

"Everything okay?" he asks.

One night. I go out *one night* and this happens. Reggie has been back for days and he's already making trouble. Who knows how quickly he'll end up back in jail?

"Everything's fine, no thanks to you, Prince." And my heart lodges in my throat as Reggie gives Bo a shove. "Get out of my way."

It doesn't really move him, but still. "Big man," Reggie's friend taunts. "Thinks he's so tough. All of them royals do."

"Not really, but... sure." Bo glances down at me, his jaw tight. "Let me help."

"It's my problem."

"No." Bo grips Reggie's arm. "It's ours."

There's a short lineup to get in, so Bo steers Reggie down in front of Coffee for the Sole. It's dark inside but I still imagine I can smell coffee even from outside.

I shiver in my short skirt and wrap my arms around myself. I can't even be in town for one night before one of my brothers ruins it. I was having fun and then Reggie—

Reggie is being Reggie and I reacted. I need to stop doing that because my brother is not going to change.

But I can.

"Let's make this quick." Bo pulls out his wallet. "I've got—"

I push Bo's hand before he can do anything else. "You are not giving him money."

"Hey, you said—"

"I said that to get you outside so you wouldn't get into more trouble. Mabel told me you just got out of jail. Do you want to go back? Were you planning on starting a fight? Because Amy McKibbon in there would be all too happy to call her brother and get him over there to drag you out and back behind bars. Is that what you want?"

Either Reggie is too drunk or too surprised to hear me lay into him like that because he drops his head.

"Not getting into trouble," his friend says. "You should mind your—"

"I would think before you say one more thing to her." Bo folds his arms in such a way that his muscles bulge. I'd be happy to take another look if I weren't so angry.

"You need to get out of here." I point to the friend. "I don't know who you are, and I don't care, but you're not helping. Go home and sleep it off."

Even with Bo's intimidating stance, he still steps forward. "Who the hell do you think you are?"

"I'm Mabel Crow's little sister and you need to be gone."

That was the right thing to say. Reggie jerks his chin at him, and the friend ambles off, muttering curses.

"Nice," Bo says under his breath.

"You think you're so fancy now," Reggie snaps. "You think you're all that, but you're not. You're just a Crow like me."

"I am a Crow, but I'm nothing like you, Reggie. I know how to hold my liquor. And Fenella's not going to risk you busting up the place because you've had too much to drink."

"I wouldn't do that." I stare at my brother. "Anymore," he concedes. "Parole officer gets snippy about stuff like that."

"And you don't want to go back to jail," Bo says with a nod. "What are you doing for work?"

"What's work?" Reggie gives a nasty laugh. "Nobody gonna hire me. They won't even give me a beer."

"Maybe around here. But I could use you up at my place up north."

36

Bo

Y OU JUST OFFERED HIM a job?" Hettie asks with disbelief. Then, "You offered him a job?" in a quieter voice.

"I did." Bo turns to Reggie. "But we're not talking about it here. It's too cold and I need to get your sister inside before she freezes."

"Go inside then," he says to Hettie with a wide sweep of his arm. "No business of hers."

"If you think I'm going to waste one minute with her talking to you, you're not as smart as I gave you credit for," I tell Reggie.

He snorts. "Nobody gives me credit for being smart."

"Maybe they'd start if you went home. Sleep it off instead of threatening to bust the place up."

"I said I wouldn't." Hettie shakes her head because her brother whines like a child. Hopefully Tema never sounds like that. "Don't do that no more."

"Good. Come see me tomorrow and we'll talk about finding you a place with the wildlife reserve up north."

"Really?" I can tell Reggie doesn't believe me, and I don't blame him. *I* don't believe me. But Hettie stepped in to help her brother and I'll do anything for Hettie.

"I said so, didn't I? I mean what I say." I turn to Hettie. "Always. Eventually."

That smile. Those eyes looking at me with respect and gratitude and...

Even if it isn't love I see in her eyes, I know that I am totally in love with her all over again.

Not that I ever stopped.

I reach out for her hand. "Go home," I instruct Reggie. "And stay clear of Fenella's place when you're drinking, especially if there's a McKibbon there. I seem to recall they're not very fond of you."

"I didn't do anything," Reggie grumbles, but he starts down the street with a bit of a rolling gait.

"Think he'll make it home okay?" I wonder.

"I really don't care right now." Hettie turns to me and clutches the front of my shirt with both hands. "You just offered my brother a job."

"I did. I should have done it a long time ago. I wish I'd done it a long time ago."

"You didn't have a job to offer him."

I give her a look. "I'm a prince, in case you didn't notice," I say drily. "I could have found him a job. Might have made it easier for you."

"Bo..." She burrows her hands into more of my shirt and I'm sure it's only because she's cold. There's not enough material in that dress to keep her warm, since it's basically a tiny shirt that covers her bum.

I like the way it covers her bum. I like everything about it. So instead of bundling her back inside the club, I wrap my arms around her to share my heat.

Hettie tips her head back to look at me, her hands folded against my chest. "Why?"

There's no other answer. "Because I love you. I've always loved you."

She bites her lips to keep from smiling, but her hazel eyes are shining. "Okay."

"Even if you don't want to be with me—"

"I ended things with Timothy."

All the air rushes out of my lungs. I actually feel light-headed. "Are you sure?" I mutter.

She looks incredulous and I get the hint that it wasn't the reaction she was hoping for. "Pretty sure."

"But why? I thought Tema was happy in Victoria." I don't know why I'm arguing, why I'm trying to get her to justify anything when all I want to do is pick her up and swing her around and then kiss her so thoroughly, like she's never been kissed before.

"I think she'll be happier here. I know I will." I open my mouth, but before I can say anything, Hettie gives me a mock glare. "And don't you dare ask why again. You should know why—I love you, Bo Erickson, and I never stopped. Never could and I think—"

I stop her then, and give Hettie the reaction I really hope she wanted.

Pressing my lips against hers, I give everything I've got into kissing her. I kiss her as her lips warm and part under mine. I kiss her as her body molds against mine and her arms wind around my waist and the people in line for the club start to cheer. I kiss her with eight years of pent up want and need and love.

And then I lift Hettie off her feet in those sexy shoes and spin her around until she laughs.

Then I kiss her again, slowly this time, like we've got all the time in the world. Because, maybe, we do.

There's no way Timothy has ever kissed her like that.

37

Hettie

I leave Tema at the castle the next day.

After Bo and I—I'm not sure what to call it except to say I think we're back together—we went back into the club and it was a great night. We danced, and danced some more, and Fenella brought out a bottle of champagne because apparently everyone saw us kissing and because Abigail cheered as much as the strangers in the line outside.

I felt every glass of that champagne when I woke up this morning, but I was too happy to care.

Magnus says he cleared his morning to hang out with Tema, but I still leave Mrs. Theissen in charge. The normally austere woman has a ready smile plus a twinkle in her eye whenever she sees Tema, so I decide my daughter is in good hands.

And Bo will take over after his therapy appointment.

I'm glad his first appointment was so positive. Because of him, and what happened last night, I'm going to spend the day facing my own demons.

My family.

Bo gives me the keys to his pickup at breakfast. "Be careful of the snow on the hill," he warns. "It builds up around the corners."

"I grew up around here, don't forget."

"I know, but it's been a while."

"I haven't forgotten anything about your truck. You never worried about me back then."

"I always worried about you back then, but I was just better at hiding it."

I drop Abigail at her parent's place, refusing her offer to go in to say hi, because if I don't go now, I'm not sure I will.

The house looks the same when I pull up. About ten minutes outside of town, on a dead-end road that gives my father lots of room to leave his derelict boats strewn around the house.

The drive has been carefully cleared, which means someone is home.

Walking up to the door, I debate whether I should knock. Technically, this is the family home, but it's been a long time since I considered myself part of the family.

After talking to Reggie last night, I don't think that was a good thing.

I knock as a warning and then open the door—which is left unlocked. My father would always laugh when someone asked why it was never locked. "I'd like to see somebody try to break into the Crow house," he'd chuckle.

The sounds of television greet me, along with the tangle of boots by the front door. "Hello?" I call. The smell is the same—hints of salt and fish and the stale tang of beer. Over it all is a rich, gravy-like scent. The only thing my father ever cooked was stew. He'd add whatever meat he could find, any vegetables in the house, along with a can of beer.

I ate it so often growing up that I've never once made it my-self.

Footsteps and then my younger brother Earl peers around the living room. "Hettie. Hey."

"Hi." Do I hug him? What do I say?

But Earl doesn't give me the chance. "Dad's in the kitchen," he says as he returns to the couch.

We used to have a dog when I was younger, but my mother took it with her. It was one thing for our mother to leave her family, but to take your dog? Earl loved that dog. I think he was more upset with the loss of Bear than Mom.

I haven't thought of her in years, and one step in this house, so much comes flooding back.

Making cookies, the string of curses when we burnt them. Her brushing my hair, explaining how my red hair came from her. Packing my own lunch for school, because she was still asleep.

Having Tema was the best thing I've ever done, but it also made me realize that some women should never be a mother.

Including my own.

My father is at the stove with his back to the door and doesn't hear me pad down the hall. I take him in before I say anything—broad shoulders hunched as he stirs a pot on the stove, wearing a wool sweater, threadbare and with more than a few holes.

The kitchen looks the same—a collection of dishes on the counter, both clean and dirty. It looks tired. Used. I try and drum up happy memories but all I can think about is how it was always my job to wash the dishes.

I clear my throat. "Dad?"

He glances over his shoulder, without the least bit of surprise on his face. "I heard you were in town."

"I—yeah." I don't know what to say to him. It's been eight years. I would send emails after I left, telling him where I was, how I was doing, and he never responded. It's not surprising that I fell in love with a man who had trouble communicating, because that's all I knew from the men in my life.

He gives the pot another stir before he turns to face me. I don't know if it's the years or the time spent on the boat, but my father looks old. His face is lined and worn, his hair full grey. The dark eyes are still the same, surveying me without a smile. "Are you coming in or just planning on hovering?"

"I guess. I thought I'd stop by."

"You staying at the castle, I hear."

"I am now."

"You and the prince?"

"I don't know. I married him," I blurt out. It's not the right way to say it, but I have no clue what the best way would be. My father has always been straight to the point, so maybe it's rubbed off on me.

"Thanks for the invitation," he says in a sour voice.

"This was eight years ago. I married him without telling any-one, and then the queen died. And then I left."

He turns to give the pot another stir. "I'm guessing there's more to it than that."

"There is, but that's the gist of it. No one knew. I had a baby."

He makes a noise in his throat. "Maybe you should have led with that."

"Maybe." I pull out a chair at the table, surprised to find a cat sleeping on the seat. "You have a cat. I didn't know you had a cat."

"You have a husband and a child, so I guess we're even."

"Fair." I give the cat a pet and pick another chair.

"Where is this kid?" he asks.

"Her name is Tema and she's seven. She's with her father. Bo is her father. I never told him I was pregnant until I came back here with her."

"Sounds like a lot more is going on. This kid—she's a princess." I can't tell what my father thinks of that, whether he's happy or disgusted with the idea.

"And I think she's handling it a lot better than I am." I give a huff of laughter. I've never had a conversation this long with my father, even with the fits and starts.

"Are you still married to the prince?" Just as Dad asks the question, I hear footsteps on the stairs and Reggie appears.

His hair sticks up and he's wearing sweat pants and a ripped T-shirt. I never noticed how thin he was last night.

Earl is right behind him. "What are you talking about?" he demands.

"Did I hear that right?" Reggie blusters. "You're *married*?" At my nod, he scoffs. "Didn't want to share that with me last night?"

"You were drunk and it's not common knowledge," I snap. "I came back to get a divorce but now I'm... I don't think I will."

It's the first time I said it out loud and my cheeks warm at the words.

I have a future with Bo. I don't know what that will look like yet, but it's there, looming before me, waiting for me to take the first step.

Telling my family is that step.

"You sure about that?" Dad demands. "Castle life wouldn't be easy."

"She'd be a *princess*," Reggie protests. "That sounds plenty easy. What does that make me?"

"Nothing," Dad barks. "You should stay away from her. We all should."

"No." All three of them stare down at me. My father. My brothers. My family. "I don't want that," I admit. "You're my family."

"Not much of one."

"But it can be. It doesn't have to be like... like it was. If I stay, you can get to know Tema. She's your granddaughter. And me. You could get to know me."

Dad turns, his shoulders hunching even more. "I wasn't here for you when you needed me," he mutters to the stove. "Don't know why you want anything from us."

The first step is the hardest, and then it gets easier. My father used to be a hugger, so I rest a hand on his back. "Because I'm older. And I'm a mother and I know how hard it must have been with Mom left. Granddad wasn't here, you didn't have any help with us."

"So?"

"You did your best. I know that now."

He gives a sharp nod but doesn't turn around. "She's really married?" Earl asks Reggie.

"To Bo," Reggie confirms. "I saw them last night. Was he serious about giving me a job?"

"He was. Go talk to him today."

"And you're moving back?" Earl asks.

"I am."

My father is still nodding and my hand is still on his back. I move it, because it's getting awkward just touching him. "The stew won't be ready for a while," he says over his shoulder. "You should come back tomorrow, it always tastes better the next day."

I don't bother hiding my smile. "I will. I'll bring Mabel.

"Bring your prince," he instructs. And this time when he turns around, there's a hint of a grudging smile on his face. "And my granddaughter."

38

Bo

T HE TALKING THING IS easier this time.

Dr. Patel says that it must be difficult to be a prince, and that sets off a whole monologue about what I hate about being born into a royal family.

She lets me talk myself out, and then she asks what I like about it.

I find out that I like quite a bit about being a member of this family.

After the session is over, I collect Tema from the big ballroom where Mrs. Theissen, Dad, and Duncan all watch Tema run riot across the polished floor. I bundle her up in the warmest clothes she has and take her up to the battlements.

The wind whistles and I tug Tema's hat over her ears. The air might have a hint of spring on the ground, but here, five stories up, it's still winter cold.

"This is my favourite part of the castle," I tell her, lifting her up so she can see over the edge.

"Whoa." Tema's eyes are wide with delight. "I can see all the way to the coffee place in town."

"Maybe not that far. But that roof over there?" I point to the south, between the trees, naked without their leaves. "That's Abigail's parents' place."

"Nana and Papa Locke," Tema supplies. She stares at the slice of shingled roof for a long moment, then, "I have a lot of grandparents."

"That's a good thing."

"No one I know has so many."

"Someone must. It just means more people love you."

"Do you have a grandpa?"

"Not anymore."

"That's sad, because he was the king."

I chuckle. "I think it's sad even if he wasn't the king. I never met him. He died before I was born."

"And Grandpa King became king. And when he dies—" Big green eyes stare solemnly at me. "I don't want to think about him dying."

"Nobody does."

"But you won't be king?"

I squeeze her tightly. "Not if I can help it."

"You'd be a good king. You like Taylor Swift and books and polar bears... and bubble fights!" Tema gives a surprisingly deep cackle of laughter that makes me smile. "I think I want you to be king."

"It's not really how it works, but thanks."

"You're welcome." Her arm snakes around my neck and I hoist her higher on my hip.

It feels right holding her, almost as right as if feels with Hettie in my arms.

Like she knows I'm thinking about her, my truck rounds a corner coming up the hill. I point it out to Tema, who waves and calls out like Hettie could hear us.

I really hope she doesn't see us or I might have some explaining to her why I took our daughter up to the battlements to let her look over the edge.

"Do you love Mommy a lot?" Tema asks as the truck disappears from view.

I'm not expecting that question, but then again, I don't expect half the things that come out of Tema's mouth. Like my daughter, I believe in honesty. "I do," I tell her.

Her smile widens. "Does that mean we're going to be a family?"

"I don't know what that means yet. Would you like that? To be a family?"

"With Abigail, and Mrs. Theissen to look after me?"

I laugh. "Abigail isn't going anywhere. Same with Mrs. Theissen. But I guess that means we'd have to stick around here."

"And live in the castle with King Grandpa? I'd like that."

"I think he would too."

"Would you?"

I stare off into the distance as the truck, with Hettie at the wheel reappears. "I think I might like that too." After more vigorous waving, I set Tema down, and she immediately grasped my hand. "So. Want to help me show Mommy how much I love her?"

"Yes! Can we do it with balloons?"

I laugh out loud. "I had something else in mind."

"It might be almost as good as balloons." We start back to the door, the wind trying to push us back to the edge.

"Tema?" I ask when we've almost made it.

"Yes, Prince Daddy."

It feels like my heart is about to explode in my chest. "I love you too, you know," I say.

"Oh, I know," Tema retorts with another cackle. "Love you, too, Prince Daddy."

We eat dinner later with Dad and Odin. Kalle and Edie are both at the pub, and Gunnar has plans with Stella. Spencer and Duncan are there, and Spencer keeps giving me sideways glances because he knows my plan.

I'm not worried about Hettie picking up on the looks I'm getting from Spencer because Tema is going to give it all away anyway by the way she's bouncing on her chair.

I'll put her out of her misery as soon as dinner is over.

When the dishes are cleared, I push back my chair a little harder than necessary and it sways back on two legs. Hettie opens her mouth to say something as I drop to one knee beside her chair.

"Oh," she whispers, her hand over her mouth.

Dad stops talking mid-sentence. Everyone's eyes are on me.

But after a quick glance at a grinning Tema, I focus only on Hettie. "I thought of proposing again," I begin, fumbling in my pocket for the little box I've kept with me all during dinner. "But I like how I did the first time. That came about out of love. I was honest with you, Hettie, about how I felt, and I wouldn't do anything differently. This time I have a different type of proposal for you—that we do what we should have done back then, and finally begin our life as a married couple."

Hettie's eyes are shining and she wears the biggest smile on her face. Even though she doesn't say anything, I take that as a sign to keep going. "I love you. I've always loved you. I'm sorry I wasn't strong enough to fight for either of us back then, but I propose we give it another chance. I want to be your husband, Hettie, and a father for our daughter. I want to give you the life you deserve. I want that so much and I... I just want you," I finish in a ragged voice. "For forever."

When Hettie drops to her knees on the floor with me, the cheering begins. And as my lips find hers in a promise of everything I have to give, I feel a pair of small, strong arms clutch me around my waist.

I stop kissing Hettie only to sweep Tema in my arms.

39

Hettie

I CAN'T STOP STARING at my ring.

Bo never gave me an engagement ring the first time. It was only days between the proposal and the wedding, and we kept it a secret anyway, so there was no point in flashing a diamond.

Timothy never officially asked me to marry him. We only talked about him asking me, and deep down, I think I knew he never would. I knew he wanted to marry me—as much as he wanted anything—but it would have been more of a business transaction than a romantic highlight.

When Bo dropped to his knees during *dinner* of all things, that was a highlight. And then when he pulled out the ring box—not until Tema stopped hugging him—and showed me the ring, I was happy not to have another to compare it with, because anything else would have come up lacking.

It was from Queen Selene's collection.

"I gave her that after Bo was born," Magnus tells us after he calls for champagne, even letting Tema have the tiniest sip. He gently takes my hand and lifts it to the light. "Sapphire for his eyes. I gave her something when each of them was born, all with sapphires."

"I didn't know that," Odin mutters.

"I haven't passed yours on yet," Magnus tells him. "She was in her purple phase for Bo, so it's a sapphire in the centre, with an amethyst and a purple garnet on either side." His thumb smooths over the gemstones and I see his throat work.

"It's beautiful," I whisper, closing my hand around his. "Thank you."

"I wanted her to have something pretty to know I was so happy to be blessed with a child. And I wanted Bo to give it to you for the same reason. You've given this family another blessing." He ruffles Tema's hair with his other hand.

"You're stealing his thunder, Mag," Duncan chides with a laugh.

"I can't help it." The king takes his hand from mine and wipes his eyes. "I'm so glad to see the two of you finally together, and with our newest princess."

"Me," Tema cheers.

"No," he corrects. "Your mother. Princess Hettie."

That—I'm not expecting that. I wasn't expecting any of it, but now that I'm here, as a member of the royal family of Laandia... it feels right.

Finally.

After several bottles of champagne and so many hugs of congratulations, we leave Tema for Mrs. Theissen to put to bed, and head into town.

Bo wants to tell Kalle and Gunnar in person, so Spencer sends the text to the brothers, and Odin joins us in the SUV.

"Usually we don't have females along for the ride." Odin grins, looking over his shoulder at where Abigail and I sit in the far back of the SUV.

"If you think I'm missing a second of this you've got another thing coming," I tell him.

"Me, too," Abigail cheers.

She hasn't let go of my hand since we got in the car. "Are you sure it's okay that I come," she whispers as the boys start talking.

"*Yes*," I assure her. "You're a part of this as much as I am."

"Not as much as you."

"Yeah, well... Spencer clearly wants you along."

Abigail shrugs, her gaze on the back of his dark head. "I'm not sure, but I'm having fun. Not as much fun as you, Princess Hettie." She bumps my shoulder. "It's going to take some time to get used to that."

"Like forever." I rub a finger over my new ring. That hasn't taken that long to get used to, but the title, a new way of life... "What are you going to do?" I ask Abigail. "Obviously, I'm not going back to Victoria. But if you like it there—"

"Not enough to stay by myself." She laughs. "I thought I'd go back and pack everything up. You can come with me, if you like, for a few days. Close up things."

"I have to tell Granddad," I muse.

"You could bring Bo along and then have him fly back with Tema for some Daddy-daughter time while we figure everything out," Abigail suggests.

I give her a curious glance. "Have you been planning this?"

"Since I saw the two of you together," Abigail admits with a laugh. "It was only a matter of time, Het. This is the best outcome for all of you."

"I think so, too."

"Although I'm not sure I'll let Mrs. Theissen be your primary babysitter," she pouts.

"She really wanted to stay with Tema." It had been Mrs. Theissen who insisted Abigail join us. Bo wanted me to be with him when he told his brothers, and I wanted to go so I could tell Mabel at the same time.

"I have a feeling she won't be alone for long," Odin cuts in.

"Dad couldn't stop talking about Tema," Spencer adds. "She's not going to get much sleep tonight with them watching her."

"It's two nights in a row," I groan. "I feel like a bad mother."

"You're the furthest thing from a bad mother," Abigail assures me.

Bo doesn't say anything. Bo sits, head bowed as we talk and laugh on the drive to The King's Hat. He's so quiet that I start to wonder what's wrong. Is this not what he wants? Did he make a mistake?

"What is it?" I demand as soon as we pile out of the car. I stare at his eyes, searching—

There's wetness around his eyes, and all I see in them is love.

Lots and lots of love.

"I can't believe this is really happening," he says in a gruff voice and pulls me close.

I clutch his jacket. "I was afraid you thought—"

"No." He cups my face with his big hands. "Don't ever think that. This is what I want. *You* are what I want. What I've always wanted."

And then his lips brush against mine, so warm in the cool air. It's only a soft touch, but the way Bo looks at me after…

I reach up on my tiptoes and kiss him, pressing my lips against his like there's nothing as important in the world.

That's how he makes me feel.

"Dude." There's laughter as Spencer jostles Bo's shoulder. "We doing this?"

"Not now," Bo says against my lips. I laugh as I try to pull away. Bo chuckles and finally releases me.

"Let's go," I tell him. "We've got all the time in the world for this."

"Now we do." Bo slips off my glove and takes my hand. "And I'm buying you a better pair of gloves."

"I can buy my own gloves." Bo holds the door and I slip under his arm, eyes widening when I see the wall of Ericksons at the bar.

The wall of family.

Kalle and Edie behind the bar, with Edie looking at me expectantly. Gunnar and Stella on the other side, with Stella's sister Sophie along with Silas and Fenella. Mabel is a few feet away.

And—Princess Lyra.

Lyra has the biggest smile on her face as she makes a beeline to Bo, practically pushing me aside to throw her arms around her big brother. "Did you know I was here?" she demands. "Is that why you called a meet?"

"This has nothing to do with you," Bo tells her with a laugh. "But I'm really glad to see you."

"Because you've been an idiot for too long." Still with her arms around Bo's neck, Lyra looks down at me. She's not as tall as her brothers but she has a few inches on me. "Both of you."

Three days ago, I would have dropped my gaze and walked away with my tail between my legs. Now, I stand tall, staring at the bright blue eyes and refusing to let her intimidate me. "Not anymore," I say.

"Good," Lyra says shortly. She unwraps from Bo, gives Spencer a cursory glance, and Abigail a much longer one. "What's going on then?"

"I'll tell you together." Bo grabs my hand and pulls me over to the group.

"Took you long enough to get here," Gunnar grumbles with a grin. "Spence said it was an emergency. But you look pretty happy for an emergency."

Bo looks down at me and his mouth curves up in the biggest smile. He lifts my left hand. "We're staying married."

"And we're having a big party to celebrate," I add before the cheers make it impossible to hear anything.

40

Bo

THE NEXT DAY, I meet with Kate in what will become my office.

"Where do you want to do this?" she asks. "And alone or with Hettie?"

Hettie, who is moving slowly this morning. Kalle pulled out the Screech after we finished all six bottles of champagne, the entire supply he had in the bar. Hettie admitted over her weak tea that it's been a long time since she's drank the stuff.

Not long enough, if you ask me.

"She'll be along in a few minutes," I say. "She's bringing Tema."

"You really want to introduce her now?"

"I'm not hiding anything, but I'm going to make sure to ask for them to give us privacy."

Them. The press.

Kate met us at the bar last night. It felt like half the town was there, all celebrating my marriage to Hettie, our daughter, and a second chance at true love.

Because that's exactly what this is. A second chance to get it right.

I still need to work on a lot, and I will because I've already gotten my reward. Hettie is staying. Hettie is staying with me in Laandia. And I'm going to be a father to Tema.

I already know I'm going to need help with that one.

"Your call," Kate says. "I'd recommend using the front foyer. We announced Odin's engagement in your father's big office, so let's do it differently. Because this is very different than how Odin did things."

"I'm not my brother."

"No." Kate smiles. "You're not."

Three hours later, I stand on the bottom step of the staircase, Hettie and Tema on the stair above me.

Hettie has a death grip on Tema's hand. I know she's bribed our daughter with anything she could think of to behave.

"You can smile and wave, but let's leave the talking to Prince Daddy," she implores Tema one last time.

The name has sort of stuck. I can't say I hate it, especially when Tema whispers it while she's giving me a hug.

I don't think I'll ever get tired of the hugs.

Kate stands on the floor and appraises us one last time. She motions to Hettie to tug down her shirt and gives my tie a flip. "You look perfect," she announces. "A perfect little family."

I nod because I'm not sure I can say anything. The few words Kate provided me keep going around in my mind like it's on repeat. *Thank you for coming. Eight years ago... we have a daughter...*

For about the fiftieth time I really wish I'd taken Dad up on his offer to address the press rather than insisting I do it myself.

But it has to be me. If I'm about to start on this new chapter of life, then it has to be me laying everything out in the open.

"Any questions?" Kate asks. "Because they're going to be banging the door down in about one minute."

I glance back at Hettie who gives me a nervous smile. "You good?"

"I'm perfect," she says.

Yes, you are, I mouth. With a wink at Tema, I turn back to Kate. "Let's do this."

Ten terrifying minutes later, the foyer is filled with press, and my cheeks already ache from smiling. I've lost count of how many pictures are taken.

And I still haven't said a word. Finally, Kate asks for quiet. "His Highness, Prince Bowden would like to make a statement," she says. She gives me an encouraging nod and then it's on me.

Hettie trails her fingers down my back, and I take a deep breath. "Thanks for making the trip in the snow," I begin. Even I can tell my voice is shaky, and I clear my throat, the sound amplified by the microphone in front of me. "I won't take much of your time, but I wanted to introduce someone to you. My... my wife, Hettie Crow. Erickson, now." I glance back at Hettie, reaching back to squeeze her hand that she's rested on my shoulder. "Princess Hettie."

Questions hit me like a wave, and I raise my hand. "We were married eight years ago," I say over the voices, and I wait for them to quiet so I can get the rest out. "Two days later, my mother died in an unfortunate accident, one I'm sure you all remember. After which Hettie left to live in British Columbia, Canada because I was unable to fully process my grief and guilt over my mother's death."

Hettie's hand tightens on my shoulder. "You're doing great," she whispers. I take a deep breath and plough ahead.

"My mother was the only person I told about our marriage, and since this happened only hours before her accident, I blamed myself for her death. Because of this, I wasn't able to be the husband Hettie deserved, or be a father to our daughter. Which is why she kept her birth a secret."

Another round of reactions and I pause, wishing I had taken Kate up on her offer of a bottle of water.

"I'm giving you the whole story now, in the hopes that you'll be respectful and give us the privacy to begin living as a family. Yes, Hettie and I are officially married. Yes, we'll be having a second ceremony, which you might be invited to if you stop interrupting me."

There's a smattering of laughter, and I look around with surprise.

"No, I did not know I had a daughter. Hettie's decisions are hers and I would appreciate they not be questioned or even brought up unless Hettie does it herself." I pause. "If you do, you definitely won't get an invite to the wedding."

Hettie laughs softly behind me and hope flares.

I can do this.

I glance over my shoulder again, this time at Tema who is practically dancing with anticipation. "Now, for the reason you're all here. I'd like to introduce a very important person to you. My daughter."

I smile at Tema, who wriggles out of her mother's hold and jumps down the two steps to the floor. "Hi!" She waves. "I'm Princess Tema."

Epilogue
Spencer

SPRING FLOWERS COVER EVERY available surface.

Tulips, daffodils, and tall iris. Pansies, peonies and tiny bouquets of lily of the valley. Boughs of lilacs and forsythia and even more plants that I've never seen in Laandia.

I'm not a flower person, especially since I have no reason, nor a person to gift flowers too, but even I have to admit it's impressive how many blooms they were able to collect in the six weeks they've been planning the wedding.

There are more flowers here than there was in the forest during Bo and Hettie's first wedding.

Watching them do it again is just as meaningful.

I'm not the only one smiling.

Bo can't take his eyes off of Hettie as makes her way between the rows of chairs set up in the Queen's study.

King Magnus insisted on the full religious ceremony, even though Bo fought against having it in the church. He also did everything he could to have the ceremony outside, even though with the constant rain, occasional snow and chill, late April isn't the best time to do anything outside.

Bo's theory was anywhere was better than inside the ball room, and came up with quite a few options, which included the town hall in Battle Harbour, The King's Hat pub, and Abigail's parents' house. Fenella Carrington offered her nightclub, and there was talk of one of the barns on the England's—Edie's parents—farm.

I've never seen him with that level of tenacity and determination, but every one of his arguments faded as soon as Magnus suggested the Queen's study for the ceremony.

That worked for him.

With the chairs and the flowers and the people, the room doesn't look much like the comfortable study where the Queen used to sit with friends, family, and foreign diplomats. But I know Bo has the memory of the last time he was here with his mother fixed in his head, like she's able to be there if he thinks about her hard enough.

Everyone is thinking about her, so I like to think Queen Selena is with us somehow.

Bo might have his mother in his thoughts, but he's looking at Hettie like she's the top donut on the rack and he can't wait to make her his.

It might not be the best analogy but I was in the castle kitchen before the ceremony and they had freshly baked donuts for the sweet table and they looked really good.

Tema practically drags Hettie the last few feet to where Bo and I stand. Abigail stands opposite, her hands full of tulips and delicate white blooms, her eyes full of tears. Rather than her father walking down the aisle, she and Bo decided it would be Tema, wearing a white dress with a fluffy tulle skirt over pink cowboy boots.

Why my father would buy her pink cowboy boots is anyone's guess, but I think it had something to do with Dad showing her a video of one of their concerts and Tema pointed out his boots.

She probably said they were cool, and then of course, he had to buy her a pair. I'm not sure who spoils her more—Dad or the king. I wonder how Tema's other grandfather can compete, but I've heard talk of a trip out to see the whales on his boat when the weather is warmer, so my guess is that he's biding his time.

Hettie is wearing white as well. I remember her in a pink dress for the first one, and while she had been pretty, the white gown with the tiny train makes it all seem real, rather than teenagers playing at being married.

It was the one thing I remembered from before—it never seemed *real*. It was like the four of us had been sucked into one of Bo's dreams, that we weren't really there.

I know I never realized the ramifications of the day until later, after Hettie left. It was my idea not to tell anyone about the wedding, and Bo didn't need much persuading.

I always thought she would come back. And I know I wanted Abigail to. Not going against Bo's wishes to look for them might have been my way of punishing them.

I'm not proud of that.

Abigail and I stand up for them at the far end of the Queen's study under an archway of flowers and watch Bo and Hettie say their vows to each other. The first time around was a quick service, but Hettie wanted to make this one last.

"It's the last time I'm going to marry you, so let's make it a good one," she told Bo. "Flowers. Poems. Written vows."

"Written by us?"

Mabel and Odin were selected as poem readers and did very well. I organized a five-piece chamber music group to serenade the guests, and did my best to help Bo with his vows.

Bo, being Bo, wouldn't take much help, but whatever he's stumbling through has brought tears to Hettie's eyes, so I think he's doing all right.

Bo finally told everyone about the conversation he had with the Queen the night she died. While there was the expected *"you're an idiot"* comments, there was also a lot of hugging. The consensus seemed to be that it was understood why Bo took on the blame but it wasn't necessary any longer.

He also admitted to his brothers and Lyra that he would be seeing a therapist for some time and everyone, even Kalle with his reluctance to discuss emotions, or even admit he felt them, decided that was a good idea.

All this divesting of emotional turmoil hasn't seemed to have changed Bo in the last six weeks. He's still quiet, still hates talking to the press, and still hopelessly in love with Hettie.

But anyone who looks at him can easily tell how happy he is.

Just watching him watch her walk down the aisle, in her simple gown with flowers in her hair, holding Tema's hand, was enough for me to be hit with a pang of *I want that.*

I've never wanted that. The whole hearts and feelings and flowers that comes with a romance. Or a committed relationship. I think that's why Bo and I have stayed so close over the years—I knew he was still in love with Hettie and no one would come between that, and therefore, no one would come between our friendship.

Not that women come between friendship, but they do change the dynamic.

But my heart does feel like it's expanding as Hettie and Bo are declared husband and wife—again—I watch Bo kiss his bride.

Across from me, Abigail meets my eye. She's crying and smiling at the same time, and I have to wonder if that heart expansion might have something to do with her being back in town.

Since she's been back, I've seen the difference in her—but also the ways that she's exactly the same. The sameness brings back nostalgia and feelings that I thought were long gone.

Not that I had as strong of feelings for Abigail as Bo had for Hettie, but there *were* feelings.

As much as there could be with Lyra lodged in my heart for my entire life.

But Lyra hasn't been around much and Abigail has been all over the place, so maybe it's time to sublet Lyra's spot.

It's difficult to continue that thought when Lyra is here, standing right in my line of sight for the entire ceremony.

Abigail is across from me, Lyra stands with the family right where I can see her.

No wonder I'm a little distracted, and I'm rarely distracted.

They kept the guest list small with only the royal family and guests and some of Hettie's family present.

The party is tomorrow night in the ballroom, and Hettie will be crowned a princess of Laandia during the festivities.

So will Tema.

I saw her tiara today and she's going to love it.

After walking Hettie down the aisle, the little girl went straight to the king and now stands between Magnus and Edie, clutching both of their hands. She's got a huge grin on her face as she watches her parents. Magnus is devoted to his granddaughter, but a solid bond has already developed between Edie and Tema.

Tema is amazing, but I know what Edie is thinking: if something happens and Edie and Kalle don't have children, that little girl will eventually be queen of Laandia. She's going to need all the help she can get taking on that role.

It's a sobering thought for such a celebration, and I push it away, especially since the ceremony is over and Bo and Hettie turn to the families to receive congratulations.

Abigail steps to my side and tucks her arm through mine and I smile down at her. "Second time is the charm, you think?"

Her dress is bright blue and is held up with two little straps over her shoulders. It's—

She looks good. Very good. Her hair is curled and held back at the sides and she's wearing more makeup than she usually does, highlighting her brown eyes.

"You look amazing," I tell her, forgetting her question.

Abigail blinks. "Why, thank you."

"I hadn't told you yet and I wanted to make sure I did."

"You don't look so bad yourself, Mr. Laz." She squeezes my arm. Half the time Abigail sounds like she's flirting with me.

I know she's flirting with me. She's always flirted with me, like she's telling me the door to her heart is wide open and to come find a place to stay. There's always been a *what if* between us, and I know I'm the reason the question is still hanging there.

"I think second time's the charm," I agree because there's that urge to step through that open door. It's been here since Abigail got back into town.

Maybe it's finally time.

"I really hope it works out," Abigail says.

She's talking about Bo and Hettie.

"Why wouldn't it? Look at the two of them. Nothing is coming between them."

"They've got eight years to get past," Abigail reminds me. "I'm happy that this was quick, but they've got some work ahead of them."

"Aren't they lucky they've got us around to help them." I squeeze her hand as I lead her through the rows of chairs. "I'm glad you're sticking around."

Bo and I had gone with Hettie and Abigail to Victoria to close up their lives there. I met Hettie's grandfather and although I admire him as an artist, I don't think he was much of a caregiver to the girls.

The grandfather had declined the invitation for the wedding saying that he was too into his painting to leave.

Abigail told me some about the years they spent in the West Coast of Canada and I hate the thought of them going there when they were just twenty-one with no family and no support.

"There wasn't really another option." Abigail grins. "Especially with the job offer from the school. I suppose I have you to thank for that."

I shake my head. "I mentioned that there's a teacher's assistant in town who needs a job. They were happy to have you."

"Well, thank you for doing the mentioning."

I don't tell her that it wasn't just for her. It's in everyone's best interest for Abigail to stay in Battle Harbour.

It seems selfish to want her to stay just for myself.

"Are you happy being the T.A? You always wanted to be the teacher."

"I managed to get a degree but I couldn't get my Bachelor of Education working part-time," she admits ruefully.

"Maybe now."

She shrugs. "Maybe now. What's next on your schedule? Now that you don't have this to organize."

This being more than the wedding. There are a lot of legal details with Bo getting a brand-new family, as well the country getting new princesses. And I've been helping Kate with the press and luckily, they've been relatively accepting about the whole thing. Hettie had been terrified and expected hostility, but for the most part, the people of Battle Harbour recognized the eight-year marriage and arrival of surprise child with more excitement than anger.

"Can the king make anyone a princess?" Abigail asks as we wait for the waiter circulating with champagne to get to us.

"They have to be married," I explain. Technically, both of them are already princesses but they don't have the crowns."

"They actually get a crown? Tema is gonna love that. I can see her wearing it with those purple leggings."

The purple leggings in question peek out under her dress. Abigail had been responsible for getting her dressed this morning, and for once Tema hadn't complained about the formal attire—if she could wear her leggings. Given how the Laandian spring is still cold with evidence of snow this morning, an extra layer wasn't the worst idea.

Abigail has the gift to know when to stop arguing with the seven-year-old. I'm not sure I ever will.

I'm tempted to shrug out of my jacket and put it around Abigail's shoulders to fend off the goosebumps dotting her arms.

I tuck her closer instead.

Abigail looks around at the study. "It's a nice spot for the wedding, but I kind of miss the trees of the first one," she confesses. "The rose petals were a nice touch."

"Bo's idea. He'll do anything to make her happy."

"And he does make her happy," she admits. "It's just strange that after living through eight years of angst, they finally have their happily ever after."

"They deserve it."

"So do you."

I shrug as the waiter arrives with a tray of glasses. "Thank you." I take two, handing one to Abigail. "How are you doing with your own happy ever after?"

"It's off to a good start," she says lightly.

"What is?"

We turn in unison. Lyra, with my half-sister Sophie, stands behind us. "Is that for me?" She gestures to the glass I'm holding.

"Actually, it's for me."

With a lift of her shoulder, Lyra steps around me to the tray and grabs a single glass. "Wait, please," she instructs and downs the champagne without taking a breath.

What Bo can do with beer, his sister can with champagne.

Setting the empty glass down, she takes two more, giving the waiter a winning smile.

"She's a bit...unsettled... being back," Sophie tells me quietly. "Seeing certain people."

Me. She means me.

Why does that make my stomach tighten like someone's grabbed hold of it?

"Nice wedding," Lyra says handing a glass to Sophie. "I'm glad we got to share in this one."

"I didn't think you were staying." Lyra has been back and forth three times, usually only staying a few days at a time, and never giving a good answer to why she can't stay longer. Events, obligations, and parties keep her busy.

I haven't heard if there's a certain someone who is also taking up her time. I know there are *someones*, but none of them seem to last.

"And miss Bo's wedding *again*?" Lyra arches her eyebrows, her smile tight and just a little bitter.

"I wasn't in charge of the guest list the first time," I tell her. Lyra has always had the worst case of FOMO of anyone I know, and when she does miss out, she takes it hard and holds grudges.

"No." Lyra's gaze drifts over Abigail. "Nice dress."

"Thank you, Your Highness."

Lyra smiles without it reaching her eyes. She's the only one in the family who never corrects when someone calls her that.

"Abigail, I think Hettie is waving at you," Sophie says.

"She is. I better go check." She gives me a smile as she moves off, Sophie following in her wake.

"Spencer." Lyra hooks my gaze over the rim of her glass. I can't take my eyes off her. It's always been like that. She drives me crazy but I can't stop watching her. "What's going on?"

I gesture to the crowd around us, standing close but giving us a little space, like there's a pocket of me-and-Lyra in the midst of everything. "Wedding stuff."

"I meant with you and Abigail."

Did she actually come right out and ask that? "She's my friend."

"Is that all?"

"Feel like telling me what business that is of yours?" I hold my breath in the hope that maybe this time...

But no.

"I've got another wedding next week," Lyra says casually. "I wondered if you were up for a trip to Toronto."

It's not the first time Lyra has asked me to escort her to events or parties. In fact, we've always been an unofficial pair most of our lives for castle events. "Anyone I know?" I ask rather than refusing.

Am I ready to refuse her?

"My friends Tad and Demi. I think you met him, he's friends with Mase Stirling and knows Fenella. I think he was here for the grand opening."

"I met them."

"Demi was on The Suitor—"

"With Odin?"

"No, that was The Suitorette. Demi left halfway through because of Tad. It's a sweet story. You should come with me."

I study Lyra, trying to see if there's more to her invitation than a simple request for an escort. We are friends; she is my best friend's sister. And then there's her renewed friendship with my sister.

Princess Lyra is unquestionably beautiful, with her father's ability to charm and her mother's poise and grace. But there's a restlessness to Lyra that's growing over the years. She needs someone in her life to help her focus, to act like an anchor when she drifts off-course.

I always thought I would end up being that anchor. I hoped someday she would see me as more than Spencer, son of Duncan, and helper of the royal family.

For the first time, I don't feel much hope of that changing.

And then I look over at where Abigail has Tema in her arms. There's something between me and Abigail. There always has been.

Maybe it's time I find a new hope.

"I don't think I'm able to do that," I tell Lyra slowly.

Has Abigail stolen Spencer's heart from Lyra?

Find out in Royal Rebel

But first, subscribe to my newsletter to grab this BONUS EPILOGUE!

Acknowledgements

Thank you for reading Royal Reluctance!

Since I started the Love in Laandia series, I've been waiting to sink my teeth into Bo and Hettie's story. It has been there from the start—a heartwarming tale of reunited first love, and Tema! I've been so excited about that little girl.

Can you see her as Queen of Laandia someday?
Of course it's the book that I was looking forward that had the delays—first, a mini spin-off as I told Fenella and Silas's in Coffee Break with the Billionaire, part of the Cinnamon Rolls and Pumpkin Spice series.

And a gentle pause as life got a little overwhelming and I had to push back the release day for Bo.

In my 10 plus years as an author, I've never missed a deadline. I'm not proud but it had to be done for sanity's sake. But still, I feel the need to apologize to you and a thank you for sticking with me.

Thank you as well to my usual suspects—Regina for her eagle eye and my dedicated readers who manage to catch the typos we both miss. To Dylan for the figures, and all the readers on Instagram who found me, and help others find me!

And now for some fun facts!

I think it's obvious to all that Prince Bo could do with a few therapy sessions! The Don't assume advice he got from Dr. Patel is straight from the mouth of my own therapist! Shout out to Laurie and thanks for all the listening!

Hettie's last name is indigenous because that's what her background is. While I don't make a big deal out of is, I'm definitely not trying to hide the fact. Also, the family is NOT based on anyone family I know.

Tema! The unusual name means 'perfect' and 'complete' and I actually knew a Tema.

Thanks for reading!
Holly xo

READING LIST

Love in Laandia

Royal Rumble
Royal Retelling
Royal Rising
Royal Reluctance
Royal Rebel

Suitor Science

Hating the Chemistry Teacher
Falling for The Suitor
Fraternizing with the Ex
Marrying the Billionaire Best Friend
Loving the Wrong Guy
Finding the One

Don't

Don't Tell Me You Love Me
Don't Want to Be Friends
Don't Stop Me Now
Don't They Know It's Christmas

Love & Alliteration

Perfectly Played
Beautifully Baked
Pleasantly Popped

Charlotte Dodd

The Secret Life of Charlotte Dodd
The Missing Files of Charlotte Dodd
The Best Worst First Date Ever
The Hidden Past of Pippa McGovern
The Last Stand of Charlotte Dodd

Sisters in a Small Town

Coming Home
Hanging On
Stepping Up

Unexpecting
Unexpectingly Happily Ever After

STANDALONES

Cinnamon Rolls and Pumpkin Spice – Coffee Break with the Billionaire

Oceanic Dreams – I Saw Him Standing There

Absinthe Doesn't Make the Heart Grow Fonder